ALSO BY MICHELLE SACKS

You Were Made for This
Stone Baby: Stories

ALL THE
LOST THINGS

ALL THE
LOST THINGS

A NOVEL

MICHELLE SACKS

Little, Brown and Company

New York Boston London

Little, Brown and Company
Hachette Book Group
1290 Avenue of the Americas, New York, NY 10104
littlebrown.com

First Edition: June 2019

Little, Brown and Company is a division of Hachette Book Group, Inc. The Little, Brown name and logo are trademarks of Hachette Book Group, Inc.

The publisher is not responsible for websites (or their content) that are not owned by the publisher.

The Hachette Speakers Bureau provides a wide range of authors for speaking events. To find out more, go to hachettespeakersbureau.com or call (866) 376-6591.

ISBN 978-0-316-47545-7
LCCN 2018961253

10 9 8 7 6 5 4 3 2 1

LSC-C

Printed in the United States of America

For my father, Norman

ALL THE LOST THINGS

Saturday

I was rescuing a baby lion when Dad scooped me up into his arms and carried me away. Clemesta and I were in the middle of complicated surgery to deliver a cub who was stuck inside her mom's belly and couldn't get out to be born. I was doing the operation part because I am very good at all kinds of medical healing, and Clemesta was the nurse assistant, passing me things whenever I called for them, like SCALPEL CUTTER or SKIN STITCHER or CUB GRABBER TONGS. The game is called VET RESCUE and we save a lot of precious animal lives every day and make them feel better if they are sick or if they get injured from vicious fights. I said BLOOD SUCKER PLEASE but before Clemesta could pass it over, Dad had taken us out to the car and that's how the best day started.

"Where are we going?" I said. Dad plonked me down on the back seat. His face was a little shiny and he wiped his forehead with the back of his hand.

"Dad," I said, "where are you taking me?"

"You and I are going on an adventure," Dad said. His breath smelled of one hundred cups of coffee and the ghosty part of something else.

He gave me a big smile with all his teeth and a wink with one of his eyes, and then he tapped my nose twice which made me scrunch up my face.

"An adventure?" I said.

Dad nodded. "Oh yes," he said. "An adventure."

I was ONE HUNDRED PERCENT excited because an adventure was an enormous and unexpected surprise and usually those are only for birthdays or Christmas morning. That's only two days of the whole entire year which has 365 days in it usually but 366 days when it's a LEAP YEAR that jumps ahead but only every four years on the 29th of February. That's also the birthday of that boy Deacon in my class with the extra-big ears, but he still gets a party every year. Anyway, I was THRILLED IN PIECES and when Dad strapped me in with the seat belt I didn't tell him that I could do it myself since FOREVER because I was too busy spinning around in my brain thinking about where we could be going and what exactly an adventure was and how come we were taking one JUST LIKE THAT on an ordinary and regular Saturday morning with no special plans marked with a red pen in the family calendar of ENGLISH COUNTRY GARDENS that stays in place on the refrigerator with three magnets that look like cookies but taste like plastic so don't even try them.

Dad climbed in front and set a duffel bag on the seat next to him. He wiped his face again with his hand.

"Who's coming along for the adventure?" I said.

"Just us," he said. "You and me."

"And Clemesta," I said, because Clemesta HATES to be left out of anything and gets very grouchy if she is.

• • •

Dad started the car and I made sure to strap Clemesta in SAFE AND SOUND so she would also be protected if we had an accident or if the car fell off a bridge, which really does happen sometimes. I saw it on TV once. The rescue team had to tie ropes around the car to lift it out of the water. Everyone inside was already dead from drowning, which is actually the FOURTH LEADING CAUSE OF DEATH in this country. I forget what number one is, maybe heart disease or that cancer, which makes millions of people dead all the time, like the man who used to live down the street and the principal from my old school Miss Jessop who went bald from it, and Mom's mom who was my grandma, and also lots of other people whose names I don't remember right exactly now.

Dad pulled the car out of the driveway and I turned back to watch our house, which is 31-42 Crescent Street, Astoria, New York, zip code 11106, and a very beautiful and lovely house of red bricks with a whole yard in the back just for me. The yard has a big old tree standing in the middle and Dad promised to build me a tree house in there one day soon. I will call it DOLLY HEADQUARTERS INCOR-PORATED and I will sleep there some nights if there are GUARANTEED no spiders or sneaky mice waiting to nibble me for their tasty midnight snack. Clemesta will stay with me of course because she never leaves my side.

Inside my stomach, I had ONE THOUSAND butterflies. Stomach butterflies are special ones that get inside your belly when you are very nervous or very excited about some-thing. Mine were beautiful and colorful and tropical jungle butterflies and they were flying around having a big party with streamers and balloons.

I gave Clemesta a squeeze.

"Where are we going for the adventure?" I asked Dad.

He typed something into his phone while we waited at the lights.

"It's a surprise," he said.

"But tell me!"

"I can't," he said. "Not yet."

"But you have to give me a clue," I said. "So I can start to guess. Then you can say 'warm, warmer, FIERY HOT' if I get close, or 'cool, cooler, ICE FREEZE' if I'm wrong. That's how it works."

Dad scratched his chin. "Uh," he said. "Well, it's a place."

"What kind of a place?"

"A great place."

"Better than here?"

"Yeah."

"Like the best place in the world?"

"Yeah."

"That's Disneyland!" I said.

"No, it's not Disneyland."

I flopped back in the seat and made a BOO HOO face which is when my whole mouth turns itself upside down to tell everyone that I am sad and disappointed inside.

"It's better than Disneyland," Dad said. "Even more fun. You'll love it."

"How do you know?"

"I just do."

"How long till we get there?"

"A couple days," Dad said. "Not too long."

"Days?"

"Yeah." I looked at the duffel bag poking out from the front seat.

"Did you already pack all our stuff?"

"Yeah."

"All my stuff too?"

"Yeah."

"But I didn't tell you everything of what I needed."

"I guessed it," Dad said. "Because I wanted it to be a surprise for you."

"Oh. That's nice. And it's just us," I said.

"Yeah."

"You and me and Clemesta."

Dad nodded.

"What about Mom?"

Dad looked at me in the mirror with his big brown eyes that are the same exact eyes as mine. "Oh, Mom's away on her girls' weekend, remember?"

I yawned because my sleep still didn't want to go away even though it was way past wake-up time. "With Rita?" I said.

Dad nodded.

"I guess I forgot."

"She left early," Dad said. "Before you were up."

"Oh."

"That's why I thought we should have a Dolly and Dad weekend."

I nodded. "Yeah, and probably we'll have even more fun."

I remembered the Vet Rescue game and the kicked-over ambulance lying on the porch.

"I hope the lion cub is okay," I said to Clemesta.

"She'll be fine," Clemesta said. "It's only pretend anyway."

"Yeah, and we're going on a for-real adventure. That's more important."

"Yeah."

"Actually we never went on a for-real adventure before. Just that vacation of three nights and four days to Montauk with Mom and Dad."

"Yeah," Clemesta said, "but this is different."

"Exactly," I said. "Because it's a surprise and we didn't know it was going to happen until three seconds ago."

Clemesta nodded and my butterflies went whooshing again. I was very excited to have Dad all to myself.

Clemesta was full up with butterflies just like me and that's because the two of us are actual twins. We are fluent in TELEPATHY which means we can speak to each other with only our minds, and we can also read each other's thoughts and see into each other's hearts. We always feel the same way about everything, like our favorite foods or when we're sad or the people we don't like and wish we could make disappear in a puff of vanishing magic. Clemesta and I also have matching twin hair, which is called CHESTNUT BROWN and is very long and lustrous. That means thick and shiny and more beautiful than anyone else's. She brushes my hair and I brush hers with ONE HUNDRED STROKES per day to keep it this way. It's a lot of work but it is very worth it because we love our silky hair a whole lot and also that's what princesses do to keep their hair beautiful and strong enough for princes to climb up if they don't have a ladder to get to the top of your tower.

•   •   •

As Dad drove down the street, our house got smaller and smaller, and that's because of *PERSPECTIVE* which is a big word that I can spell in my head and also on paper because I have an ADVANCED BRAIN. That's what Miss Ellis says and she's my teacher so she knows all about First Grader brains. Probably Miss Ellis knows everything in the whole entire world, that's how smart she is, but she is also very kind and nice and that's why I made her a Valentine's Day card this year with a chocolate heart stapled on the front. It melted a little from being in my bag, but she didn't mind and she said it was *SCRUMPTIOUS* which is like delicious but even more tasty.

Miss Ellis has started giving me extra homework to do on the weekends which sounds like a punishment but is actually a good thing to make me even smarter and keep me STIMU-LATED IN THE BRAIN, which everyone says is a sponge that likes to soak things up and the more the merrier. Because of being advanced, I can spell very tough words like *PALE-ONTOLOGY* and *PHOSPHATES* and I know how to stop someone from choking to death and I can also make a fire from rubbing sticks together, even though I never tried it for real yet, but I can still do it anytime I might need to. I am also good at Math and remembering all the countries and I know magic tricks like making coins appear out of people's ears and I can cast spells that are sometimes good and a few times bad but only if someone deserves it like YOU KNOW WHO.

Dad turned at the lights and we drove past Mr. Abdul standing on the sidewalk outside the bodega. I waved to him but I guess he was too busy smoking his DISGUSTING CIGARETTES to wave back. Even though he smokes and will probably die from lung cancer or rot his gums until they bleed and turn black, he is a very nice man and very friendly to me whenever we go and buy something from him. Before we leave, Mr. Abdul always says, "You have a terrific day, Little Lady," and I say, *"DITTO,"* which is a word I like very much and try to use whenever I can. My other favorite words at the moment are *bumblebee, preposterous,* and *funicular.* Miss Ellis lets me take home the class dictionary on the weekends so I can learn all the words in the whole world. First in English and then maybe all the other languages too.

I know millions of words but not all of them are nice. Some of the WORST WORDS in the world are *divorce, Los Angeles,* and *depressed,* which are all very bad things. Another word for *bad* is AWFUL and another word for *awful* is HOR-RENDOUS. *Horrendous* rhymes with *tremendous* but it means something different and I know that too.

I liked being in the car just with Dad. I especially liked being in the new car, which was a shiny and fancy Jeep Renegade. Dad is very lucky, because he gets a new car whenever he wants, he just has to say NEW CAR PLEASE and there it is. That's because he has a very important job at VALUE MOTORS selling people their shiny new cars. They have HUNDREDS of them and all of the cars are nice and new-looking, and inside they smell of fresh pinecones because they have air fresheners hanging off the mirrors in the shape of real trees to make you feel like you're sitting in a forest and not a car. I wish they would make other flavors, like hot fudge sauce or chocolate chip cookies, and then you could feel like you were inside an ice-cream parlor or maybe a kitchen with a lovely mom at the oven baking your favorite treats for you.

Anyway, you have to be VERY SMART for a job like Dad's, and he is and he wears a gray suit every day along with a badge that says his name and the word *SALES EXECUTIVE* beneath it. Dad is up for a promotion soon and that means he will get an even more important badge, FINGERS CROSSED. He will also get more money and that's good news because MONEY IS TIGHT and the house is MORTGAGED TO THE HILT and that means BILLS BILLS BILLS which are the worst thing to see on the kitchen table because as soon as one goes away another one pops up and opens its greedy envelope mouth and says "feed me your money right now."

Sometimes I use my magic disappearing tricks and I make the bills vanish in my bedroom under the bed. That way Mom and Dad won't get in a cloudy mood and feel stressed out. Stress is a disease that grown-ups get when they are unhappy and it can actually kill them, so I always try very hard to keep them in good spirits. I do this with GOOD BEHAVIOR and LISTENING and BEING DELIGHTFUL and STAYING OUT OF TROUBLE and also MAKING FUN JOKES. Once I heard someone say that laughter is the best medicine and that means if someone is sick or sad you can cure them with a joke but it has to be extra-funny and not too rude or else they will get mad.

Today was the first time I was getting to drive in the new Jeep because Dad only brought it home last month. Maybe it was before that, but anyway he didn't have a chance to take anyone for a ride yet.

The Jeep was beige inside and spotlessly clean, and the seats were soft and squidgy smooth, like a very comfortable sofa in your living room. I pressed the button to open the window, and then close it, and then open it again, until I found the perfect amount of *VENTILATION* which is air and another word I can spell if I concentrate hard. *Ventilation* rhymes with *nation* rhymes with *station*. That's another thing I am excellent at, is making rhyming words. Miss Ellis has a reading game where you have to call out a rhyming word at the end of every sentence and I always win it because I always have a very good word sitting in my brain waiting to make a match. That's not bragging, it's just FACTUALLY TRUE, like the fact that the earth is a round ball or that it's bad luck to step on sidewalk cracks because little invisible trolls live there and they will eat your toes if you cross the line. Also you shouldn't talk to black cats, that's bad luck too. Sometimes if I see one I say, "Sorry, Beloved Cat, I wish we could chat, but we can't." They always understand because they are used to people saying that, even though they don't feel unlucky.

Being in the Jeep on an adventure was an extra-special treat, like ice cream for breakfast or finding a five-dollar bill on the street, and it was a double treat because Dad was all for me and that ALMOST NEVER PROBABLY EVER happens.

In my head I made up a song called "Adventure," which went like this:

We're going on an adventure, ho-ho-ho,
Dad and Dolly and Clemesta, off we go!

I sang it for Dad and he smiled. He didn't sing along. Probably he didn't know the words yet and he was concentrating on the traffic which is your job when you're the driver. It's the same as if you're in an airplane. You can't distract the pilot with songs or he'll go the wrong way in the sky and crash into all the migrating birds.

Clemesta and I watched out the window as we passed the tire shop and the funeral parlor where dead bodies are kept until they go into the ground, and we saw all the building sites which everyone says are TAKING OVER the neighborhood. I watched a man with a plastic bag over his hand bend down to pick up his poodle's poop and I was happy that he was being responsible because everyone knows IF YOUR DOG POOPS, YOU SCOOP. When I have a dog, I will train him to pick up his own poop so I won't ever have to touch it because that would be disgusting and then I bet my hand would stink all day long and no one at school would want to play with me. I will also train him to fetch snacks from the kitchen and do cartwheels, because you can train dogs to do anything except probably drive a truck.

Dad gave the steering wheel a whack with his hand.

"Come on," he said, but we didn't move, we just stayed trapped in our traffic jam with all the other cars trying to get somewhere. I bet nobody else was headed for an adventure, I bet they were only going to buy groceries or get blood tests at the doctor.

"LUCKY DUCK," I said to Clemesta. "We are two lucky
ducks."

Dad took a sneaky turn down the next street to try and get
out of the traffic.

"Look," I showed him, "that's Savannah's house down there."

"Hmm?" he said.

"Savannah," I said.

"Who's that?"

"She's my best friend."

"Oh."

"Maybe I forgot to tell you."

I gave my lip a chew in the meaty part. Clemesta poked
me in the ribs.

"Hey!" she said.

"She's only my best friend when I'm at school," I told her.
"The rest of the time you're my best friend ONE MILLION
PERCENT."

Dad came to the end of Savannah's street and turned left.
We were right back in the traffic and it was still jammed.

"Goddamn," he said.

Another car tried to slide in front of the Jeep but Dad
wouldn't let him. The man threw up his hands and shook his
head. Dad squeezed his hand into a fist like you do when
you're getting ready to make a punch. I do punching exercises
too to get strong and fit and IN SHAPE like Mom, but also for
SELF-DEFENSE which means you can protect yourself from
bad guys when they come up behind you on the street and you
just whack them HI-YAH like that with your elbow. They fall
down on the ground and you run away as fast as you can.

"My second-best friend is Casey," I told Dad. "She has a pet snake. But it lives in a big glass box. It can't escape unless you take it out."

Dad didn't say anything.

"It eats rats," I said. "They keep them in the freezer. Not where their regular food is, but in a special one just for frozen rats. I think it's in the basement. They also have a gerbil but she lives in a different cage."

Dad was tapping the wheel with his fingers and staring ahead. I guess he was trying to keep every bit of his attention on the road so he wouldn't get us lost. Being lost is the SECOND WORST THING in the world and I would know because it happened to me once. Mom and I were at the Queens Zoo which was a special treat for me getting ten gold stars on my GOOD BEHAVIOR CHART on the back of my bedroom door. You get a gold star for being polite and getting good grades or for doing chores and not complaining about stuff and also sometimes for keeping important secrets.

Mom and I had been looking at Mrs. Puma and then next thing she said she looked around and I was gone and she was in a FLAT PANIC. I was also in a panic as soon as I realized I was lost, which was when I was talking to the Andean Bear and he said, "Dolly, where's your mom?"

I tried to remember everything about not talking to strangers and finding a grown-up to help and not climbing into the animal enclosures even if they invite you inside for a chat and say PRETTY PLEASE. I found the security lady who was walking around near the entrance and I gave her Mom's phone number which I keep stored in my brain for emergencies. Inside I was shaking like Jell-O because I thought maybe I'd never ever find Mom or see Dad or go home to my house, and then I'd have to live in the zoo or get adopted by the security lady who had bad breath and a lot of flaky white pieces on her scalp which I bet would fall into all the food she cooked and then I'd have to eat it.

Luckily, Mom answered her phone right away and said, "DOLLY DON'T YOU EVER DO THAT AGAIN," and I didn't and I won't.

Sometimes Mom has good advice and sometimes she is only full of STUPIDITY.

Dad's eyes in the mirror were popped wide open like he was doing a staring contest. We do them on nights when he comes back home early from work. We lock our matching eyes together and try not to blink. Most of the time I giggle and blink first. That's losing the contest but actually winning, too, because it's fun and I'm laughing at the end.

As Dad drove, I was trying to keep all the things I wanted to tell him safe in a list inside my head. I wanted to remind him about all the IMPORTANT FACTS about me in case he didn't remember, like that my favorite flavor of ice cream is RASPBERRY SORBET, and that I can do hip-hop dancing and ballet and tap and that I'm not scared of spiders, except a tiny bit if they are very enormous and hairy, and that I am saving up all my money to buy a jewelry box that is made of red satin with real gold beads sewn on the top. Inside there's a beautiful ballerina who dances to music every time you open the lid and it's the best treasure I have ever seen.

I also wanted to tell Dad about Miss Ellis and the new class assignment which is called KINDNESS WEEK where you have to try and do nice things for strangers, like picking up litter on the sidewalk or giving someone a hug if they look lonely and sad. My list was getting so long it was starting not to fit in my head and I wished I had a notepad outside my brain for writing it all down instead. My handwriting isn't as advanced as my brain but Miss Ellis says if I keep practicing it will be perfect in no time.

I sang the "Adventure" song again but softly and only to Clemesta.

"Your voice is lovely," she said, "like an angel or a world-famous pop star."

"Thank you," I said. I combed my fingers through her hair. It was as soft as velvet.

Dad took the exit for the tunnel and I knew that was the way you go to get to Manhattan because I have been HUNDREDS of times with Mom. Mostly we take the N train from home and we get out wherever is nearest to the place Mom has marked on her map. The trips sometimes used to be fun but not anymore. Now they just put me in a THUNDERCLOUD mood for the whole day. That's not Manhattan's fault, it's hers.

One thing I like a lot about Manhattan is looking at all the buildings in the city because they go up to the sky and probably the moon. The shape of them is called the *SKYLINE* and once I had a whole coloring book full of all the different ones in the world. For Manhattan, I made the colors look like nighttime and it was very beautiful.

I recognized some of the streets we were passing, and the big shops with the bright flashing signs and the street vendors and the MILLIONS of people who were all in a great big hurry. There were hundreds of dads walking around Manhattan and I felt sorry for their kids that they weren't going on an adventure. Probably the other children in my class would call me a *SPOILED BRAT* but I didn't care because we were going to the best place in the world that's even better than Disneyland, and it was a special adventure just for us.

"Anyway, you deserve a special treat," Clemesta said, "and maybe they don't. Maybe they are bad or rude or ungrateful."

"Exactly. Especially Neshi. She is all of those things."

We passed a homeless man pushing his shopping cart. He had a sign around his neck and I turned my head to read it because I like to read everything and I am always looking for new words to collect.

HOMELESS HOPELESS VETERAN is what he had written and I tried to remember what VETERAN was. I hate seeing homeless people on the streets because they always look so lonely like no one ever talks to them or gives them a hug and probably that's just what they need to feel better. Hugs are another good medicine, like jokes and Zarbee's Cough Syrup.

Dad checked his watch and made a face.

"Is the adventure in Manhattan?" I said.

"No," Dad said. "We're just driving through."

I read a sign for CASH LOANS and looked at Clemesta. She put a hoof to her lips.

"I know," I said. "I'm glad we're leaving Manhattan. It makes me reminded of BAD STUFF."

Dad had gone quiet again but actually he doesn't usually talk a whole lot anyway. I don't think he likes to. Probably some people are born that way so you shouldn't get mad at them if they are silent most of the time.

We drove into the Lincoln Tunnel and everything went dark.

"Lincoln like Abraham Lincoln," I said. "He was the president. He built all the tunnels in America, probably the world too."

"Mm," Dad said.

"I know all the presidents' names, like John F. Kennedy and Theodore Roosevelt and Thomas Jefferson. He's on the two-dollar bill. Benjamin Franklin is on the one-hundred-dollar bill because probably he was nicer. In Aruba they don't put dead presidents on their money bills, they have shells and turtles and snakes. Can you turn the radio on?"

Dad pressed the button and flicked through the stations but it was crackling because of the tunnel. It was dark and noisy and it reminded me of the movies, when the bad guys chase after the good guys and sparks fly on the road and sometimes one of the cars flips over but no one is hurt and they just crawl out and start running away from the flames.

We came out into the regular world again and Clemesta squinted her eyes to adjust them to the light. Her eyes are very sensitive because they are so sharp and good at seeing things. She can see things that people can't see. It's called X-Men vision.

If you don't know Clemesta, I should probably tell you that she is an exquisite red-brown horse with a long beautiful mane, and a long beautiful tail, and eyes that are black and deeply soulful because they are POOLS OF KINDNESS

AND WISDOM. Clemesta is made of plastic that's covered in horse fur and everyone thinks she is only a toy horse but the secret truth that no one knows except for me is that she is actually a WISE HORSE QUEEN descended from fire and kings and magical fairies and exploding stars and the moon's dust and angel kisses. I know this because she whispered the whole story to me one night under the covers. I was supposed to be asleep so that Mom and Dad could have one of their GROWN-UP DISCUSSIONS which are always noisy and give me a funny feeling inside my heart, but instead Clemesta was telling me about her life as a pretend-toy horse and a real-life horse queen with many special gifts.

Of course, I promised that I would never tell A LIVING SOUL and I will keep that promise until my most DYING BREATH because that is what true friends should do. I got Clemesta for my fourth birthday and she used to just sit up there on the top shelf in my bedroom, but that night when she told me everything, she flew down with her magic horse wings and landed on my pillow and after that we were BEST FRIENDS AND TWINS forever.

I tell Clemesta everything, and she is always very wise if I need her help with something. Sometimes Mom tries to speak to her but then Clemesta pretends she's only a plastic horse and I don't force her to reveal her true identity because that would be cruel. I am better than Clemesta at Math and Reading and Coloring and Words, as well as my own special SECRET BRAIN POWERS and some other stuff too. She is better at Magic Spells and Curses and Mind Reading and Remembering Stuff and Guardian Angel Duties like protecting me from danger and making sure I am never scared.

We will be best friends forever because we promised that we would be and we also swore in HUMAN BLOOD when I cut my finger on a knife in the kitchen sink at Thanksgiving and then pricked Clemesta with a fork and mixed our blood so we would be bonded together FOR ALL OF LIFE.

I nuzzled Clemesta in her mane and she yawned. She likes to take naps on car rides, so she snuggled up in my lap while I kept watch outside trying to guess where we were going. I scratched inside my brain to remember all the places nearby to Manhattan, like Long Island and Newark and Staten Island. I didn't remember more but I know all the states of the United States of America, and also all the other countries around the world, like Sweden and Ireland and Canada and Spain where they are so crazy and mean that they make bulls fight a guy inside a stadium until one of them is dead. That's called ANI-MAL CRUELTY and it's the worst because animals can't even defend themselves or go to protests in the streets. Miss Ellis says we should practice ANIMAL KINDNESS and that's why Clemesta and I do Vet Rescue whenever we can to help.

WELCOME TO NEW JERSEY, it said on the billboard.

"Dad!" I said. "We've left the state!"

"Yeah," he said.

"I never left the state before. Did you?"

"Yeah," Dad said.

"How many times?"

"A few," Dad said. "I used to travel sometimes—for work."

"When you and Mom lived in Florida?"

"Yeah."

"Clemesta also comes from out of state," I said. "Actually from another planet. Well, kind of another planet, but she's made of magic, from lots of different special things. Fairies and queens, that's in her...in her bloodline. Her grandparents were magical. Not like Pop."

"Sounds neat," Dad said.

"Yeah. It is."

I tried to think of other interesting things to talk about so Dad would say, "Gosh, Dolly, you are EXCELLENT COMPANY," and then he would realize how great it is to be with me. Usually he is very busy and he works very hard and that means most of the time it's just me and Mom together and Dad somewhere else.

Most nights when he comes back home from working all day he is not in a CHATTERBOX MOOD and he doesn't do a whole lot of talking to me before Mom says "Time for bed, Sleepyhead." Sometimes I'll say, "How was your day?" and he'll shrug and say, "Same, it's always the same." If there's time we can have a staring contest and if there isn't I just go to bed without giggling.

I wish he could spend hundreds of hours playing games with me and telling me stories and taking me swimming and teaching me how to do tricks on my bicycle and helping me memorize new dictionary words and a bunch of other stuff too. But now we were on the best treat of an adventure and he was paying me all of his attention and it was MARVELOUS which is like *excellent* but way better.

I sucked my arm with my tongue to try and make a love bite. Savannah taught me that last week. You have to suck a lot until it leaves a mark and then it means that some-one loves you very much. My skin tasted salty and a tiny bit soapy. The mark was red but it was a circle instead of a heart.

We drove by a stretch of strip malls and fields and trees and trucks, and a billboard that said DISCREET GIRLS. It had a woman holding her finger to her red lips, which meant she was good at keeping secrets too.

I remembered something to tell Dad. "Guess what?" I said. "There's a boy in my class, Ross, who once went in a helicopter. He had a medical emergency because he hit his head one day when he went out sledding. He's fine now. He didn't get any of that brain damage."

"That's good," Dad said.

"And do you know there's another boy in my class who can do an air split? He can jump and his legs go straight out and he doesn't even practice a lot. He'll probably join the circus." I checked the love bite but it was already almost gone. "Why do you keep rubbing your eyes?"

"I'm trying to wake up," Dad said.

"Are you sleeping still?"

"I'm sleepy."

"Me too. Because I think last night I slept too hard. Like I wasn't ever going to want to wake up. But then I did. But I was very fuzzy."

"Mm."

"Were you fuzzy?"

"Yeah, I didn't sleep much."

"Anyway," I said. "Do you know who the smartest kid in my class is?"

"Who?"

"It's ME!"

"Really? The smartest?"

"Yeah," I said, "I'm really the smartest."

Dad smiled at me in the mirror and that made me feel happy inside but also a PINCH of bad for telling a white lie. White lies aren't like real lies, they're just teeny tiny ones for keeping people's feelings unhurt or showing off a tiny amount to impress your dad.

I'm not actually the smartest in the class, but number three.

"Yeah but that's only because stupid Verity gets all those extra lessons," Clemesta said.

"And an au pair," I reminded her.

"Silly old pear," Clemesta said, and we collapsed into STITCHES, which is when you laugh so hard you burst open and need to be sewn back together again. Both of us think Verity is the most annoying girl in the school. She doesn't eat any candy and she is learning to play the violin and she definitely isn't invited to my next birthday party even if she begs on her knees and cries two buckets.

I looked at the clock in the front of the car and read the time, because it wasn't one of the round clocks with two hands but the kind that gives you the numbers right away. It was 1:47 which was after lunch and before dinner and I was very hungry suddenly because I hadn't eaten anything since a bowl of Cheerios before we started Vet Rescue.

"Clemesta is very hungry," I said.

"Who's hungry?"

"Clemesta," I said. I held her up so Dad could see and

Clemesta humphed, which is horse for being irritated that someone forgot your name AGAIN.

"She's hungry?" Dad said.

"Yeah, I can actually hear her stomach growling right now."

Clemesta's stomach does make very loud noises when she hasn't eaten for a long time and also sometimes when she needs to go to the toilet for a NUMBER TWO.

Dad nodded. "All right," he said, "I'll find somewhere."

WELCOME TO PENNSYLVANIA, said the sign and I looked at Clemesta with my eyes popping out of my head. Her mouth was on the floor. "Two states," she said.

"That's because it's an adventure," I said. "You have to go far into the wide world. Or is it wild?"

"Wide and wild, I guess," Clemesta said. She turned to look out at all the green fields.

At the next gas station, Dad pulled up the car. I hopped out and took his hand because he forgot to hold mine. His hands are big and sometimes they squeeze too hard, but I like holding hands with him very much so I keep it there no matter what until he has to let go. I skippety-skip jumped and my hair bounced off my shoulders and probably looked very pretty in the light.

Inside the store, there was a lady behind the counter with long lovely braids and orange lipstick. She was reading the gossip magazine that Mom likes to buy so she can see which famous actresses are getting fat and old. She likes best the pictures that say *HORROR BODY* or *SUMMER BLUBBER.*

The lady didn't say hello to us even though being friendly is probably part of her job.

I stood at the top of the aisle. "We can't get lunch here," I said. "It's just snacks and junk."

"Well," Dad said. "I'm sure we'll find something." He walked around and picked out a bag of beef jerky and held it up.

I shook my head. "Yuck. I hate that stuff."

"What about pretzels?"

"Yeah. But not the spicy ones. Just the ones that are a little bit salty-flavored."

"You like cookies?"

"Yeah," I said. Dad picked out chocolate chip which is my third favorite flavor after oats and then peanut butter, but I didn't remind him of these important and interesting DOLLY FACTS.

I took a Twix off the shelf, and Peanut Butter Cups for Clemesta.

"Can I get these too?"

Dad nodded.

"But they're also JUNK."

"Mm," Dad said.

"I won't tell Mom," I whispered.

Dad poured coffee from the machine and stirred in three packets of sugar. He got a couple of sodas from the refrigerator and also bottled water and two Red Bulls which are FORBIDDEN for kids because they will get too much energy and fly away.

"Do you want a soda?" Dad said.

I shook my head. "I'm holding in a pee."

Dad scrunched up his eyes at me. "Don't do that," he said. "Go on and use the restroom. We won't stop again for a while."

"Will you guard outside?"

Dad nodded. He balanced everything in his arms and kept one hand free to drink his coffee.

The smell inside the restroom burned my nostrils. Whoever had cleaned it had used BUCKETS of disinfectant, but at least all the germs were good and dead so they wouldn't be able to jump on me.

I sat down and waited until I was empty. It took forever. I remembered to wash my hands with two squirts of the soap, and I dried them on the hot-air machine on the wall.

Dad wasn't waiting right exactly outside the door, but he was still close enough to run and grab me if any bad guys tried to get me. I went over to him, and we walked to the counter.

Dad handed his credit card to the checkout lady to swipe through the machine. She had earrings going all the way up her ears, plus one sparkly stud pierced into the bony parts. I bet she cried when she got that one. I cried the day Mom took me to get my ears pierced because the lady shoots you with a real gun and doesn't even say sorry afterward.

"Thank you, sir." The checkout lady handed Dad his credit card and his receipt. He looked at the card and mumbled something to himself which might have been a curse word that rhymes with DUCK.

"Hang on a minute," he told me. He went to the machine that gives you piles of money if you know the SECRET PASSCODE. I saw him give the machine a fat WHACK with his hand. "It's broken," he called to the lady in his VERY IRRITATED voice.

She shrugged. "Guess so."

Dad walked back over to the counter and grabbed his coffee and the bags. He glared at the lady, who was back to looking at all the SIZZLING SUMMER BODIES.

"Fix your goddamn machine," he told her, and he stormed out. Some of the coffee spilled.

I followed him but I didn't take his hand. "What a stupid woman," I said, when we climbed into the car.

Dad didn't say anything, he just gulped his coffee down and then drove to the next gas station. He pulled up the car like he was mad at it. He slammed the door when he got out, and the whole car wobbled.

While he stood at the second cash machine I concentrated on laying all the snacks out on the back seat. I put them in neat rows, like I was running a store and you could choose whatever you wanted.

I ate one finger of my Twix and Clemesta ate one of her Peanut Butter Cups. Peanut butter is very healthy for horses. It helps their teeth stay strong for chewing grass and biting bad guys. Dad came back to the car and opened his Red Bull. He drank it down in two great thirsty gulps and then we set off again.

"How's that Twix?" he said.

I licked my chocolatey fingers. "It's very delicious."

Dad opened the window and let his arm hang out in the breeze.

"Isn't this the most fun?" I said to Clemesta. She smelled of peanut butter and I wanted to lick her but I didn't.

"I guess so," she said.

"Why aren't you more excited?"

She shrugged. "I don't know where we're going. Maybe I won't like it."

"It's the best place. Obviously you'll love it."

Out the window, we passed lots and lots of fields and trees with pretty pinky-purple blossoms. The sky was very blue and very high, like it stretched all the way to outer space.

"Dad," I said, "probably this is the best day of my whole entire life. And Clemesta's. Is it yours too?" He smiled at me and his eyes crinkled at the corners.

"Yeah," he said. "Mine too."

That made me warm inside my heart.

I ate a handful of chips and one of the chocolate chip cookies.

"That's enough," Clemesta said, "or your stomach might burst."

"Yeah." I ate one more cookie. Then I laid my head back against the seat and used my fingers to comb through Clemesta's silky mane. On days when I braid my hair, I like to braid hers too. That way people can tell immediately that we are twins and sisters.

"But they don't know we are magical," Clemesta said. "That's our special secret."

"Yeah. But a good secret. Not a bad one."

"Yeah. I don't like the bad ones either."

"I like Pennsylvania," I said. I slipped Clemesta's second Peanut Butter Cup into my mouth and let it melt away on my tongue. I knew she wouldn't mind because we always share everything and my stomach is bigger than hers anyway.

PENNSYLVANIA I said inside my head. I tried to remember the spelling from the billboard but I hadn't concentrated hard enough. There were MILLIONS of trees everywhere, maybe more than I ever saw before in my life all at once. I bet all the kids around here had their own private tree houses.

"Oh, isn't Dracula from Pennsylvania?" I said.

"I don't think so," Clemesta said.

"He is."

Clemesta scratched her head. She does that when she thinks very hard. She uses her front hoof. "No, he's from the other place. Transylvania."

"Oh," I said. "Well, you're very good at geography."

"Yeah, but you're excellent at words and Math and millions of other things."

"Yeah."

We rubbed our noses together, which is a special kind of secret kiss just for us two twins.

Dad switched on the radio and turned it up to listen when the news came on. I don't like listening to the news because it's only ever talking and BLAH BLAH BLAH and boring like when Principal Hanson at school gives her lecture on how all of us are the same even if some of us are Hindus or Muslims or Catholics and especially if we are like Alex in the class below mine who was born a girl but is actually a boy and wears boy clothes.

• • •

I watched the back of Dad's head. I shifted my legs to try and stretch them out. I pointed my foot like a ballet dancer and I lifted my leg like I was going to do a pirouette, which I can do for real anytime but not in a car sitting down. All the other girls in my class go to after-school ballet but I can't go because of the BILLS BILLS BILLS. It's very unfair because even Shira goes to classes and she doesn't like ballet one bit, she just has to go because her big sister takes the class after hers and she has to KILL TIME with dance steps.

Anyway, Clemesta and I practice our own private ballet every day for HOURS and one day we will probably be so good that someone will walk past the window of the living room and spot us dancing and make us the leading dancers for *Swan Lake,* which has the best and most beautiful costumes of all the ballets in the world. All the girls from my class will come and watch me and they'll feel pretty silly for wasting so much money on dance classes for no good reason. Afterward, they will throw roses onto the stage while I curtsy and they will give me a standing elation. Verity won't stand and clap, because she will be too green with jealousy to get up from her seat.

Dad will be there too. He'll be clapping the loudest because he hasn't seen me dance ballet in a long time and he will get a big surprise and a gigantic burst of PROUDNESS to have such a graceful and talented daughter called ME.

After I finished stretching my legs, I checked my teeth with my tongue. They are very busy at the moment. My front tooth has been missing since before Christmas, my back molar tooth is poking through, and my bottom tooth on the left side is loose. I like to wiggle it. If I poke it in far enough I can feel the slippy slimy gum part underneath and the sharp parts of the tooth's roots where it's still trying to stay attached. I bet it's going to fall out soon, maybe even on the adventure.

"Dad," I said, "can the tooth fairy visit you even when you're in another state?"

"What?"

"The tooth fairy."

"The tooth fairy," Dad said. "Huh. Well. I guess if she's a fairy she can go anywhere."

"That's what I thought," I said. "Are we still in Pennsylvania?"

"Yeah."

"How much further is the adventure?"

"Uh, we have a way to go still," Dad said. He peeked at something on his phone.

"Are you sure I'll like the place?" I said.

"Yeah, I'm sure, Doll."

I smiled. I love it when Dad calls me Doll, which isn't my real name but a name you make up for someone you love very much. Dolly isn't really my name either, but it's what everyone calls me because Adaline is a funny name for a child and Mom only chose it because she liked an actress once who was called Adaline, and then she decided she didn't like her anymore after all and I became just Dolly, or Doll when Dad loves me especially much and wants to tell me in one special CODE WORD that we both understand.

Dad's real name is Joseph Rust and Mom's name is Anna Rust but her name before she married Dad was Anna Kalina and that's the name she uses when she's being a famous actress. I like her name a lot because it stays the same even if you write it backward. My name backward is just a nonsense word.

Probably I am very lucky to have a famous and beautiful Mom instead of an ordinary and boring one like everyone else has, but sometimes I don't feel lucky at all. I just feel FED UP to my eyeballs.

Outside the window, the sun had gone to bed and the sky was turning blurry.

"How many hours have we been driving?" I said.

Dad sighed. "A lot. We'll stop soon."

"The adventure is very far away."

"The good ones are." Dad smiled.

At the next exit, he turned off the interstate and I read the sign on the side of the road that said WELCOME TO CHAMBERSBURG.

"Is this where we're stopping?"

"Yeah."

"Is it the place for the adventure?"

"No, but it's getting late," Dad said. "And we need a place to sleep."

We drove by an Arby's and a Burger King and a Taco Bell all in a row and I really hoped that Dad would say something about stopping for dinner but instead he drove a little further and pulled up in the parking lot of a CVS. He checked his phone and typed something into it. Clemesta tugged at my shirt.

"We never spent a night away from Mom before," she said.

I shrugged. "She's on her girl weekend. And anyway I'm

still mad at her so actually it's GOOD LUCK and GOOD NEWS not to have to see her right now."

Clemesta scratched her head. "I guess so."

"I absolutely know so."

I breathed my breath-steam onto the window and made a nose print in the glass. "Did you see that fox in the trees?"

"Where?"

"Over that way, before we took the exit. She waved to me. Like this." I showed her with my arm, pretending it was the fox paw.

"I didn't see anything," Clemesta said.

"Probably it means excellent luck."

"I hope so."

Dad started up the car again and we drove a few minutes more. Then we pulled up outside a hotel called the CHAMBERSBURG COMFORT LODGE and Dad grabbed his duffel bag off the seat.

"Come on," he said.

I took Clemesta and we all went inside a bright and sparkling lobby with a big arrangement of plastic flowers sitting on a table. It was very glamorous, like a ballroom in a movie with very shiny floors and music playing out of the walls.

The woman at the front desk smiled at us.

"Welcome to the Chambersburg," she said, in a loud voice that sounded like she was singing instead of talking.

She had a pretty face with blue glassy eyes like a doll, and her skin was creamy and smooth like it was made from butter. Dad asked if there was a room for two and she said the only available one she had was a JUNIOR SUITE, which she could give us for a special price, since it was already so late.

"To the right and up the elevator to the fourteenth floor," she said. "It's actually the thirteenth floor, but we call it the fourteenth on account of thirteen being unlucky."

"Got it," Dad said, and he took the key which was really a plastic card.

Inside the elevator I pressed the number *14* button and frowned.

"How can you just pretend something is something else?" I said. "It's lying."

Dad shrugged. He looked like all the air was running out of him, like balloons the week after your birthday.

"Is this the end of the adventure?"

"No, Doll."

"That's good."

The elevator opened and we found our room. I was feeling sleepy too, but as soon as Dad opened the door, I jumped WIDE AWAKE.

"It's so fancy," I said. Dad gave my shoulders a squeeze. The room was huge and beautiful and there were a MILLION different wonderful things to explore. Like two giant beds next to each other with a wooden table and a white lamp in between, and an enormous TV and a bathroom that had a hair dryer stuck on the wall and two bars of soap that were wrapped in plastic like tiny presents. There were lots of white towels in all different sizes and also a refrigerator hidden inside a cabinet and a desk with writing paper and a small pencil in a green leather folder in case you needed to write someone an important letter from the CHAMBERSBURG COMFORT LODGE.

But the best part was the real-life bathtub in the middle

of the room, just stuck right there on the carpet opposite the bed. It was a round tub and very deep, and there were lots of nozzles and taps and Dad said those were for different kinds of water to spray you while you soaked. I BEGGED him to have a bath and he rubbed his head and said, "Sure, Dolly, you go ahead."

I jumped up and down and Clemesta squealed and reared up on her horse hind legs and danced her happy dance, which she only does when she is extremely delighted about something. I tied my hair back into a ponytail and I threw off my clothes in split seconds of speediness. Dad was figuring out the knobs and running the water, which could come in either a soft trickle or a great powerful whoosh like a fire hose. There were three little bottles of bubble bath on the side and we poured them in until the tub was full up with foamy white water. I jumped in and grabbed at the bubbles.

"Get in," I said to Dad. "It's so much fun in here, you'll love it."

He looked at me and made a face.

"It's okay," I said. "I won't look at your private parts." That made him laugh.

"Dolly, you are such a great kid," he said.

I did see Dad naked once, coming out of the shower with his PRIVATE PART very pink, and Mom was in the bathroom still and when she came out later her cheeks were very rosy and she was being FLOATING MOM which is when she is so happy and smiley it's as though she is dancing on air and there is music playing that only she can hear. That must have been a long time ago because she hasn't been like that with Dad for a while.

"Come on," I said, "get in!"

Dad shook his head. "You have fun," he said. He sat on the bed and switched on the TV.

I watched him flick through the channels until he found what he was looking for. He took the remote and used it to scratch his back.

I sighed. "Probably he's a little bit shy in front of me," I said to Clemesta. "That's what it is. That's why he isn't playing."

"Grown-ups are ridiculous sometimes," she said.

"Never mind," I said, "I've invented a brilliant fun game."

We used the glass cups from the bathroom and pretended that I was a grown-up lady with creamy-colored skin who worked in an ice-cream parlor that was inside a hotel. There were ONE THOUSAND flavors to choose from and also hundreds of toppings like sprinkles and caramel chunks and M&Ms, but also crazy stuff like snail shell crumble and cockroach confetti. Clemesta had to order and then I scooped up the bubbles and she ate it.

Savannah says we are too old to still be playing games like this, but she was at home in her boring old house in Astoria and I was in the state of Pennsylvania at the CHAMBERSBURG COMFORT LODGE on a private DAD AND DOLLY ADVENTURE so I decided I could do whatever I wanted. Even pee in the water. Clemesta peed too but it wasn't gross or unhygienic because of us being twins and pee being like water anyway. Once I peed into a cup so I could smell it and feel how warm it is when it comes out of your body. Also once I tried to pee standing up but it doesn't work, it only makes a big mess if you have the girl parts.

•   •   •

When the water turned cold, I asked Dad to work the taps for more hot water, even though I was turning into a wrinkly prune from so long in the tub.

"I think it's enough," Dad said.

"Oh." I didn't make a fuss because it's best not to PUSH IT or grown-ups get cranky and use up all their patience and they don't even have a lot to start with, more like a pinch.

Dad handed me the biggest white towel and I stepped out of the tub onto the carpet. My feet left behind two wet puddles. On the bedside clock, the red numbers said 8:46.

"It's very late," I said. "We didn't get any dinner."

Dad rubbed his head. "Yeah."

"I guess we still have some snacks left over from earlier," I said.

I sat on the bed in the bath towel. Dad finished the bag of BBQ beef jerky and I ate the pretzels which cut up the top of my mouth with their salt. I licked my fingers and felt the soft prune wrinkles with my tongue.

"Actually this is better than a regular dinner," I said. "Because this is an adventure BANQUET."

Dad smiled. We passed our last bottle of water back and forth until it was empty. I only backwashed a tiny little bit, but that was an accident.

Dad lay back against the pillows and put a hand on my back. He turned up the volume on the TV to watch the national news and then the local news and then some other news and then a commercial for something that helps you go to the toilet. The man in the commercial laughed a lot and was very happy when he was no longer BACKED UP. He worked as a builder and his friends were happy too, maybe because he didn't hog the restroom anymore. Dad read something on his phone and then set it on the table.

Clemesta yawned and I yawned so wide that my whole mouth dislocated out of my skull.

"Let's get you to bed," Dad said. "It's been a long day."

"Do you have my pajamas?"

Dad looked inside the bag and then pulled out one of my T-shirts.

"You can wear this for tonight."

"Oh." The T-shirt wasn't even one of my favorites and actually it was getting a little tight at the arm parts. "You said you packed everything I needed."

Dad sighed. "I must have forgotten the pajamas." He looked sad, probably because he felt silly for being bad at packing.

I slipped the T-shirt over my head. "It's fine," I said. "I'm not mad."

I looked at the bag.

"But are there toys for me? And my books?"

Dad knocked on his head with his fist and made a kind of groaning sound. "Yeah," he said. "I forgot a bunch of stuff." He stared at the bag on the bed like it was the bag's fault for forgetting.

"Oh," I said. I pulled at the T-shirt so it would cover more of my stomach.

"We'll pick up anything you need tomorrow," Dad said.

"Like toys too?"

"Whatever you need."

"Promise?" I said.

Dad nodded.

"Pinkie promise." I held up my little finger.

Dad looked at me with his BLANK FACE so I had to show him.

"Shake with your little finger," I explained. "That's called a pinkie promise and it's a very strong and UNBREAKABLE FOREVER promise."

"Got it," Dad said. His finger was very big against mine.

I was very, very sleepy and my eyes were already trying to close themselves. I climbed under the covers. The bed was gigantic, like an island made out of a mattress but only for me. Above the bed there was a painting of a man in a field holding a gun. The sky behind him was black and full of clouds. The sheets were pulled tight and felt clean and lovely against me.

Dad lifted the covers of his bed.

"Wait," I said. "You have to tuck me in first or I won't fall asleep."

He came over and held a hand to my cheek. "Haven't done this in a while, have I?" he said.

"Why haven't you?"

Dad tucked the covers up around my arms. "I guess..." he said. "Mom always does it."

"You can do it whenever you want," I said. "It doesn't always have to be Mom. I like it better when you do it, actually."

That wasn't a white lie, it was true. Sometimes Mom is my favorite and sometimes it's Dad, but it was definitely Dad now, because he was being the nicest and most fun and Mom had been SILLY and BAD so she didn't deserve an adventure trip with a sleepover in a Junior Suite with a bathtub in the middle of the floor.

Dad brushed a piece of hair off my forehead. His hand was

warm and smelled like the bubbles from the tub. I breathed in the soapy smell and wished he could keep it there all night long so I could fall asleep with him watching over me.

"Dad," I said. "What if I have the bad dream from last night?" He looked at me and pinched his lips.

"I don't think you will," he said.

"How do you know?"

"Because we're in a different place," Dad said. "The bad dream won't follow you. It's over."

"Well, it was A STUPID one," I said. "And my dream catcher is meant to send all the bad ones away." My dream catcher was a gift from Savannah last year for my birthday when I turned six. She has the same one in her bedroom window but hers is silver and mine is white and blue and probably nicer.

"I bet tonight will be fine," Dad said. "I bet you'll have a good sleep."

"Are you going to bed too?"

"Mm," he said. "I'm exhausted."

I watched as he climbed into the bed next to mine and kicked off some of the covers so his feet could hang off the edge.

"Is your bed the same as mine?"

"Exactly the same."

He sighed and I watched him squeeze his head.

"It's been a long day," he said.

"Ditto," I replied, even though it wasn't exactly right.

I closed my eyes and stroked Clemesta's mane. She smelled of bubbles from the tub, too, sweet and flowery, like spun sugar. I remembered that we hadn't brushed our one hundred strokes of chestnut hair, and I wondered if Dad had packed my hairbrush.

I pulled the covers under my nose.

"Today was the best day," I whispered to Dad. "Wasn't it?" The air-conditioning made a pat-pat-pat sound and the refrigerator sighed.

I heard Dad swallow. "Yeah," he said. "It was a good day."

Sunday

Clemesta and I snapped our eyes open very early. We were all ready to RISE AND SHINE but Dad was still fast asleep in his next-door bed, spread out like a star with one hand covering his eyes.

Probably he needed extra sleep because in the middle of the night he shot up like a bolt of lightning and cried out. Clemesta and I got woken up and I looked at him in the bed and said "DAD!" very loudly to get him out of his bad dream. He was sticky and shivery at the same time and he looked at me with wild eyes like an animal trapped in the forest who has to chew off its own paw to get away. I saw that once on a nature show I wasn't meant to be watching. I think it was a coyote.

Anyway, I said "DAD!" again and he looked at me and wiped his face and took some deep breaths. "Sorry," he said. "Go back to sleep."

I guess dads need dream catchers too, or maybe my bad dream from the other night followed us to Pennsylvania after all.

I stretched my arms and wiped the crusty crumbles from my eyes. Clemesta did the same. Even with the bad dreams, I liked being in next-door beds with Dad because that's another thing that never happened before in my life, except maybe when I was a baby and then I wouldn't remember it anyway. *Hello adventure partner,* I said to him in my head and to Clemesta I said, "I wonder where Dad is taking us today?"

"I don't know." Clemesta frowned. "I wonder where Mom went with Rita."

"I don't care," I said.

There were voices coming from outside and I hopped out of bed to take a look. I tried to open the window but guess what? It was glued shut. Probably some DUM-DUM did it by mistake, like if he spilled that very strong glue that can stick your fingers together FOREVER if you don't use it carefully and responsibly. Dad has the glue in the garage but only he's allowed to touch it and probably I won't be able to until I am at least eighteen years old.

I made a head-note to show Dad the silly glued-shut windows when he woke up, and also to ask him if we ever slept in next-door beds before, and also if he knows that French people eat frogs' legs and think they taste delicious.

I went into the bathroom to use the toilet and decided not to flush in case it woke Dad from his fast-asleep sleep. I opened one of the gift-wrapped soaps and washed my hands. Then I opened a little box that had a sewing kit inside, and two white cotton balls, and a very small nail file. I thought Mom would like the nail file, because she is always painting and unpainting and shaping her nails. Her favorite shade is a dark red polish called *SCANDALOUS,* which is a word that means very naughty and usually secret things.

"Should we be scandalous today?" Mom likes to say, and the answer is always yes.

I pinched the nail file between my fingers and broke it in two. Then I threw it into the trash.

On the bedside table the little black clock said it was 7:11 and that was not yet human time for grown-ups, so the rule is you have to let them keep on sleeping and AMUSE YOURSELF until they are good and ready to wake up. I was feeling thirsty and hungry and probably almost dehydrated, which means you can die soon if you don't drink water URGENTLY. Miss Ellis told us that our bodies want to drink eight glasses of water every day or they won't work properly and our brains will shrivel up and stop being smart. I love my brain very much because it is advanced and full up of useful stuff and it is getting smarter all the time. Miss Ellis says there is NO LIMIT to how much you can fit in there and that's why I try very hard to remember about the water drinking.

I spotted the glasses by the bathtub and filled one with water from the tap.

I gulped everything down and felt the water sinking into my stomach.

Dad was still sleeping. I ran my tongue over my teeth. They felt furry. Doctor Harold would not be pleased that I forgot to brush them last night. He is my dentist and he always tells me about GERRY GERM who likes sweets just as much as kids. He burrows into your teeth making cavities when you don't brush the sugar away TWICE DAILY PLEASE.

Doctor Harold is always happy to see Mom. Probably because she is so pretty and she always wears short skirts or super skinny jeans so you can see what her figure looks like even without taking off all her clothes. She is very beautiful, with her long yellowy hair that she pulls straight every morning and her skinny-lovely figure with bones sticking out in the proper places and her very green eyes the color of shining emeralds and her lips which sit like a perfect red heart on her face. Sometimes she lets me wear her lipstick and then I look a teeny tiny bit like her, but in my secret heart I know that I will never ever be as pretty as she is.

"At least you have good hair," Mom says. I think she is disappointed that I came out looking too much like Dad and not enough like her. She always tries to make me more beautiful, like when she plucks my eyebrows with the metal pincher thing so they aren't one caterpillar line across my face, or when she makes my hair straight with the special hot iron. One day she will take me for a nose repair job to take out the wonky bit but not until I'm sixteen or maybe fifteen. She says that's when girls should start to change their faces.

I walked over to the bed to look at Dad up close. I wondered how long he would stay asleep. His breath had the MORNING MOUTH smell, which is when your breath is stale from being cooped up in your mouth all night long and needs freshening. I stood looking at Dad's eyes for a few minutes more, because sometimes if you stare at someone who is sleeping, they will feel your eyes burning them and wake up.

He stayed asleep.

The carpet under my toes was soft and squishy, not like the one at home which is old and scratchy like Pop's scraggly beard used to feel on my cheek. That carpet is full of stains and in places it is actually coming apart in patches but we can't buy a new one because of the bills.

I wondered if my Vet Rescue game was still set up on the porch at home or if the wind had blown it over. I bet the lion cub was happy it got born. It was probably spending the morning cuddling its lion mom. Lion moms are very nice. They always look after their cubs and they never do selfish and SPITE-FILLED things.

I clicked the remote.

Dad opened his eyes and I turned the volume down to whisper-loud so he wouldn't get disturbed.

"You okay?" he said in his sleepy voice.

"I'm watching TV."

He turned over and pulled the covers up around his ears. I clicked through the channels to get away from all the talking people, and stopped when I found a show about elephants, which are my third-best animals after wolves and then tigers.

Once, when I was playing outside in the yard, a wolf crept up to me and I thought for sure he would want to eat me but instead he whispered in my ear that he was my friend and I should not be afraid of him. He showed me the secret wolf greeting that all wolves and friends of wolves know by heart, which is a sniffing of noses and a tapping of paws and then a nuzzling of ears against each other. He said any time I met another wolf, I should do the greeting and communicate that I am ONE OF THEM and then they will not want to eat me or feel they have to defend themselves. Obviously, I taught it to Clemesta too, and it saved her life one day last year when she went trotting in the woods and came upon a pack of hungry wolves who hadn't eaten anything all winter. Lifesaving is part of twin best-friend duties so it wasn't even a big deal.

Clemesta nodded. "Exactly."

"Of course, my horse."

She kissed my nose and we watched the show, which was explaining how elephants are MAJESTIC AND MARVEL-OUS creatures. They have excellent memories and never forget anything, like which other elephants are their friends and where to find food and the place where their loved ones are buried.

"That's like you," I said to Clemesta.

She never forgets one single thing. That's another of her special powers. I have lots of my own, but I do not have an elephant memory because things like to slip out of my head and disappear forever.

Actually sometimes I also push them out or store them in the NOT NOW box in my brain which is where things go if I don't want to think about them just yet.

Sometimes things also go into my SECRET-SECRET BOX which is a real shoebox that I keep inside a drawer and hidden underneath a pile of my old clothes that Mom keeps meaning to drop off at the thrift store. My secret-secret box is full of actual secrets, which I write down on tiny scraps of paper and then fold ONE MILLION times and then stick back inside the box so that no one will ever find them except for me. It's a very smart invention but right now I'm not thinking about it and no one can make me.

• • •

The show on the elephants finished and I picked up Dad's phone. He has only one game on there for me and I only get to play it on special occasions when he doesn't need to make calls or wait for someone to call him. I saw one message on the screen from someone called Bart who wrote that he wanted to make an offer on the Honda and another one from someone called Diego which said TELL ME WHAT YOU NEED. I clicked it by accident. Then the other messages came up and I saw Mom's name but no new messages from her.

"We could send her a message and say hi," Clemesta said.

"No, I don't want to."

Dad opened his eyes and sat up in the bed. His hair was squashed flat against his scalp in some parts and sticking out like he had an electric shock in others.

"Morning," he said.

"Morning, Dad," I replied. I was very glad that he was awake FINALLY.

"You sleep okay?"

"Yes," I said. "It was a very comfortable bed. Like a cloud or maybe a marshmallow."

He smiled.

"You had a bad dream," I told him.

"Did I?"

"Yeah, but then you went asleep again." I set his phone down. "Are we still going on the adventure today?"

He rubbed his eyes. "Yeah."

I hopped up on the bed and bounce bounce bounced and Dad laughed at me because I was making crazy faces and when I was all bounced out I flopped down.

Dad patted the bed. "Come on," he said. "Let's get dressed."

"Wait," I said. "I have to show you my dancing. Watch."

I did my best ballet hip-hop dance concert and I waited for Dad to clap so I could do a curtsy and an ENCORE BOW.

"Dad!" I said. "Did you like it?" I was out of breath from all the dancing.

"It was great," Dad said.

"Then clap," I said. "And yell ENCORE but loudly so I can do more dancing."

Dad clapped and then he stood up and picked his clothes up off the floor.

"We should probably get some breakfast," he said. He looked at me standing on the carpet waiting to curtsy.

"You didn't do it right," I said. "You never did the encore part."

"Do you like pancakes?" he said.

I flopped onto the bed.

"Yes," I said. "Everyone knows they're my second-best breakfast after French toast."

Dad clicked on the news channel and watched the TV for a few minutes, then he went into the bathroom to take a shower.

While I waited, I did more of my excellent dancing in front of the big mirror which showed my whole body from my head to my toes. I did a pirouette and the hip-hop CHEST POP that Jordan taught me, and also the CAT DADDY one with the arm, arm, circle arms, circle arms, scoot your hips. I'm very good at all the kinds of dancing and I wish with all my heart that I could do real classes, especially since Mom gets to spend LOTS OF MONEY THAT DOESN'T GROW ON TREES for stuff like hair salon visits and new clothes and Pilates classes and new headshot photo shoots and that thing where she comes home with puffy shiny lips or a very stiff face. She says it's different because all that stuff is part of her job and it's not wasting money because it's an important investment in her career of being a FAMOUS STAR. I wish she had a different job, actually, like Sasha's mom the lawyer or Trinity's mom who works at the magazine. Mom calls them both SNOBS and doesn't talk to them when we run into them at the store or the park. She says she doesn't like any of the moms at school, probably because they never invite her to their lunch parties. I think they are jealous of her for being the prettiest mom of all the moms and because all the dads look at her with ridiculous KOWABUNGA eyes popping out of their heads any time she walks by and especially at Halloween. She always dresses up as a nurse or a very sexy cat and then she takes me trick-or-treating in the neighborhood and the dads give me candy and they give her all their attention and that makes her very happy like she's the one with a bag full of treats.

Actually I think the other moms don't like Mom because she can be a SHOW-OFF and a SELFISH BITCH sometimes. Dad called her that before, but she deserved it because of her BAD BEHAVIOR. A lot of her behavior is bad, like when she has a bunch of CAN'T GET OUT OF BED days and she just lies around crying and staring at the walls. Or other stuff that's EVEN WORSE.

I did twenty jumping jacks for my fitness and then one more dance routine with a little tap-tap footwork and I sang:

YOU KNOW WHO is a stupid head, I wish wish wish he was good and DEAD.

Clemesta opened her mouth to say something but then Dad came out of the shower in his towel. His chest was wet and all the hair was stuck down and his belly was poking out over the top. That's called LETTING YOURSELF GO and Mom says it's a very bad thing.

Dad pulled out clean clothes and handed me a pair of my leggings and a long-sleeved shirt with red stripes that makes me look like a candy cane. Sometimes I lick my arm when I'm wearing it but I still taste like a person.

"I love this one," I said. "That was a good one to pack."

"I'm glad," Dad said.

"Did you remember my toothbrush?" I said. Dad pulled it out of the bag, along with a tube of Crest.

"Actually I wish you forgot this. Then I could get a new one. Because the spikes on this are very old. Like one hundred years."

Dad peeked out the window. "We can pick up a new one."

"Do you have my hairbrush?"

"Uh, I couldn't find that."

I shrugged. "Sometimes I forget to put it away. I can buy another one."

I went to brush my teeth, and fix my hair. I used my fingers like a comb and then I tied it in a ponytail and then I made it loose again.

When I came out of the bathroom, Dad was still peeking out the window at the cars below. He looked at his phone and slipped it into his pocket.

"Let's go," he said.

Downstairs at the front desk, the creamy-faced lady asked if we had enjoyed our stay.

"It was scrumptious," I said, and she gave me a big smile.

Dad forgot to say goodbye and thank you, SILLY DAD.

"He has bad manners," Clemesta said.

"He just forgot," I said. "Sometimes grown-ups have A SIEVE in their heads and it lets out all the things they are meant to remember. Probably it's a side-effect of the stress disease."

Dad pulled out of the parking lot and drove down the main street. It was funny-looking, like an olden-day town from the movies and not like anything at home. Dad said I should keep my eyes peeled for a diner so when I saw a sign for The Hop Inn I yelled STOP. There was an American flag at the entrance, next to a garden gnome with a red hat who was busy cooking pancakes. They weren't the real ones for people to eat, they were the ones for gnomes. Inside they cooked the ones for people.

We chose a booth at the window so we could look out onto the street. I gave Clemesta the best view, because she likes to watch people and also look out for any IMPENDING DANGER so she can warn me and keep me safe. She usually does a very excellent job of it too.

The waitress came over to our table and handed us each a menu. Her name was BETHANY and she had hair the color of ketchup and a pretty bracelet made of tiny white shells and she smelled of strawberry perfume. I liked that she gave me my own menu, instead of thinking I was a baby who needed someone else to read to me. Probably she could tell I had an advanced and watery brain.

"You visiting?" she said.

"We're on an adventure," I told her.

"An adventure?" she said. "Well, you're a very lucky lady."

I gave Dad a big smile so he would know how happy I was to be on our trip. He was reading the menu and he didn't see.

Bethany poured him a mug of coffee from her silver pot and took our orders for TWO HOUSE SPECIALS which were pancakes made from buttermilk and full of chocolate chips.

"Good choice," Bethany said.

Dad took his phone out of his pocket to look at a map. He kept making it bigger and bigger with his fingers, which is actually easy to do once you know how. Mom lets me play on her phone when we are on TOP SECRET trips to Manhattan. She doesn't usually like me messing with it but on those days she lets me do whatever I want until it's home time. That's called BRIBERY and it means I get something nice in exchange for keeping my mouth SHUT UP and the secret inside the secret-secret box.

"We're co-conspirators, Dolly, aren't we?" Mom says. We pinkie promise and Mom giggles. "Naughty us!"

I don't like being naughty but Mom doesn't even care and that's another reason why she gets the name *SELFISH BITCH*.

Dad was concentrating on the map but I couldn't see much. I dipped my finger in the sugar and licked off the white dust. Dad started looking at the news on his phone, scrolling through all the words very quickly.

"Where are we headed?" I said.

"You'll see."

"But where, though?"

"Um, Virginia."

"But that's another whole state!"

"Yeah. Because this is a real adventure. We aren't just going across the street."

I was very excited and I jiggled in my seat and looked around at the other people who were for sure not having an adventure. Dad drank his coffee but it wasn't making him perky like it's meant to. He still looked very sleepy, actually.

Bethany came over with two plates piled high with pancakes and two small silver jugs of maple syrup balanced in her hands.

"You're very good at balancing," I said. "How did you learn to do it?"

Bethany made a funny snorting sound with her mouth. "Well, darlin'," she said, "I've been doing this twenty goddamn years is how."

"That's nice," I said, but she wasn't smiling when she walked away.

"Virginia," Clemesta said. "That's very far."

"Yes," I told her. "It's the adventure."

She scowled. "Why can't we have an adventure closer to home? Like Long Island."

"Because that's obviously not the best place. Here, have some pancakes."

Clemesta shook her head. "I'm watching my figure." I smushed the syrup with the whipped butter and made a special sauce. The pancakes were delicious.

Dad was gobbling his down in big mouthfuls and he was finished before me. He drank more coffee.

I tried to eat delicately LIKE A LADY with my mouth shut like Mom always reminds me. If she was here I wouldn't be allowed to eat pancakes at all because she is obsessed with healthy food and she doesn't like me to eat anything that will make me fat. She is already CONCERNED ABOUT MY SHAPE, because I am not skinny-small like she is, I am wobbly-soft like a marshmallow. She says there is an EPIDEMIC OF CHILDHOOD OBESITY in this country and no one picks the fat kid in life, which means you will always be sad and alone. I don't want that to happen. I want to be like Mom, who will never be alone because of how pretty she is.

I would like to be less squishy but it's very hard to always watch my diet and skip dessert and say no to candy treats that the other kids can eat whenever they want. In the bath, my belly makes three smaller bellies and my thighs are ON THE LARGE SIDE. Clemesta says it doesn't matter and it's better to be a kind-hearted marshmallow than a string bean with a lump of black coal for a heart. Mom says all it takes is DISCIPLINE, like when I brought home a cookie that I specially baked at school for her Mother's Day treat and she shook her head and said, "Really, Dolly, you know I don't eat any sugar." She threw the cookie straight into the trash and I tried not to cry with my broken feelings. Later, when she was taking a bath, I fished it out and ate it myself. It was sweet and chewy and delicious.

Mom spends a lot of time working on staying pretty but I didn't get her same discipline, like I didn't get her figure or her hair. There are some days when Mom forgets her discipline too, usually on the CAN'T GET OUT OF BED days but sometimes also on the BEST MOM days when she says, "To hell with it all" and spends the whole day making the house spotless and cooking big dishes of her world-famous macaroni for us to eat on the rug with no plates just forks. She wears sweatpants and no makeup and we're allowed to bake on those days, because Mom doesn't hate sugar anymore, and we make cupcakes, which I decorate with frosting and sprinkles, and Mom says, "Isn't this the best?" and I say, "You bet," and we lick the runaway frosting from our lips.

Sometimes on those days Mom will look at me and stroke my cheek and say, "Dolly, I think being your mom is the best job in the world." That makes my heart want to explode and I always say a wish for Mom to stay BEST MOM forever. But she never does.

Right now she is WORST MOM. WORST MOM is the opposite of Best Mom and she should be fired from her job of Mom or punished VERY STRONGLY. That's not being kind but sometimes it's okay if you take a break from kindness for a short while and go back to it later when you're ready and the other person has learned all their lessons. Like after a TIME-OUT when you come back into the room with sorry in your eyes and REPENTANCE in your heart.

I stabbed my fork into the last pancake on my plate.

"Do not make me fat," I told it. I stabbed it again and then put it in my mouth.

Bethany brought over her coffeepot and refilled Dad's mug AGAIN. He was drinking coffee like it was water and he needed eight glasses for his brain.

"How was that?" Bethany said.

"Delectable," I said.

She smiled at me and I saw that she had those special dimple-holes in her cheeks that I wish I had and sometimes try to make by pushing my fingers deep into the skin until they leave a mark. They always disappear again unless you're born with them but only very lucky people get that. They get to stay adorable forever, not just until they turn seven when suddenly everybody says you are old enough to understand EVERYTHING and also please STOP BEING A BABY.

Dad asked Bethany for the check and forgot the magic *please* and *thank you* words AGAIN.

Clemesta rolled her eyes. "It isn't that hard to remember."

"Yeah, he wouldn't get any gold stars on his chart for manners. Probably only one for driving," I said.

When we walked back out to the car, Dad forgot to hold my hand but I didn't remind him because my hands were greasy from the maple syrup and I didn't want him telling me to go wash up. The pancake gnome tipped his hat as we passed him. He told me that his name was Gerhard and he came from Germany on a ship.

"Auf Wiedersehen," I said.

I learned that from a movie.

Dad stopped by an ATM that was not far from the car, and I watched him fold more bills into his pocket. Clemesta made her eyes big and I shrugged. "Maybe we're actually very rich."

Before Dad drove off, I made Clemesta comfortable in the back with her head looking out the window.

"Did we win the lottery?" I said.

"What?"

"Yesterday was Saturday. Did we have the lucky ticket?"

Dad shook his head. "I never got one."

"But you keep getting piles of money from the ATM. I thought you won."

Dad laughed. "No, sweetheart."

"Oh. Well, I hope yesterday wasn't our very lucky day and we missed it."

Dad buys his FINGERS CROSSED WINNING TICKET from Mr. Abdul every Saturday. We always choose the same numbers and we kiss the card and make a shopping list for when we win. If Dad's treated me to a candy bar I have to finish it before we get back home so Mom won't get mad. Sometimes I choose a fifty-cent toy from the machine instead because toys can't make you fat. Mom says lottery tickets are a waste of money but she wastes way more money all the time. Besides, when Dad wins then she won't have one single more thing to complain about and she won't be able to yell at Dad to BE A GODDAMN MAN and she won't have any reason to be a WORST MOM.

A good trick for when Mom is being WORST MOM is the vanishing trick. I shut my eyes and Mom goes away and then I say, "Now you are gone and I am somewhere else, and you will miss me and cry and be mad at yourself for making me go away."

"Maybe Mom vanished from us this time," Clemesta said. "She had a bag packed. Remember, we found it hidden in the back of the closet?"

"That was for the girl weekend with Rita."

Clemesta made a face. "Are you sure?"

"Yes. Surely sure."

Dad tapped his phone so he could hear the lady tell him where to turn. Her voice was very friendly and I bet she was pretty.

"Are we driving all day again?"

Dad looked at me.

"Because that isn't so much fun." I bit my lip. I didn't want Dad to get mad or think I was ungrateful.

"What about we do the shopping trip?" Dad said. "That will be fun."

"Yeah." I looked out the window. Everywhere felt empty of houses and people, not like back home where you are always knocking into someone. Some of them don't even say sorry.

"Where is everybody?" I said.

Clemesta shrugged. "Maybe they left."

"To go where?"

"I don't know. Mexico. Or across the oceans."

"I like our ocean," I said.

"Me too."

"It's called the North Atlantic."

"I know. I remember Miss Ellis teaching us."

"The other side of the country gets the Pacific Ocean. It's warmer for swimming, but we have much friendlier sea creatures."

Clemesta nodded. "The other side of the country is where YOU KNOW WHO lives. In Los Angeles."

"Do NOT say his name," I said. "It makes me want to throw up my guts."

• • •

I folded my arms and looked at Dad. He has dark hair like me, apart from the middle bit on top which likes to hide in the drain of our shower. I always feel sad looking at that part of Dad. And sometimes I just feel sad looking at Dad PERIOD, because once upon another time he was smiling all the time, and now he mostly never does. I saw a video once from when Dad lived in Florida and worked as a Mortgage Broker. I don't know what job that is, but Mom says it was much better than the one at VALUE MOTORS. She calls this one BENEATH HIM and HUMILIATING, whatever that means. Anyway, in the video, Dad was laughing a lot and smiling and making a CHAMPAGNE POPPING TOAST, and he was looking very shiny and fancy, and Uncle Joshua was there, and Mom was next to him in a beautiful floaty red dress and they were having a party on a yacht with all their friends and everyone looked very, very happy, like they were in a movie or a reality TV show.

Dad and Mom don't look like that anymore, and Uncle Joshua doesn't look like anything because he's dead. Actually Dad's whole family is dead and that's a shame because it means I don't get so many gifts at Christmas and for my birthday. Probably if they were alive I would already have the jewelry box and a Lego Grand Hotel, which Savannah got in the mail from her uncle Richie.

I picked at the skin around my nails. Mom says that's a bad and unhygienic habit, like nail biting and nose picking. Sometimes I don't care, or I forget. Clemesta bites her hoof-nails too, but only when she is an EXCESSIVE BUNDLE OF

NERVES. Probably she should take those same little white pills that Mom eats after breakfast.

I touched my loose tooth again and tasted the leftover syrup that was sticking to my fingers.

Dad took the next right turn off the ramp and pulled up in the parking lot of a Walmart. As we climbed out of the Jeep, an ambulance came screeching by and stopped right behind us. Two men burst out of the back and vanished into the alleyway behind the store.

"I wonder who they're coming to rescue?" I said. "Maybe it's another lion mom with a cub stuck in her belly."

Dad squeezed my hand.

Inside, the Walmart was as big as a whole city and very bright like you were standing in the sun.

"Pick out whatever you need," Dad said.

"Just stuff for today?"

"A couple of days," Dad said.

"And toys?"

"Anything you want. Go wild."

I looked around the aisles but actually there was hardly anything to pick out. The store was full of big red signs saying HALF OFF and STORE CLOSING SALE and REDUCED TO CLEAR, and a lot of the shelves were empty.

Dad went off to find the things he forgot to pack for himself, and I picked through the girls' clothes. I found a purple ballet tutu and pulled it over my head. I couldn't find a mirror to see what I looked like. I lifted it off and went to get everything else I needed. I walked up and down, up and down, looking at the empty shelves. Soon the whole store would be cleared out and you wouldn't be able to buy anything at all.

I passed the aisle with books and magazines. A man in a big green coat stood holding a magazine called CONCEALED CARRY. There was a gun on the cover and he closed his eyes and rubbed it against his jeans, right by his PRIVATE PARTS. I ran down the aisle away from him. I wished Dad hadn't left me alone.

I found more clothes and picked out underwear and a pair of white shorts and a dress with flamingos on it and white shoes that were like fancy grown-up pointy pumps and spotty purple pajamas that said *NIGHT NIGHT* on the pocket. I found a small flashlight for emergencies and added it to the pile. In the toy section I found a box of colored pencils and a blank notepad for drawing and a pink comb for Clemesta's hair, and a new toothbrush for me with a glitter handle and a hairbrush for keeping my hair IMPECCABLE, and a box of chalk sticks for writing on the ground because I always wanted to try those out.

I did not want to be a SPOILED BRAT like Lina in my class who gets whatever she wants from her Mom and also $200 every week for her allowance. Maybe it's only $200 every month, but she is still a brat and a show-off and once I made her cry when I said her new sneakers were stupid. It was only because inside my heart I was feeling jealous. I never get brand-new sneakers, only hand-me-downs from our neighbor Caleigh who is eight and growing out of all her clothes. Her mom bundles everything up and gives it to Mom. She hands it to me and says, "See? Now you have everything you need," and then the next day she comes home with bags full of new clothes for herself, even though her closet is already FULL UP with sparkling beautiful dresses hanging in plastic to keep them fresh. Those are the clothes she wore in Florida when she went to parties all the time but now Dad and her don't go anywhere fancy, so the dresses just stay in the closet. She brings them out on CAN'T GET OUT OF BED DAYS because she likes to put one on to cry in.

Actually Mom shops a lot for new clothes but most of the time she returns them after she's unpacked them and tried them on and snapped a photo in them and pretended they are hers. Some stores won't take the clothes back and then she has to hide them from Dad so he won't get mad at her for being so *IRRESPONSIBLE* and *DELUSIONAL*. Those are bad words too, and her clothes are another secret I have to keep in the secret-secret box.

Anyway, I was very responsible and I stopped putting things in the basket. I went to find Dad, who was waiting for me at the start of the checkout line.

"I'm all done," I said.

He had grabbed stuff for himself, like a stick of deodorant and a pack of navy blue boxer shorts and a plaid shirt.

"You could have packed those at home," I said. "Then we wouldn't have to buy all new stuff."

Dad rubbed his face with his hand like he wanted to wipe away invisible dirt.

"I could have packed for both of us," I said. "I'm good at making lists and then I could have ticked it off and that would have been very EFFICIENT."

• • •

The checkout lady said hello and I saw that she was missing two of her front teeth.

Dad loaded everything onto the counter. It was a huge pile.

"We're on an adventure," I said, in case she was wondering why we needed so much new stuff or thinking we were spoiled brats instead of regular nice people.

Dad grabbed a six-pack of water, a box of mints, and a pack of headache tablets. He paid for everything with bills he pulled from his jeans. The checkout lady yawned and I saw that she had some of her back teeth missing from her mouth too. I bet Gerry Germ ate all of them. He can be a real greedy guts sometimes. Probably Gerry Germ is also obese.

At the car, Dad set the bags in the trunk.

"Now what do we do?" I said.

"Now we drive," Dad said.

"Oh. For how long?"

"A while."

"Do we have far to go?"

"Kinda."

"That's good. I like being away from home. And from Mom."

Dad didn't say anything. He shut the trunk and got behind the wheel.

We went LEFT RIGHT LEFT out of the parking lot and then we were back on Mr. Interstate 81, heading south.

I laid my head back to watch out the window. I read a sign that said MARYLAND WELCOMES YOU and then another one that said WELCOME TO WEST VIRGINIA and that was two more states ticked off our list. It was a sunny and blue-sky beautiful day, and there were trees all the way along, nothing but trees. And not just a few browny-turning-a-little-green trees like the ones on our street at home, but extra-green trees and purple blossom trees and orangey-fiery trees all showing off their spring colors. I opened the window because fresh air is good for you and I wanted to suck it all up into my lungs.

"I'm glad we aren't home today," I said. "It's so stinky there."

That's only half-true. Our house is very lovely actually. It has lots of different rooms and a basement and a yard and a bunch of hiding places and my bedroom, which has all my stuff inside, like my craft projects and my closet full of clothes and my dream catcher on the window and my Legos for building and my doll's house on the floor, and a pretend microphone for playing AMERICA'S GOT TALENT which is Mom's favorite game since she likes singing and winning talent shows. She likes to be the BEST and she even has a whole list of sentences printed out on a page and stuck to the mirror in her closet which she says out loud every day to make her life perfect. Like "I am beautiful and talented" and "I have money, power, and joy in abundance" and "I am a successful actress." Probably it's stuck up but maybe it's helping. Like the other things she says aloud to practice sounding fancy and to make sure her Queens accent STAYS AWAY. Otherwise it might ruin her chances for parts.

Our house is actually the exact same house that Mom grew up in when she was a little girl like me. She spent her whole life there until she graduated from high school and moved to Hollywood to be a star and then moved to Florida to be a wife. After Dad's mortgage company went BANG and she got me in her belly, she and Dad moved back to Queens to live with Pop, who is Mom's dad. Pop's friend Tommy Marsden found Dad the job at VALUE MOTORS which was only meant to be until he got BACK ON HIS FEET but now it's his forever job.

Mom says she didn't want to move back to where she started because she always said OVER MY DEAD BODY would she live in Queens again. She liked living in their fancy beautiful house in Florida with a pool and a cleaning lady and a whole closet full of beautiful clothes. She liked their Florida friends and their Florida parties and she liked taking trips to Italy in the summer and trips to Aspen in the winter, and most of all she liked Dad because he was very successful and happy and rich, and she says that's what he was always destined to be because he worked so hard and ROSE FROM NOTHING and that's what being a real winner is all about.

Sometimes Mom gets so mad about living in her old house again that she throws things against the wall or slams doors or just bursts into pools of tears for no reason.

"It's a nice house," I say, but she just sobs.

Some days after she picks me up from school, we walk down to Socrates Park, which is on the water. Mom stands at the edge looking across at Manhattan on the other side and her eyes get misty.

"I'm always in the wrong place, Dolly. My whole life I've been stuck here and there's no way out."

I don't know what to say to that.

I feel very heavy when I think about everything going wrong, like a bad magic spell that makes a curse on your whole life. Mom hated living with Pop and said he was a mean old bastard. Probably because he was mad at her. He wanted her to be full of brains and a doctor or a lawyer, but instead she was just beautiful. He always looked at her and shook his head and said something in a sad voice in his strange Bulgarian language. Everything sounds sad in Bulgarian, but he was extra upset with her for disappointing him.

I didn't mind living with Pop. He never did much except sit in front of the TV all day and drink beer and make bad smells, but if you stayed out of his way it wasn't so bad. The only times he made me really mad was when he said he hoped I didn't get Mom's birdbrains and also when he said STOP TALKING TO THAT STUPID HORSE, CHILD. After that, Clemesta put a curse on him and soon after he went to the old people's home with the disease that eats your brain and six months after that he died and now he is in the ground at the cemetery next to Mom's mom, who was Grandma, who died before I was even born.

We visit them sometimes and bring white peonies for Grandma because she loved those the best when she was alive. We don't bring anything for Pop because probably you can't bring dead people beer.

Outside the window I could see ONE MILLION American flags. They were everywhere, stuck in the ground and flying from poles and painted onto buildings to remind people which country they were in. Clemesta and I made up a counting game to pass the time. You had to yell FLAG! when you spotted a flag and you got extra points if it was a particularly giant one or if it was two flags next to each other.

We counted thirty-two flags and that was just in one hour of the clock. Dad wasn't playing along even though I explained the rules VERY CLEARLY.

We passed a long stretch of trees and I could see apples hanging from the branches.

"Red apples are my second-best kind of apple," I said. "My first-best is green because they make your mouth go juicy from the sour. Green apples are called Granny Smiths because she's the lady who grows them. Look," I said, "like this. Look at my face. It goes juicy if I just think about green apples."

Dad looked at me and then back at the road. He was VERY FOCUSED so he couldn't tell me about his best apples.

We passed by a row of houses, and some of them were fancy like from a TV show where a big family lives inside one house and laughs a lot, but others looked like they were falling apart with broken front steps and smashed windows. None of the houses looked like the ones back home.

I waved to some of the horses and cows but Clemesta HATES other horses so she would only greet the cows and the dogs. She says that other horses don't believe she is a magical horse queen. They think she's just making up silly stories and they tease her and that's why she hates them and won't even say hello.

"Dad!" I said. "I'm so bored I might crack." I was using my whining voice even though nobody likes a whiner. I couldn't even help it. "My legs need stretching. My neck is stiff from staring out the window the whole time." I kicked my legs to shake them out. They had needles and pins stuck in them.

"Actually my bones are stretching again. That means a growing spurt. I bet I'm going to be really tall like Mom." I closed my eyes to make that into a wish. *Tall and beautiful,* I said in my WISHING VOICE. That's the voice that stays in your head so you can hear it but no one else can, because if you say a wish out loud it gets JINXED and then it won't come true. *Tall and beautiful, tall and beautiful,* I said. That would make Mom happy and then she wouldn't have to do the other stuff.

I stared at Dad's head, which wasn't moving. I sighed and folded my arms and sighed again. "You said this was supposed to be fun."

Dad rubbed his eyes and checked the time.

"Sorry, Doll," he said. "You're right. We should have some fun."

"Yeah."

"I'll pull over soon as I can. We'll find somewhere."

"Somewhere fun."

"Yeah."

Clemesta and I went back to flag counting to pass the time.

Flags are PATRIOTIC and that means everyone loves America a whole lot, like Pop who always said AMERICA IS THE GREATEST NATION IN THE WORLD. He and Grandma came to America because where they were from was full of bad guys who kicked Pop's Dad out of his big house and took away all his money and stole his job and left him with NOTHING, not even the watch on his wrist. When Pop was twenty-five years old, he met Grandma at the movies and said, "I love you, let's go to America," and they saved up all the money they could find until they had just enough to leave.

In America, Pop worked in a bakery even though he was actually a very brilliant engineer. He learned English and he drank a bottle of Coca-Cola each morning with his breakfast. Every day he kissed the ground because he was so happy not to live in Bulgaria anymore. Probably he ended up with mouse droppings in his mouth but he didn't care.

Dad kept looking out his window but we weren't passing by anything except flags and churches, flags and churches. Clemesta and I made a new game out of reading all the church names very quickly as we zoomed by.

ACTORS FOR CHRIST.

CHURCH OF GOD: SERPENT-HANDLING.

HIS FAMILY SAVIOR GOSPEL.

If you didn't get all the words you couldn't get any points.

I was winning but Clemesta wasn't mad because she isn't ever a SORE LOSER.

Dad pulled up at a gas station. It was called LIBERTY and there was a flag hanging out front. The roof was painted to look like the flag too.

"That's two points," I told Clemesta. "But I'll share them with you so it's one each."

"Dolly, your heart is an ocean of kindness," she said.

"Yes, it's for Kindness Week," I said.

The parking lot was big and empty. Part of it was for trucks but there weren't any around. On the other side, there was a diner but it didn't look like anyone was inside.

"Why are we stopping here?" I asked.

Dad popped the trunk and scratched through our Walmart bags. "Well, there's nothing around here for miles, so—"

He pulled out my brand-new chalk sticks and held up the box. "We'll make our own fun, for now."

I followed him with my eyes and then also my feet. He walked across the parking lot and then bent to the ground and started drawing with the chalk.

"You're making hopscotch!" I said. "I love hopscotch."

"So, go ahead," Dad said. "Let's see you."

I hop hopped wobbled hopped and Dad watched and then I went back the other way and he took out his phone to read something.

"Why are you checking the news the whole time?"

"I don't know. In case anything happened."

"Like what?"

Dad shrugged.

"Probably something bad," I said. I hopped twice more with wobbles and once without and then I stopped. "It's your turn."

I watched Dad jump and he almost fell over and then he made himself straight again with his hands. "You're better than me," I said. "But I'm faster. Let's make another game. Like an obstacle course. You have to, um. Make symbols. And each one is different and I have to do the right move. Like a circle is a jumping jack and a star is a twirl. No, probably that should be the other way around."

Dad bent down and made some marks with the chalk. He wiped his hands against his jeans and squinted against the sun. He was sweating through his shirt at the armpits and over his back. I bent down and drew a heart with the pink chalk. That was for a pirouette, because I love ballet so much. I wiped my forehead which was also feeling sticky and then I made up moves for all the rest of the drawings. I did a frog jump onto an X. The gravel nipped at my hand when I landed and the game ended.

"Now let's race," I said. "Draw a start line and a finish line and then we say READY SET GO and race. Probably I'll be faster than you."

Dad drew the lines and I retied my laces. When I stood up my head was spinning.

We did three races and I won two and Dad lifted me up in his arms and danced me around and said I was a champion. I put my hands on his head and covered his eyeballs.

"I wish we could have fun days like this every day," I said. Dad set me down very gently on the ground.

"Me too, Doll. Me too."

"Why can't we, then?" Dad rubbed his face on his sleeve to mop up the sweat. "I don't know. Too much work. Too much..." He shook his head. "Sometimes dads aren't too smart."

"You are smart!" I said. "The smartest. Like me."

Dad laughed. "Wanna grab an ice cream?" he said.

"For lunch?" I snickered behind my hands because Mom would be so mad at us for all this MISCHIEF.

Dad collected up all the chalk pieces and slipped them back in the box. I picked up Clemesta, who had been waiting on the curb.

Inside the store, there was a man wearing shorts and he had one real leg and one robot leg made from metal. He was paying for beer at the counter.

"Don't stare," Dad whispered.

"What happened to him?"

"He must have gotten hurt."

"How?"

"I don't know."

"I think his leg was eaten by a shark. They like leg meat."

I picked an Oreo ice cream out of the freezer and Dad chose a popsicle. By the time we got to the counter, the one-leg man was gone. The lady behind the counter gave Dad back his change and said, "Have a nice day."

"Thank you," I told her, but Dad didn't say anything.

I leaned in close as we walked back to the car. "You didn't say *thank you*. You keep forgetting to say it."

Dad frowned, and then nodded. "You're right," he said. "I keep forgetting."

"Why do you keep forgetting?"

"I have a lot on my mind, I guess."

"Me too," I said. "My mind is full of stuff, like questions and information FACTS and the times tables and spelling for the hard words and a bunch of other stuff too."

"But you always remember your manners."

"Yeah, my brain is advanced, probably that's why."

Dad shook his head and smiled at me and his eyes were full of MILLIONS OF LOVE-HEARTS just for me. My ice cream was running and I tried to lick it all up.

Dad and I sat on a patch of spiky grass near the Jeep.

"What happens to that checkout lady when the Walmart closes?" I said.

Dad shrugged. "She loses her job, I guess."

"Like when you lost yours."

"Right."

"But you found another one. So she will too."

"Maybe," Dad said. "I hope so." He looked at the tires of the Jeep.

It wasn't Dad's fault that he lost his job and his whole entire company. It was the fault of the big crash that made everything fall apart. MILLIONS of people lost their jobs and their savings and their houses, and everyone was sad for ten years. Mom says that's called HARD LUCK but she says you have to make your own luck in life and that's why she goes to every single casting because you never know and this country is built on lucky breaks. I hope Dad gets another one soon. Then he'll cheer up and he won't just come home from work and turn on the TV and be too tired to play with me.

"Look, that cloud is the shape of a diplodocus," I said. Dad looked up.

"Diplodocus is my third-best dinosaur, after Velociraptor and Dilophosaurus. Everyone says Tyrannosaurus Rex is their best but actually they were very dumb and their brains were tiny like peas and even smaller than their tiny hands."

Dad smiled. He scrunched up his popsicle wrapper into a tight ball. I licked my mouth all around with my tongue to get out all the flavor. Dad had gone quiet.

"This is so much fun," I said. I scowled. "Mom didn't even call yet to speak to me," I said. "She doesn't care. She doesn't miss me. She only cares about having her own fun AS USUAL."

"That's not true, Doll," Dad said. His voice was heavy and his eyes looked at me with their sad spilling out.

"She's just…enjoying some time with Rita this weekend. Sometimes…sometimes moms need a break."

"From what?"

"From…well, probably from me."

"Well, she hurt my feelings. And she makes me mad sometimes. A lot, actually."

Dad sighed. He scrunched the wrapper some more in his knuckles and then he stood up and stretched his arms over his head. His shirt lifted up and I could see his hairy bear belly underneath.

"Stay away, Mr. Bear," I warned.

"Come on," Dad said. "Time to get back on the road."

"Are we still going to the place?"

"You bet."

"That's good."

We climbed back inside the car and Dad set his phone on the console. My shirt was damp and I lifted it off my skin.

"Can you turn on the air-conditioning?" I said. "I'm melting into a puddle."

Dad turned up the dial, and we drove off.

Clemesta and I went back to looking out the window for a stretch, while Dad listened to the radio and the Jeep ate up the road. It never ran out.

"What time is it now?" I asked Dad. It felt like hundreds of hours had passed.

"Two forty-five."

"How much longer to go?"

"A while," Dad said.

"But how long till we stop again?"

Dad sighed. "I don't know. A while."

"Like minutes or hours?"

Dad put his hand to his forehead. "Jesus, Dolly, I don't know. Later. Stop nagging, will you?" He switched the radio up so it was too loud to talk.

I clamped my mouth shut and sewed up my lips with invisible thread.

"He's trying to stay focused," I told Clemesta. "We can't bug him." I sat very still but Clemesta fidgeted.

"Dolly," she said. "I have the worried-feeling in my horse stomach."

"Why?"

"I think it's all that stuff with YOU KNOW WHO."

"I don't remember anything," I said.

She bit her lip. "I think I do."

"Well, I want to forget everything about him. He has the ugliest heart in the world and I wish it would stop in his chest and make him die on the spot before anyone could call an ambulance to save him. He is the WORST person in the world and that isn't EXAGGERATING it's very, very true."

Clemesta nodded. "I know."

I made a face. "I bet he's covered in warts all over his body."

"I bet he has lice, and DIABETES."

"What's that one, again?"

"It's when your blood turns into sugar and you have to get injections every day."

I looked at Dad's nice head and tiny-bit balding hair. YOU KNOW WHO has silver hair and a lot of it. He always wears a black suit and fruity aftershave and a gold watch, and Mom looks at him like he is the best thing she has ever seen.

"That, Dolly, that's the kind of man your dad used to be."

Well, WHO CARES, because Dad is more handsome and delightful than YOU KNOW WHO, even when he's being silent and a tiny bit grouchy.

I watched him as he floated his arm out the window to feel the breeze on his skin. The hairs went goosey and prickled up. I opened the window in the back and did the same, and the sun made a block of light on my arm.

HOLY FATHER.

CRACKER BARREL.

SALVATION METHODIST. ALL WELCOME.

BEST DANG FRIED CHICKEN.

I yawned.

Dad changed radio stations. We drove by a truck carrying a whole row of new houses, all ready to be planted in the ground like spring flowers. "That means you can move any time you like and your house always goes with you," I said. "Like a snail or a turtle."

"Or a periwinkle," Clemesta said.

"You are the REMEMBERING QUEEN," I said. "But you shouldn't become a show-off."

We did more and more driving. I made faces out the window but no one was paying attention. In the mirror, I made faces too, so Dad would look up. I put my fingers up my nose and pulled them out again. One had a slimy booger on it and I wiped it under the seat.

"No one will find it," Clemesta said. "So it isn't gross."

I set her on my lap and braided her mane to pass the time. I tried to do my hair too, but the pieces kept falling out. I tried not to get upset at my INCOMPETENCE.

• • •

I leaned forward to talk in Dad's ear.

"I'm not nagging, I'm just saying hi," I said.

Dad smiled. "I'm sorry, Dolly," he said. "I'm a little preoccupied today."

"It's okay," I said. "I can zip it and throw away the key and not bother you."

"You don't have to do that." I looked down his collar at the black hairs poking out. They were curly and damp and I wanted to pet them like fur.

"Where are we sleeping tonight?"

"We'll find something," Dad said.

"Something lovely. Like with a Jacuzzi instead of a tub. And a bed in the shape of a heart, with velvet walls. And remote-control drapes."

"Mm."

"Another word for *drapes* is *curtains*."

"Mm."

I shut up my mouth again.

Outside, the sky with its shadowy colors was warning us that it would soon be night again, which meant TWO NIGHTS away from home. I was happy to have a new hairbrush and new pajamas, and actually a whole bag of new stuff just for me. I rubbed my eyes. All the sign reading was making them tired and blurry. I probably need glasses like that girl Farrah in my class but whenever I tell Mom about my fuzzy eyes she says, "Oh no, we don't want you to be a four-eyes, Dolly."

She hasn't taken me for the eye exam yet even though Miss Ellis said it was RECOMMENDED. Probably it's because Mom thinks smart isn't everything you need to be in the world, so she doesn't mind if I can't read the board without going squinty.

Dad took a turn and then another one, and then we were driving through a very empty-looking town, with the mountain behind it and the streets quiet like everyone was already asleep in their beds.

"Where are we?"

"It's called Clifton Forge," Dad said. "We'll sleep here tonight."

"Clifton Forge," I said. It sounded mysterious and magical. Dad told me that a forge was a special fire that could burn hot enough to bend metal.

"Will we get to see the fire?"

"I'm not sure," Dad said. "It might only be something they did a long time ago."

We drove in the almost-dark and pulled up outside a house that was actually a hotel, called THE RED CARRIAGE INN. Dad left me in the car while he went inside to see if they had any room for us.

I didn't like being alone in the car in the night, but Clemesta was keeping extra-special guard to protect us. I lifted her up and gave her a kiss.

"Don't distract me," she said. "I'm keeping watch."

"Oh, sorry." I set her back down.

"Dolly," she said. "Aren't you worried? We are very far from home."

"Yes but we're with Dad," I said. "You can go anywhere with a dad or a mom because their job is to look after you forever. That's how it works."

"But what if we go so far that we can't ever get back home?"

I rolled my eyes. "Clemesta!" I said. "You are stealing all the fun out of this day. Now stop."

Dad's head popped out from behind the front door and he gave me a double thumbs-up sign which is what you do for good news.

We had everything from the shopping spree to carry inside but Dad took most of it and his duffel and I just held onto Clemesta.

The woman at the front desk was the manager and the owner and she also lived upstairs right next to where we would be sleeping, which is a very good idea for a hotel. Her hair was purply with the white roots on top trying to take over.

The house was like an old-timey house, with furniture from hundreds of years ago and lots of pictures of black-and-white old people on the walls and dried dead flowers tied with ribbons on the shelf.

The woman said her name was Darlene and she said it like *DAAAARRR-LIYAN* and I liked very much how it sounded in the air.

"Just you two?" she said, and Dad nodded.

"Lucky Mom," Darlene said. She laughed and her whole face scrunched up and made four rolls of chins under her neck.

Darlene had a bunch of different kinds of porcelain dogs sitting at the front door. There was a bulldog and a poodle and a German shepherd all crammed to one side, and then on the other a terrier and an Airedale and one of those huge Saint Bernards. They took up almost all the space in the room.

I know all the dog breeds by heart because the library has a series of the best books in the world called ENCYCLOPAEDIA

BRITANNICA and each one has a million different facts inside, with pictures and stories and every time I visit I read from a different section so I can discover something new. As well as knowing all the dog breeds, I know all the horses, like Palominos and Lipizzaners and Missouri Fox Trotters, and I can name the planets and the flowers and dissect a human body, which is another of my favorite pages of the encyclopedia even though some parts of it where they show all the veins and muscles are a little gross and make my stomach do a flip-flop.

"I like your dogs," I said to Darlene. "The Airedale is my favorite."

"Well, aren't you a smart little lady," Darlene said. "You can go ahead and pet them if you like. They won't bite."

I petted the bulldog and I was glad he wasn't drooling like a real dog because then my hand would get covered in spit. The Airedale didn't want to get petted because he was from a noble family and you aren't allowed to touch them or their greatness will rub off on your hands.

The poodle said his name was Roger. He told me he had run away from the circus because his mean owner had made him stand on his hind legs all day long juggling balls.

"I'm sorry," I said, but then he told me that the tiger ate the owner one day during rehearsals and unlocked the cages for the other animals and they all escaped together.

"It's a happy ending," he said. "And Darlene doesn't make me do tricks."

A girl came out of the other room with a baby in her arms.

"This here is Jolene," Darlene said. "And my grandbaby, Dorie."

Jolene's teeth were weird-looking like they'd all fallen over and her voice sounded very sleepy. She looked the same age as my sitter Lucy at home, who is fifteen and a spelling bee champion who has won lots of prizes. She can't come around to look after me anymore because of the BILLS BILLS BILLS but sometimes I see her in the park babysitting other kids whose dads make more money and we wave and say hello.

Jolene's belly was very round and sticking out, like there was another baby inside waiting to come out. The one in her arms cried and Jolene bounced her on her hip like she was dancing.

Dad paid Darlene and listened while she explained the HOUSE RULES.

I tickled Dorie's foot through her faded pink socks.

"I wish we had a baby at home," I said.

"No brothers or sisters?" Jolene said.

I shook my head. "Mom didn't want to lose her figure again after me. She's a famous actress, that's why."

"Is that right?" Jolene said. She switched Dorie to her other hip.

"Yeah," I said. "She was on a TV show a long time ago and she does commercials now. And she has a new show coming soon. But that's meant to be a secret," I said. "Don't tell anyone."

"I won't," Jolene said. "I was in a pageant once," she said. "Miss Clifton Forge."

"Did you win?"

She shook her head. "If I had, I wouldn't be standing here."

"Where would you be?"

"Probably Orlando," Jolene said. "I always wanted to be one of those dolphin trainers at SeaWorld."

"I love dolphins," I said. "They're very smart. They have advanced brains, so they are much smarter than the other sea creatures."

Jolene yawned. She had very pink skin, like someone had rubbed it with sandpaper. Her eyelashes were blue.

Dorie grabbed my finger and stuck it inside her mouth. It felt hot and gummy in there, and her teeth scratched my skin. "She likes me," I said.

Jolene frowned. She opened Dorie's diaper and sniffed it. "She's always taking a dump or about to," she said.

"Yuck."

"Tell me about it." She made a face.

"Is that another baby in there?" I pointed to her stomach.

She nodded, but she didn't smile. Probably she didn't like being fat.

Dad called out to me and I patted Dorie on her bald head.

"Time for bed, little sleepyhead," I said.

I followed Dad up the stairs. At the top of the landing, a gray cat was taking a nap. I quickly looked at Dad because he HATES all cats and usually pushes them out of the way with his foot, like that time the neighbor's cat Felix came around to our house and he got a big fat kick in the guts with Dad's boot.

"Otherwise he'll come back every day," Dad said.

Felix yelped and I felt bad that he had to get taught a lesson that hurt so much.

Darlene's gray cat scooted away before Dad could kick him, LUCKY CAT.

Our room had two small beds sitting next to each other. There was no tub in the middle of the room and no refrigerator, but Darlene said she'd made the curtains and the quilts herself, and they were very pretty with red and pink stripes. Two pictures made of stitches were framed on the wall. One said GOD IS LOVE and the other said GOD BLESS AMERICA. On the desk, there was a BIBLE WORD SEARCH puzzle book and a stack of little booklets called HAVE YOU BEEN SAVED? with a picture of Jesus on the cover.

Dad sat on the bed and did that thing he does where he clicks his whole jaw out of its place and it goes CLICK CRACK. Mom hates it when he does it. She hates other stuff too, and so does he. That's why they have to yell at each other, and why Clemesta and I have to go hide in our HURRICANE STORM SHELTER, which is a secret safe place in the house just for us. We pretend a storm is happening outside but we are safe inside with hot cocoa to drink and marshmallows to eat and all our favorite books to read and all our coloring books and also there's a kitten inside who's lost but we help her stay safe until the storm is over. Then we find her mom and dad and everything is perfect again and that's the end of the game.

Once or maybe three times, we fell asleep in the hurricane storm shelter because the fights went on the whole night.

Dad looked around the room and sighed. I stood with Clemesta, waiting for him to say what we should do, but he just picked up his phone and flicked through the news.

"Did anything happen yet?" I said.

He shook his head and set his phone down. His screen had

a photo of the three of us on it. We all look very smiling and happy, even Dad. I don't remember when we took it. Maybe last year or the one before that.

Outside, I could hear dogs barking. Or maybe it was Darlene's porcelain ones from downstairs coming to life at night. In the yard outside the trees were mostly bare, except for one that had its spring blossoms peeking out.

Dad sat on the edge of the bed and chewed his nails.

"I'm hungry," I said. "We didn't eat any dinner. Or lunch."

Dad picked through the Walmart bags and pulled out a bag of jerky and some Doritos.

I made a face. "That's more junk."

"It's all we have," Dad said. He spat all his chewed-off nails onto the floor and I hoped the cat wouldn't choke on them.

I sighed. Maybe Dad didn't even know that kids are meant to eat vegetables and not just candy the whole entire time. No wonder he never makes dinner or we would all be very obese and Mom would be REPULSED. Already she thinks that everyone in our neighborhood is gross because they don't take care of themselves and all they do is sit on the sofa watching TV and eating candy.

Dad ate a mouthful of jerky and then he stood up.

"We should wash up," he said, "and get to bed."

In Darlene's bathroom across the hall, he helped me figure out the faucet and make sure the water was not too hot or too cold but just right, like Goldilocks from the book Mom used to read to me before bed. We have stories every night except when I say GO AWAY and LEAVE ME FOREVER

ALONE. That was last week and I lay in bed feeling mad until I fell asleep.

In the shower, I used lots of pumps of Darlene's soap, which smelled of lemons. Then I wrapped myself up in her soft and peachy towel and I brushed my teeth with the new toothbrush until they were sparkling clean and minty fresh and very untasty for Gerry Germ. Then I went back into the room.

Dad was lying on top of the bed with his eyes closed. I thought he'd fallen asleep already but then I saw that his eyes were watery, with little streams running down his cheeks. I bit my lip.

Probably that was how he looked the whole year that he was in bed after the HARD LUCK of his company going BANG and Joshua dying. Mom said he was like that every day, with the door closed and the curtains pulled shut and he might have stayed like that forever if she hadn't told him about the BEST SURPRISE. Me being born is what cured him from sadness and made everything better and that means I am the most ESSENTIAL thing he needs and also his LIFESAVER. When you save someone's life even once, you are responsible for them for their whole life, and that's why I have to try extra-hard to be Dad's best girl.

I crept over to the Walmart bags and fished out my new pajamas. Dad opened his eyes and sat up. He wiped his face with his hands. His eyes were red.

"Let me go take that shower," he said.

"What's wrong with him?" Clemesta said.

"He's fine."

Clemesta brushed my hair with the new brush and made it beautiful.

"I think maybe it's the bad thing," she said.

"I don't remember anything bad," I said. "So THERE-FORE and ERGO it can't be important."

Clemesta sighed and I picked up the booklet about Jesus. It said he would forgive you if you REPENTED but you could also send $12 for extra-quick forgiveness.

"Do we have twelve dollars?" Clemesta asked.

"Maybe back home. But we don't need any forgiveness."

Clemesta frowned. "I don't know," she said. "Maybe we do."

Dad was still in the shower. I could hear the water running. I lay down on the bed nearest the window and climbed under Darlene's handmade quilt. The sheets smelled like rose perfume and outside the window I could see the pale silver moon.

I wondered if Mom was seeing the same moon wherever she was. "Probably she's starting to miss us now. I bet she wishes she was here instead of on her girl weekend with Rita."

Clemesta blinked her wide worried eyes and shook her head. "I don't think she's with Rita, Dolly. I think she's somewhere else."

Monday

Dad was already dressed and ready to go when he woke me up from my dreams. He rubbed my cheek with the back of his rough hand and I opened my eyes. For a tiny moment I forgot where we were and whose bed I was sleeping in.

"It's Darlene's house," Clemesta reminded me. "The Red Carriage Inn."

"Morning, Dolly," Dad said. I wiped my eyes.

"Are we going home now?"

Dad shook his head. "We still have that surprise to get to."

"Yeah," I said.

"Come on," he said. "We have a long drive."

I groaned. "But I don't like all the driving."

Dad zipped up his bag and slipped some bills in his back pocket. "Yeah," he said. "But driving is the only way to get to where we're going."

"Why couldn't we fly? Like in an airplane or a helicopter or a hot air balloon?"

Dad picked at something in his teeth. Probably jerky hiding there since last night. "Yeah. Flying would have been quicker," he said. "But...I couldn't find your passport. Mom must have hidden it somewhere new. Or something."

I had a memory of Mom giving YOU KNOW WHO a

pile of papers in a folder but I shook my head hard from side to side to shake it loose.

I slipped on my new flamingo dress along with my new very white pointy shoes. In the bathroom, I splashed my face clean and brushed my teeth twice to show Gerry Germ that I meant business.

"Good job," Clemesta said. "Dental hygiene is of very essential importance." She brushed her mane but her teeth can't get cavities so she just licks them clean.

We went downstairs and Darlene came over to me clucking like a chicken. "Don't you look a picture," she said.

"It's from the shopping spree," I told her. "Dad left all our other stuff at home."

Darlene had prepared a pot of coffee for Dad and a glass of orange juice for me. She said we could choose anything we wanted from her breakfast cupboard, which had all kinds of food inside it, like boxes of cereal and Pop-Tarts and waffles and cream cakes in plastic wrap. She had baked a fresh batch of snickerdoodles which she colored with red food dye to make them pink. I chose Cheerios and a snickerdoodle but Dad wasn't hungry. He drank a second mug of coffee and then number three, even though he already looked full of JUMPY JITTERS and probably didn't need any more coffee bolts to wake him up. Darlene was talking to him about the weather and he was scrolling through the news on his phone.

Jolene was sitting on the sofa in the other room watching a TV show.

"No one can come to the Father, but through the Son," the man said.

His name was Jewish Jesus but his hair was cut short and he didn't have a beard and he was wearing a suit and tie like the one Dad wears to work every day.

"I don't think that's Jesus," I said.

Jolene didn't say anything, her eyes just stayed on the screen, staring at the picture. Dorie was on her lap wearing a very stinky diaper. She was sucking on a plastic bottle of soda and getting spit everywhere.

"Lord, Jolene," Darlene yelled. "Will you change her already?" She rolled her eyes. "She's going to sit there all day," she said.

Dad set his mug on the counter. He picked up our Walmart bags and threw his duffel over his shoulder. His hair was still wet from the shower and the bald part was peeking through. "We'll head off now," he said.

Darlene walked us to the door. "You enjoy the rest of your trip," she said. She crouched over and pinched my cheeks with her long pink nails. "Bless you, sweetheart."

No one ever did that to me before and I liked it. I took the blessing and put it in the pocket in my heart. That's where lovely things go, like love and cuddles and giggles and kindness. The pocket is very big and it never gets too full.

Dorie screeched from the other room and Darlene went to get her.

"Goodbye," I said to the dogs. They all stood up straight and saluted me with their paws like soldiers.

•　•　•

In the daylight, Darlene's house looked different. The walls were crumbling around the back, and the yard was covered in dead brown grass. All the flowers were dead too. I kicked my sneakers into the gravel drive so they could crunch the stones *crunch, crunch,* like they were munching up a delicious breakfast. I crunched again and I almost kicked a baby bird lying near the wheel of Dad's Jeep.

I crouched down to look at her.

"She's dead," I said.

Dad peered down. "I think it probably fell from the tree."

I reached out my hand so I could give the baby bird special farewell blessings like FLY AWAY TO HEAVEN PRECIOUS CREATURE OF NATURE AND WONDER but Dad yelled, "Jesus, Dolly, don't!"

"What?" I said.

"It's full of diseases," he said. "Don't you know not to touch dead animals?"

"I only wanted to send her to heaven," I said very softly.

I climbed into the Jeep and held my arms tight against me to make myself a cage that you couldn't get inside. My throat felt lumpy as I watched Dad. He climbed in and shut the door with a loud bang.

"You don't have to get so mad," I said.

"What?"

"It was an accident. I didn't mean to do anything bad."

Dad stared ahead. I pinched my nails into the squishy skin under my thumb. It's a good trick for making you hurt in a place that isn't your heart.

Dad sighed. He shook his head. "Sorry," he said. "I'm sorry for yelling at you. I just . . . it's been a rough . . ."

A girl wheeled a stroller toward Darlene's house. Maybe she was Jolene's friend, coming to visit. She looked fifteen too. She wore a lot of makeup around her eyes and her legs were like two very long poles.

"It's fine," I said. "You didn't mean it either."

"No. I never want to yell at you." His hands were holding the wheel, squeezing.

Clemesta nudged me. "Hey," she said. "It's Monday."

My eyes popped. "I'm missing school today," I said.

Dad rubbed his eyes. "Yeah," he said. "I already called Miss Ellis to tell her you won't be in class."

"When did you call?"

"Earlier. You were still asleep."

"Is she mad?"

"Not at all," Dad said. "She's happy you're on an adventure." He took his phone out of his jeans. "That reminds me," he said. "I should call the office too."

He got out of the car again and shut the door. I bit my fingernail and SO WHAT about bad habits that Mom doesn't think are LADYLIKE.

"Are you nervous?" Clemesta said.

"No, it's just a little tiny snack."

Clemesta narrowed her eyes at me.

"Yeah, Ahmed," I heard Dad say, "I guess it's a bad flu."

Ahmed is the Junior Manager at VALUE MOTORS and a very nice man who always lets me choose a bar of candy from the special candy drawer in the office. Ahmed comes from Pakistan which is very, very far away and his wife still lives there with his four children. He is trying hard to earn enough money to bring them all to America which is their dream but so far he hasn't seen them in TWO WHOLE YEARS. Being away from home is the first-worst thing in the world so I feel VERY SORRY for him and I am always extra-friendly when I see him so he is cheered up for a while before being sad again.

I couldn't understand why Dad was telling Ahmed that he had the flu, because he wasn't sniffling or coughing or throwing up.

"He does look a little clammy though," I said. "Like he isn't one hundred percent perfectly healthy."

Clemesta shook her head. "I don't think so."

I watched Dad walk around the car, kicking at the tires.

"And Ahmed?" he said. "No one's called looking for me or anything, have they?" He tapped the roof of the car with his hand. "No, no reason," he said. "It's nothing. Just...just someone from the bank. I thought he might call."

He said goodbye and climbed back in the car.

"You don't have the flu," I said. He nodded.

"Yeah. But I want to go on our adventure. I had to say it so I wouldn't be stuck at work all day."

Clemesta frowned.

"He shouldn't be telling lies," she said.

"White lies," I told her. "They're different."

We left the town of Clifton Forge and we didn't find any fires. The main road just had a bunch of empty stores with nothing to buy inside them. They looked full of dust and probably rats. There was nowhere to go to the movies, no bookstore or toy store or cupcake store or anything fun like that.

A lot of the houses had their windows shut up with

cardboard so you couldn't even see into them. It made me think of our house, which Mom keeps very tidy and lovely, even though she hates it. She has a book beside her bed that says a clean house is like a clean mind, and she wants one of those badly. I thought of her waking me up in the morning for school, creeping into my bedroom on tiptoes and then giving me a hundred soft kisses so it feels like angels are batting their wings against my cheek.

"Good morning, Dolly Delicious," she says. That's one nice thing she does.

I looked over at Clemesta.

"Maybe I'm starting to miss her now," I said. "But just a tiny bit. I'm still mad at her. More mad than missing."

Clemesta nodded. "But remember what I told you last night? I don't think she's on a girls' weekend. I think we should call her."

I shrugged. My new white shoes were biting my toes like real teeth that were sharp and mean and hungry. "Not right now," I said.

We passed by railway tracks that were grown over with weeds and trash. One of the old cars was sitting right in the middle, like it was meant to be going somewhere but instead the world stopped and it stayed there forever, rusty and broken. Probably a family of raccoons lived inside. They ate berries and grew vegetables to sell at the weekly farmers market.

"Someone should fix that train," I said. "So people can use it again."

"Mm," Dad said.

· · ·

We drove a stretch of the way being silent again, and I watched the trees and the fields out the window. Once we were away from the town, the sun was high and shining and the sky was big. Everything felt fresh, like you'd never run out of sky or air or mountains or trees or places to have picnics. And America was so enormous, like probably you could fit the whole world inside and everyone would still get a yard and a tree for building a tree house.

I was already getting bored with the driving.

I tried singing the "Adventure" song but I forgot the words and I was not in the mood to make up new ones. The mosquito bite on my leg from Darlene's house itched and I dabbed spit on it, which is a magic trick to make it stop.

Dad's phone on the seat next to him started to ring.

"Fuck," he said. Then he hit his forehead and said IDIOT and both of those are bad words.

Clemesta made eyes at me.

"Who's an idiot?" I said. The phone kept ringing but Dad didn't answer. "Is that Mom calling?"

"It's not Mom," Dad said.

"Who's the idiot?"

"Me. I forgot to do something."

"What?"

He didn't answer. He drove a little further and pulled up at an empty picnic spot. There were a few wooden tables with lots of trash lying around, like empty soda cans and McDonald's wrappers and someone's backpack with a sweater lying in the dirt. Dad hopped out of the car and scratched around for something in the trunk.

"What are you doing?" I said.

"Just . . . never mind."

He sat back down in front and used a screwdriver to break into part of the dashboard. He grunted and pulled out a small black box which he looked at for a second before he hurled it into the trees like it was a football.

"Dad!" I said. "What was that?"

"It's the—it's a part of the car we don't need."

"Why?"

"Because."

"Because why?"

"It's just, it takes too much fuel. It's bad for the environment."

"Oh. Then that's good you're throwing it away."

Dad chewed his lip.

"He's a climate change warrior like us," I said. Miss Ellis told us all about caring for the planet and looking after nature and the animals and recycling and not using plastic straws and not burning lots of coal.

Clemesta frowned. "I don't like this," she said.

"Well, I like it a lot. Dad cares about our very precious Miss Planet Earth."

"I think it's something else," Clemesta said.

"Oh, you little worrywart. You are always worrying. Like that time you said 'Do not climb all the way to the top of the tree or you'll get stuck up there forever,' and I did it anyway and I didn't get stuck. That's just one example," I told her. "I have lots of other ones in my head."

I pointed to her mouth. "Now turn that frown upside down."

She snapped at my hand with her teeth.

Dad stood at the car door but he didn't get in. I could smell the grass and also the new smell of the morning before the day melts it away. I watched Dad.

I knocked on the window. "Let's go."

"Just a second," he said. He reached into his pocket and took out his phone.

He tapped on it with his finger and looked at the screen, and then he reached back his arm and threw it into the same trees where the black fuel-eating box was lying.

My mouth fell TO THE FLOOR.

"Dad!" I yelled. "Are you crazy?"

"I think he might be," Clemesta said.

Dad climbed back in the car and shut the door. "That phone was broken," he said. "Piece of junk."

"But you just used it to call Ahmed."

"Yeah, but it hardly worked. So. Better to get another one."

"You could have gotten it fixed at that repair shop next to the pizza place."

I watched him. He did that thing with his jaw again. CLICK CRACK. I folded my arms.

"You shouldn't have thrown it away," I said. "I could have played games while you spent all day DRIVING. It's so boring back here, like I could literally die from boring. And I wanted to call Mom. She needs to hear my voice. Dad!"

He rubbed his eyes. "Yeah, sweetheart. We can find a pay phone."

"When?"

"Later."

I groaned. "Where are we even going for this dumb adventure? It's so far."

"It will be—you'll like it once we're there."

"Aren't you excited anymore?"

"I am."

"You don't look it. You look the opposite of excited. Like when we used to go and visit Pop in the old people's home."

Dad laughed. "Yeah, those weren't the most fun trips, were they?"

I shook my head. "Except when the nurses gave me Jell-O. That was nice. Jell-O, Jell-O-O-O."

I wobbled like Jell-O and then I went back to being a girl. My thighs kept wobbling and I squeezed them together.

Dad started the car. I pulled my dress over my knees. The flamingos stretched and their necks got even longer. I showed Clemesta.

"See? It's a magic growing trick. I just invented it right now."

"No wonder everyone tells you you're advanced."

"I know." I did it three more times and then the birds got worried about their necks being forever broken and asked me to please stop.

"I guess we'll have to play the SIGNS game again."

Clemesta sighed. "It's not THRILLING FUN."

"Yeah, but it's all we have right now."

"Look," Clemesta said. "That attraction board is blank. There isn't even one single fun thing to do here."

"The adventure is fun."

"It's not an adventure, it's only driving through America."

"I bet the fun is coming. Have some patience, you impatient impossible impolite horse."

Patience is a good word to know. It's also a very important trick to have. I need lots to help Mom with being an actress

99

and sometimes I run out and she gets mad. First I need it for all our trips to Manhattan, because that's where she goes to audition for new shows and acting jobs.

Last year she won a part in a TV commercial for diapers. She plays the Mom's hands and she has to unfasten the diaper and hold it up to show how it doesn't spill even when it's very full of baby pee which was actually just blue water for the commercial. Up until last year Mom used to take me to castings to try and see if I could be a CHILD STAR. But the ladies behind the desk always sighed with disappointment at me being all wrong and said "NEXT PLEASE." Now we only go for Mom's famous-making roles.

Dad doesn't like Mom being an actress because he thinks it's a waste of time and there's no money in it and she does nothing but bring home bills and she should get a real job and give up her RIDICULOUS DREAMS ALREADY. That's why our trips have to be another secret for the secret-secret box. But nowadays they are a DOUBLE SECRET because of YOU KNOW WHO.

I need patience for other stuff too, like watching the episode from when Mom was a star. She plays it ALL THE TIME and she doesn't like it if I don't pay all my attention. On the show, she had to pretend to be a girl called Sally who was a kindergarten teacher in love with the principal, Mr. Hughes. They didn't get to kiss ever because Sally had to move away and go teach kids in Korea and then Mom wasn't on the show anymore.

Mom says she had to stop being an actress because she moved from Los Angeles to Florida to be with Dad after he met her and said, "I LOVE YOU AND MARRY ME." Dad was visiting Los Angeles for work and Mom was being a part-time waitress while she waited to get famous. He thought she was the most beautiful of every woman he had ever laid eyes on before in his whole life and he told her that and she was very happy to hear it and he was very handsome in his suit and he invited her back to his fancy hotel and they fell HEAD OVER HEELS into fairy-tale love and that's the story and happily ever after is how it ends.

Mom does have another job that she does on the side of being famous and that needs patience too. It's called JEWELRY MAKER and she makes beautiful necklaces and bracelets with special stones and crystals that can do magic things like HEAL and FIND LOVE and BRING PEACE and CHANNEL ENERGY. She makes the jewelry and writes little cards to explain their powers and then she sells them to a shop in Brooklyn. A lot of afternoons I have to help her sort the stones with my fingers because they are smaller than hers. I don't like doing it because I would rather play other games that I like better like BALLET STAR or ANIMAL SAFARI PATROL GUARD, but those are for days when Mom is BEST MOM and looking at me with LOVE-HEART EYES that will do anything to make me happy.

Mom says the jewelry-making is silly and only something to do until she is famous again. That's why she doesn't spend much time on it and some days she rolls her eyes when she gets a new order and says, "Some people are so goddamn gullible."

Before the jewelry-making, Mom made greeting cards, and then before that she sold that magic Herbalife powder for making you skinny and rich, and before that I was too little to remember so I don't know.

A bunch of other stuff needs patience, too, like the time Mom took off all her clothes and stood naked in the hallway in only her underwear, and made me take the camera and snap pictures of her from every single angle so she could see all the parts of her that were ugly. That way she would know what to work on even harder, until she's perfect all over.

It took a long time, and I had to take all the ones of her legs a second time because the shadows of me got in the way.

I touched my wobbly tooth. When it wiggled my stomach wobbled. I let my tongue roll onto the leather of the seats. They tasted smooth and a little smoky. Clemesta was watching out the window and practicing her patience.

"Good girl," I said. "You will get a gold star when we get home."

"Dolly, I don't think we're going back."

"Clemesta, of course we are. Home is where we belong."

I put her at my feet where it was shaded from the sun. "Have a nap. Sleep off your weary and your troubles."

I counted three churches and a sign for a gun club. *Gun* rhymes with *fun* but they aren't. The churches here didn't look like the ones back home, with colorful windows and beautiful towers and bells for ringing when the bride gets confetti thrown over her head. Most of them were just boring old trailers or flat white houses with a fat cross stuck on the roof. We never go to church, except on Christmas to hear the carols or if we get invited to weddings, like when Rita married Terence. When they stopped being married, Rita got a pet dog instead. The dog is a very adorable pug and his name is George Clooney and he farts all day long and in the winter he wears a pink fur coat because Rita says he is gay just like all the best men in her life. I love George Clooney and whenever I see him, he faints with happiness and I have to tickle him back to life.

The biggest truck I ever saw came creeping past.

"I bet that's a truck full of Skittles to feed the cows," I said. "I saw that once on TV. The farmers buy up all the Skittles that come out in the funny colors that people don't want to eat, and they give them to their lucky cows for breakfast."

That was an interesting fact but Dad didn't say so.

"Maybe you should throw something at his head, so he pays attention," Clemesta said. She was awake from her nap.

I sighed. "Let's just invent a new game."

We called it DEAD ANIMAL SIGHTINGS and you had to shout out DEAD ANIMAL whenever you saw one squashed on the side of the road, and you also had to guess what it was when it wasn't dead, like RACCOON or DOG. Lucky for us, there were a MILLION dead animals. Sometimes they were squashed flat and all you could see was blood and red guts and it was impossible to say what kind of animal they had been when they were alive. Other times you could still see their faces and the color of their fur and then it was easier to call out DEAD POSSUM or DEAD SQUIRREL or DEAD DEER.

"Dad!" I said. "Play."

"Mm," he said.

"But try."

"Not now, Dolly."

Clemesta looked at me and rolled her eyes.

"It's because he's distracted with driving and focusing," I said. "He can't do all that and play games at the same time."

She shook her head. "No. I think I remember what it is. And it's something bad."

I turned my head all the way away from her.

"Dolly."

"I can't chat right now, Clemesta," I said. "I'm too busy focusing on the road. Look, we just missed that dead thing and we didn't even get to figure out what she was."

Clemesta made a face. "I don't think I can play anymore. Those dead animals are making me nauseous."

We passed a very tall tree, called Mr. Majestic Oak. He had good long branches for climbing and building tree houses. I wished Dad would hurry up and build mine like he promised. Maybe he would do it when we got back home. Maybe he would be full up with energy and fun and happiness after the adventure. He would be like the man in the TV commercial who has a before picture of him looking sad and then an after picture of him looking OVER THE MOON. Or he'd be like Ezra's dad, who is always laughing and throwing him over his shoulders and who always stays after class to see what Ezra did that day. Ezra is browny-skinned and lovely and probably one day we will be boyfriend and girlfriend but we are too young for that RIGHT EXACTLY NOW.

"Why don't you climb to the top of my tree and live here a

while?" Mr. Majestic Oak said as we passed. "You'll be away from everyone except good-natured squirrels."

"I wish I could," I called.

Mr. Majestic Oak waved his arm. "Too bad," he said. He was sad to say goodbye.

"Mom was fed up with wishing Dad was different too," Clemesta said. "That's why she was meeting YOU KNOW WHO in hotel rooms and bars in Manhattan. Because he's the opposite."

"Hush," I said. "I WILL NOT think about that man. If I do I get FLAMING and FURIOUS inside like I am burning with fire."

"I know," Clemesta said, "but it's true. 'You deserve so much better, Anna.' That's what he said. Then he said, 'You don't have to stay and suffer. You don't need to waste the best years of your life.' Do you remember?"

I took my fingernail and pressed it into my mosquito bite. I held it there until I popped the skin and the watery stuff oozed out. It was the mosquito poison, which is very dangerous in your body. If you don't squeeze it all out you'll get sweaty and die from MALARIA.

I poked my finger into my stomach. It was hard and stiff and a little sore.

GOD'S LOVE IS RELENTLESS.

"What does *relentless* mean?"

"It means it won't ever stop," Dad said.

"That's good, right?"

"For love, yes," Dad said. "It's good if love is relentless."

I wished he would say MY LOVE FOR YOU IS

RELENTLESS, but instead he said a curse word under his breath.

"What happened?"

"I took the wrong exit. I probably need to get myself a map."

"Your phone had a map," I said. "But you threw that into the trees."

At the next gas station, Dad pulled up the car. "Want to come inside?"

"It's only another gas station," I said. "They all look the exact and exactly the same."

"Yeah," Dad said. "But you can stretch your legs."

I looked at my legs. "These need real stretching, not just gas-station stretching." I sighed. "I guess I'll just go pee."

Dad was already walking ahead. He rubbed his head which looked like it was hurting him. Probably he was stressed from planning the adventure and looking after me the whole time alone. Usually that's Mom's job and not his.

I ran to catch up and my flamingos went flying.

The man in the store was sitting behind glass so you couldn't touch him. You had to hand the money through a small hole.

"Why is he in a cage?" I said.

"To stop him getting robbed, I guess."

"Or shot dead. But actually someone could break that glass if they had a glass-blaster torch or a destroyer flame or something."

"Mm," Dad said. He flipped through all the different newspapers on the rack. Most of them had the same face on the cover.

"Hello, Mr. President," I said. I stuck out my tongue.

Dad asked the man behind the counter for a map.

"I'm going to pee," I said. Dad nodded. "Don't forget to watch out," I reminded him.

I found the door to the restroom and went inside. The floor was wet and the toilet seat was covered in someone else's pee. I pulled toilet paper from the roll and made a cover for the seat, which is a smart trick that Mom taught me. I tried to hold my breath against the bad smells.

When I came out, Dad was over at the ATM getting some more money. He had a map and two Red Bulls in his hand.

"Pick out some snacks for the road, if you like," he told me.

I walked down the aisle looking at candy bars and cookies. None of those would help me fight scurvy, which is another thing I learned about from Miss Ellis. She told the class how the sailors in the olden days got sick and died, and all because they weren't eating enough fruit, which gives you vitamin C. That's why you have to have your FIVE A DAY and make sure to get all your vitamins, but Dad kept forgetting about all that important stuff. I bet no one around here ever eats GREEN SMOOTHIES for breakfast which is what Mom has every day after her exercising. Sometimes I have one too, so she can be proud of me for trying to stay healthy and pretty. They taste disgusting but I like the part where Mom smiles at me and says, "That's my good girl." Everyone likes a good girl but sometimes it's hard to always be her and I give up trying.

I set a Twix and a pack of Twizzlers on the counter. Dad picked out something called a Moon Pie, and I took one too.

When the man behind the counter spoke, I saw that he had teeth made from gold. I bet that was why he was behind the glass.

As we were leaving, another man walked inside with a dog on a leash. He bumped Dad and Dad said WATCH IT ASS-HOLE even though it looked like it was just an accident.

"You say that with a kid right by you?" the man said. "Who's the asshole?" He shook his head.

"That was a pit bull the man had," I told Dad. "They are very good SAVAGER DOGS. They can kill bad guys if you tell them to. Lucky he didn't set him on you. Like this," I said, and I showed him my SNARLING teeth.

Dad pulled the tab of his Red Bull and finished it before we got back to the car. On the ground, I spotted a postcard. I bent to pick it up because it wasn't a dead animal with hundreds of diseases, it was only paper.

The picture on the front was a pile of silver coins and it said INVEST WISELY.

"What's that?" Dad said.

"It's a secret message for me," I said. "I can't tell you about it." I held the postcard against my chest to hide the picture.

Dad hopped in the car. I opened up the bag of Twizzlers with my teeth while he read his map, folding it and unfolding it across the passenger seat until he could find what he was looking for.

"Actually I'm very good at reading maps," I said. "I can help be the NAVIGATOR MAN. That's the person who tells you where to go so you don't get lost. We can be a team," I said. "We can pretend that we're sailors on a ship but it's really a road. That doesn't matter though, it's only pretend so you can make up whatever you like."

"Maybe later," Dad said.

"When later?"

Dad held the map up close to his face and squinted.

"Do you need glasses too?" I said. "Miss Ellis says I do the squinting thing with my eyes when I look at the board."

"Mm," Dad said.

"Will you take me for that eyes exam when we get back home, the one where you have to read the letters of the alphabet but they're all mixed up so you can't cheat?"

Dad nodded. "Yeah, sweetheart. We'll do that."

He pulled out of the gas station and then we were BACK ON THE ROAD.

Roads, roads, roads, we are always on the road.

Driving, driving, driving, I'm so bored I might explode.

I sang the song again, but louder so Dad could hear it. He turned the radio on and listened to the newspeople talk about the student who took a gun to college to shoot eight of his classmates till they were dead and the world's tallest building that you can see from outer space.

"Is *asshole* a curse word?" I said.

Dad nodded.

I held up my hand and made the sign with my finger that Savannah had taught me. "Is this a curse word?"

Dad looked up and smiled. "No, the other finger."

"This one?"

Dad shook his head. "The middle one. But don't do it. It's rude."

I put my hand under the seat and practiced.

Then I showed Clemesta the secret message postcard. "It means there is treasure waiting for me. Probably at the end of the adventure."

"Like the pot of gold at the end of the rainbow?"

"Exactly."

She nodded. "I guess our secret-secret box is like a treasure chest. Because secrets can be like treasures."

"Only if they're good ones," I said.

"I guess. Do you remember what we put in there last?"

I shook my head.

"Can you try? I think it's important."

"Okay, but later. Right now I'm busy."

"Doing what?"

"Being on the adventure. And I have to help with the navigating."

I pressed the button to open the window and the wind came in and made a big noise. That reminded me of the stuck windows in the Chambersburg Comfort Lodge and I told Dad.

"Isn't it dumb? Because windows are for opening!"

"Yeah," Dad said. "Normally. But in hotels, I think they have to do it like that."

"Why?"

"I think so people don't fall out of the window, or, or—"

"Or jump," I said.

"Maybe."

"It's called committee suicide."

"Committing suicide, yeah."

"Like Uncle Joshua."

Dad didn't say anything.

I wasn't meant to hear the GRIZZLY BEAR DETAILS about how Uncle Joshua died but one day I overheard Mom talking to Rita and she said, "He went up to the eighteenth floor of the apartment complex they were building and he jumped right out the window. Joe had to identify him by his appendix scar."

Dad did the fist-making with his hands on the steering wheel.

"Sorry," I said. I bit my cheek between my teeth.

Dad swallowed. "I just don't like thinking about that."

"Because it makes you sad."

"Yeah."

"Dad's always sad," Clemesta said.

YOU'RE DEPRESSED, JOSEPH is what Mom yells when she CANNOT TAKE IT ANYMORE. I can spell DEPRESSED but I forget sometimes what it means exactly. Probably that you miss your friends and your old job, because Dad got very sad that day two Christmases ago when we bumped into his old work friend from Florida called Pete.

We were in Manhattan for the very special treat of seeing the holiday lights at Rockefeller Center. We were having lots of fun and Mom and Dad were holding hands and sneaking secret smooching kisses and I was holding Mom's other hand and it was dark out but the lights were sparkling and we were about to go ice skating but then Pete said JOSEPH RUST! and we had to stop to talk to him. They shook hands and he asked Dad lots of questions and it was very boring so I didn't listen to everything but then I heard Pete say "Jesus, VALUE MOTORS?" and then he said he could HOOK DAD UP and why didn't he ever turn up for that interview he set up for him because he was a shoo-in for the job?

Anyway, after we said goodbye and Happy Holidays to Pete, Dad was in a black and cloudy mood and we had to skip the ice skating and just go home in the car in silence. Later, Mom slammed a lot of cupboard doors while she was making dinner and said "YOU WANT TO SUFFER, DON'T YOU JOE? IT'S THE ONLY WAY YOU FEEL PUNISHED ENOUGH." In my bedroom, Clemesta and I built an ice-skating rink out of aluminum foil and Lego bricks and sent my dollhouse family out for a special Christmas treat, which they enjoyed very much.

I already have two things on my Christmas list for this year but I wrote them in pencil in case I change my mind.

Outside, I spied an American flag twisting in the wind and then a roadkill animal splatted on the ground.

"DEAD WOLF," I said.

"I don't know if there are wolves around here," Dad said.

"Are too! I love wolves. I think that dead one was a Mom wolf and she was probably defending her cubs because they don't let anyone mess with them. They are very fierce."

Actually human moms are fierce too, because once when I told Mom about Neshi being mean to me and calling me TERRIBLE NAMES, she got so mad that she went up to her at the school gate and hissed at her like a snake.

"You're a real little cunt, aren't you?" she said, and Neshi ran off shaking in her boots. Later, her mom tried to call but Mom tapped *DECLINE* on her phone and made her go away. Fierce moms are a little scary but not when they are on your side.

I cupped my hands and blew into them. "That's called wolf whistling. It's how you call wolves. Or moms sometimes, like on the street."

Dad smiled at me in the mirror.

"Let's do a staring contest," I said.

"Can't when I'm driving."

I flopped my head back. "Will there be any fun parts today or is it only driving?"

Dad opened another soda. "Fun, too," he said.

I sighed. "It feels like we are driving to the END OF OUR WORLD." I closed my eyes and tried to use telepathy to find out what Miss Ellis was teaching the class. I hoped she would be missing me and my smart answers and advanced sponge brain soaking up all her GIFTS OF KNOWLEDGE. I tried to think of Kindness Week ideas. Maybe I could give the homeless lady on our corner some money from my piggy bank. Or maybe I could tell Mom I forgive her. Forgiveness is kindness too.

I tapped Dad's shoulder. "Is Mom back home from her girls' weekend?"

Dad coughed. "Yeah, I think she is."

"Oh." I chewed all the white moons off my nails and dropped them on the floor at my feet.

"Shouldn't we go back home now, too? So Mom doesn't miss us."

I pressed the mosquito bite on my leg, which had already grown a rough scabby piece on top to keep the blood from leaking out.

Dad looked at me in the mirror and his eyes were a tiny bit worried-looking.

"Don't you want to see the surprise? The place?"

Clemesta squeezed my hand. "Think, Dolly, think," she said.

"The best part is coming up," Dad said. "You don't want to miss it, do you?"

"I guess not."

Dad swallowed the last gulp of his Red Bull and the empty can rolled to the floor. "Good," he said. "You're going to love it."

I nodded. "Yeah, I know."

MINISTRY OF HOPE.

CHURCH OF SAINTS.

HEART OF CHRIST OUR LORD AND SAVIOR.

God was everywhere around here but the people didn't look like they were happy about it. They all seemed sad.

I turned around in the seat to look out the back as we passed a sign.

WELCOME TO TENNESSEE, it said.

"That's another state for America," I said.

"Dolly, I don't like this," Clemesta said. "Not one bit."

"Stop it," I said. "You're spoiling my adventure with Dad with all your NAGGING and GLOOMINESS."

"I don't think it's an adventure," she said.

"It is too, now ZIP IT already."

Dad turned left and pulled the car up on a patch of road that went into a field.

"Give me a minute," he said. He pulled up the map and traced his finger along the squiggles. I laid my head back against the seat. The car didn't smell of pine trees anymore.

Now it smelled of our empty cans and wrappers. Mom wouldn't like the mess. Her mind would be very unclear and unhappy.

Dad drove off and I waved to some horses we passed in a field. They were from Tennessee and they told me they were the fastest racehorses in the world, faster than cars or lightning.

"DEAD DOG," I said. "Wild dog. They make angry ghosts. They howl at the moon and spread fleas."

"Look ahead," Dad said. "Those are the Appalachian Mountains. Aren't they beautiful?"

"I guess," I said. "They look like ordinary mountains to me."

I ate my Moon Pie. It didn't taste of the moon, just regular chocolate and marshmallow. I pressed my stomach again. It felt hard, which Mom calls BLOATED and that happens when you don't eat nutritious food and also when you don't go to the toilet. I counted the days without a number two and there were three of them already.

"That's from all the junk food," Clemesta said.

"I know."

"You didn't go to the toilet since Saturday."

"You didn't either. I can try a magic spell, maybe that will work."

"I don't think it will," Clemesta said. "I think our magic is broken."

"Nonsense, you goofy goofball," I said.

REAL CHRISTIANS OBEY JESUS.

BEAUTIFUL HEART GOSPEL.

WE BUY AND SELL GUNS.

Dad turned on the radio to listen to the news. It was the

same stories as before, just in a different voice. The song that came on afterward was called *Lazarus Rising*. I never heard it before so I couldn't sing along.

I rubbed my eyes. "Are we getting closer?"

"All the time."

I kicked off my shoes. I watched the fluffy hairs on my legs as the sun lit them up. One day probably soon, I will have to get rid of them with the pink strips Mom keeps in the bathroom. I will yell *FUCK* every time I yank one off but my legs will be lovely and smooth.

Tennessee was full of flags but not just United States ones. Some houses had another kind of flag that Dad said was called the CONFEDERATE FLAG and that's the old flag they used to have when the South wanted to be separate from the rest of the country and made everyone fight a war.

"Because they wanted to keep having slaves," I said.

"Yeah."

"Why are they still hanging the silly old flags?"

Dad shrugged. "I guess they want to remember."

"Remember what?"

"I don't know," Dad said. "Other times. How things were before."

"But that's stupid. It's the wrong flag."

"They feel like it's their flag."

"But it isn't. They didn't win the fight."

"Yeah," Dad said. "I guess a lot of fights can't be won. Everyone just loses in the end."

I thought about something. "Like when you and Mom fight," I said.

His eyes stayed on the road.

"I guess you're winning now."

The road and everything around it was the same no matter how far we went. Trees, mountains, churches, flags, old flags, farms. I tried to remember the word for when caterpillars change into butterflies.

MENNONITE CHURCH.

MOUNT GLORY BAPTIST.

CROSSROAD CHURCH OF CHRIST.

I brushed out Clemesta's knots and then we switched. I looked out at the houses along the way. They reminded me of the places you see on the news, all broken down and ruined after a very big storm. A *tsunami* is a big storm. It's a SLY FOX word because the *T* is a trick and you aren't meant to say it out loud. I don't like SLY FOX words or SLY FOX people. Those are people who trick you into thinking they are helping solve all your dreams but actually they are making everything terrible. Like YOU KNOW WHO.

"You have to leave, Anna, or he'll drag you down with him."

That's what he told Mom.

"You should have left him years ago. Really, you never should have married him. I always said that, didn't I?"

He said that in the Nomad Hotel. He had that special kind of room with a door that connects it to another room. I was in one room and Mom was in the other. I was meant to be sitting with the headphones on watching *Minions* on the iPad but I took them off and listened at the door.

"It can be an open-and-shut case," he said. "You just...embellish. Those bruises she has from falling in the park, you take a couple of pictures, you make your eyes wide, you say, 'Yes, Your Honor, he's always had a bad temper.' You're an actress, Anna. It won't take much."

"I guess I'll do whatever it takes," I heard Mom say.

"There's the other stuff too," YOU KNOW WHO said. "You have that option, of course. If he...if it happens again."

Mom went quiet.

"Either way, Anna, my advice is: find something. You don't want some endless battle where you can't leave the state, you can't move. Your life will be on hold. It'll be a nightmare."

"I know," Mom said, in her saddest and softest voice, in the voice she uses on CAN'T GET OUT OF BED DAYS.

"Paul and I will help," YOU KNOW WHO said. "Whatever you need, we've got you."

They stopped talking after that. I guess they got busy with OTHER THINGS.

"I hate that man. I hate him so much I wish he would explode."

"Me too," Clemesta said. "I think maybe the wish came true."

"Did it?"

"Well, he's nowhere near us now."

WAFFLE HOUSE.

LOVE THE SINNER HATE THE SIN.

CHEROKEE SOUVENIRS.

"Cherokees are Native Americans. Miss Ellis says we stole America from them."

Clemesta tugged at my dress. "Do you think Mom knows we're in Tennessee?"

I shrugged. "Moms know everything."

"I don't think she knows this."

"Well. Then she should try harder and pay more attention."

We sat in silence. A bug flew into the car and I waited for it to land on the window. It was a fly.

"I wish you were a ladybug," I told it. "That would have been GOOD LUCK. This is just regular luck."

Right then, we passed a big billboard that said THIS WAY TO DOLLYWOOD THEME PARK. I flipped my head around to read it again.

"Dollywood!" I said. "Is that the surprise?"

"You bet," Dad said. "It's a theme park and it's even got your name. How about that?"

I squealed and high-fived Clemesta and planted a million kisses on her head.

"You see," I said. "I told you that Dad wasn't telling WHITE LIES. This is a one hundred percent real adventure just for us. He wasn't lying," I said again. "He was telling us the truth the whole time."

Dad parked the car and we waited for the special Dollywood tram to collect us and take us up the hill to the theme park, which was like a magical special place hidden high up on top of the world.

"How come it's called my name?"

"Well," Dad said, "there's a famous singer and actress from around here, called Dolly Parton. It's her theme park."

"Famous like Mom?"

"Well, Mom only made one episode of a show. She isn't such a big star."

"She will be. She said so."

Dad made his hands into two tight fists but he didn't say anything else.

The tram arrived, and we climbed aboard with three other families. We had to listen very carefully as the lady called Jan told us about the rules for STAYING SAFE and HAVING FUN, like no standing up while the tram was moving and checking you were tall enough for the rides.

I watched a pair of sisters who were sitting in the row in front of us. They were wearing matching dresses and shoes, and they both wore their hair in long braids tied with red ribbon, so they looked like twins even though they were just regular sisters.

"We're real twins," I whispered to Clemesta.

"Exactly," Clemesta agreed. "Not like these ugly sisters."

"Jan," I said. "My name is really actually Dolly. Dolly Rust."

"Well, isn't that nice," Jan said into her loudspeaker. "We have a real Dolly here with us today, folks."

The sisters looked back at me like they were GREEN WITH ENVY which is what happens when you are so jealous it makes you want to throw up. I made a face at them behind their backs and imagined how it would feel to snip off their yellow braids with Miss Ellis's giant pair of craft scissors, which no one can use except for her because they are so sharp and TREACHEROUS.

Dad put his head in his hand and rubbed his eyes.

"Don't do that, okay?" he said in a soft voice into my ear.

"Do what?"

"Tell everyone your name."

"Why not?"

"Because," Dad said. "I could get in trouble."

"Why?"

"Uh, for taking you out of school."

"Oh."

"Does Mom know you're doing it?"

"Yeah."

"Is she mad?"

"Nope."

"I won't tell anyone my name," I said. Dad patted my leg.

"Good girl," he said.

Clemesta poked me in the ribs.

We hopped off the tram and lined up to buy tickets, and then we were inside Dollywood, which was like being inside a fairy tale that gets made into the real world. But not the Disney one, another kind. Anyway I was very excited with the butterflies back inside me, because it was a whole entire village of fun stuff, like restaurants and popcorn shops and slushy parlors and candy stores and there were people everywhere and balloons and delectable chocolate-marshmallow-spun-sugar smells and kids screaming with all the fun in their lungs.

Dad and I sat at the ice cream parlor and ordered sundaes. We watched the families pass by on their way to get food or stop by the gift shop for souvenirs. Everyone looked like they were visiting with their whole entire family and that made me feel bad for Mom that she wasn't with us.

I finished the last scoop of melted ice cream. Lots of people were riding around in those wheelchair-bikes for people who are so big they can't walk anymore. Mom wouldn't like that part. She'd say, "Honestly, some people just make such bad life choices."

I put a hand to my puppy-fat belly. I made a head-note to do my jumping jack exercises later, because that would help get me in good shape before we got back home.

Dad pulled out the special treasure map the lady had given us at the entrance, which showed you how to find everything in the park.

"It's like the map of America you have in the car," I said. "Except America isn't a theme park."

"Mm," Dad said.

"But imagine if it was, and every place was actually a very fun ride. Or a scary one. Or maybe somewhere you could win something. It could be called Americaland or Americawood."

"Mm," Dad said. He tapped my head. "You've got quite an imagination in there, don't you?"

I nodded. "It came with my brain."

I read out the list of the places you could go and the rides, like DAREDEVIL FALLS and DEMOLITION DERBY and SKY RIDER, which all sounded sort of scary. I don't like scary things, which maybe means I am a SCAREDY-CAT but who cares because I am only just new to being seven and not ten years old or something like that.

Dad stood up and slipped the map into his pocket. I was a pinch mad that he folded it up and made it all crumply inside his jeans, but I didn't tell him.

"You should probably hold my hand so I don't get lost," I said.

He took my hand and gave it a squeeze and I held on tight and I made sure not to do anything annoying like swing arms or ask to be swooshed up into the air, which makes grown-ups irritated and gives them sore shoulders.

The first thing we passed was the EAGLE MOUNTAIN SANCTUARY where real American bald eagles were perching in trees behind giant nets to keep them inside so they wouldn't fly away and get lost in the sky. They were enormous and strong and MAJESTIC and that's obviously why they got chosen to be on everything from the United States of America, like the coins and the buildings and T-shirts.

There was another dad next to us with his son and he told him, "That, son, is the symbol of American freedom." He was wearing a T-shirt that was very tight against his muscles and his son was carrying a huge stuffed tiger. He didn't have muscles. He had a wobbly belly and very pale skin like he got dipped in flour.

The eagle spread his gigantic wings like he wanted to fly but he only went as far as the net. Then his wings flopped down and he flapped back to his perch.

"They clip the wings," Dad said. "That's why they can't fly."

The eagle looked at me with his black eyes. He was fuming.

"I'm sorry about your wings," I said.

He tossed his head. "Me too," he said. "And you are a kind-hearted treasure, Dolly Rust."

"Thank you," I said. "But don't tell anyone else my name." I put my fingers to my lips and zipped them up.

The boy with the tiger looked at me. He was jealous that I could talk to the eagle and he couldn't. He made his hand into a gun and pointed it at my head. Then he pulled the trigger three times and shot me dead.

"Never mind," the eagle said, "he will probably die young from falling into a tar pit."

Dad and I left the eagles in their cage and went toward the rides. Before you could go on any, you had to first check that you were tall enough by standing next to a stick measure. You also needed to check that you weren't too fat to go on the ride by sitting in a special plastic seat. I sat and wiggled around and there was plenty of room so I was very happy, but there was another girl standing nearby who was crying. I guess she was too obese to have any fun so HARD LUCK for her. I stared at her but only very quickly.

Dad and I went on two rides. They were medium-scary but everyone screamed so I wasn't the only scaredy-cat. We all got wet and afterward we got to dry off in the special family-drier which is like a clothes drier for wet people. After that we walked around. There was that old-timey accordion music playing and lots of people screaming their lungs out and different smells of food. I watched all the other families walking together and I saw Dad watching them too. We didn't look like them. They looked like they were having fun but our fun was only half fun and half something else.

Dad rubbed his head and popped two pills out of the plastic bottle and into his mouth. We came across the shooting range booth and I spotted a row of the stuffed tigers hanging up, next to pandas and eagles and polar bears. I locked eyes with the tiger in the middle of the row.

She said, "I am Louisanda and I will be yours." I turned to Dad.

"Can you PRETTY PLEASE win me that tiger?"

"You bet," he said.

He took the gun but he only popped two balloons and you had to get all three for a prize. He paid the man for another round but this time he only got one of the balloons popped.

He rubbed his eyes. "One more," he said, but his face was red and I could tell that he was getting mad. There were two girls next to us and they laughed behind their hands because they had already hit all their balloons and were choosing their animals to take home.

Dad shot again, but he missed everything. "Fuck," he said. "How much for a tiger? Let me just buy the damn thing."

"Can't do that, sir," the man said. He was an old granddad with a big bushy gray beard that he stroked with his hand like it was a pet cat.

Dad slammed his gun down. "SHE WANTS A GOD-DAMN TIGER," he said, "so let me buy that toy off you."

The granddad shook his head. "Rules are rules."

"Fuck your rules," Dad said. He took me by the hand and we stormed off together even though I wasn't in a bad mood, I was trying to be nice and polite with lovely manners, and especially to old people who can die of fright if you are too rude in front of them.

"Asshole," Dad said. He was squeezing my hand very tightly and I tried to pull it away. We walked like that for a while. I was shaking a little in my shoes and my heart was going THUMPITY THUMP.

"Let's just get some food," Dad said. At the pizza place, he bought a couple of hot and cheesy slices that left big grease marks behind on the paper plates. I touched the pizza and the oil made a pool around my finger.

Dad's hand squeezed into a punching fist. That's the fist that breaks things in the house sometimes when he's really mad. It isn't his fault, it's Mr. Angry Bear who lives inside him and wakes up in a bad mood if someone does something silly. Sometimes Mr. Angry Bear gets into fights with other dads and then he comes home with black eyes. Mr. Angry Bear makes Mom cry but afterward Dad is always very sorry and full of love and they hold their heads together and say lots of gentle whispers and Mom glows from happiness. "I need you," Dad says. "I need you to help me be better, my shining light." Mom always looks extra beautiful on those days. I think because the tears are good for her skin.

Slowly, slowly Dad's fists came undone. He rubbed his head.

"Sorry," he said. "I lost my temper. I just hate it when I can't give you what you want. When I disappoint you."

His voice went scratchy and high, not like Dad's regular voice but like a little boy's voice instead. He swallowed. "We'll get you a tiger," he said. "I promise."

I pulled the crust off the pizza. "I don't want one anymore," I said. "They're for babies."

I watched the ride opposite us. It made my stomach flip-flop. The roller coaster went all the way into the sky, taking the people slowly slowly up to the top and then stopping for a moment, dangling them in the air and then tipping them right over the edge. They fell down but you couldn't see anything after that, they just looked like they vanished into the air forever and never came out again. Maybe they didn't and you had to go home without someone you came with.

I swallowed a bite of pizza. My throat was dry and it hurt going down the pipe.

"I don't want to go on any more rides," I said.

Dad bunched up the napkins and threw everything into the trash.

As we walked to the exit, I held Clemesta close. She was very quiet.

"Did the cat get your tongue and eat it up?"

"Dad scares me sometimes," she said.

"He doesn't mean it," I said. "It's just Mr. Angry Bear. We woke him today."

"I don't know, Dolly," Clemesta said. "I don't think it's really a bear."

I watched Dad's chest move in and out, in and out. I squeezed his hand so he would be reminded of our BEST LOVE. Best love helps to keep bears sleeping.

Jan didn't take us on the tram back to the car. The new lady's name was Felicia and she was talking on her phone.

"Yeah, Carl, that's what I'm telling you," she said, "it isn't right."

Dad's knee was bouncing up and down like it was itching to run away.

"Where are we sleeping tonight?" I said.

"I don't know yet. This place is a tourist trap. It's probably all a rip-off."

"And money doesn't grow on trees."

"Right."

"Maybe if it runs out at the ATM you can just get a loan. Mom got a whole pile of money from that place in Manhattan."

Dad frowned and then he let out a long sigh.

Clemesta hoofed me in the side. "That was meant to be a secret," she said.

I clapped my hand over my mouth. "It fell out."

Clemesta humphed. "That's not the only one, is it?"

There was a man standing at our car. It was a police officer and his radio was crackling and his badge was shining in the sunlight. He watched us as we walked toward the doors to open up, and he very slowly tipped his police officer hat.

"You have a good time?" he said. He was standing very close to my side. I looked over at Dad, who was not moving or opening the door or saying a word.

"Yeah," I told the officer. "It was fun." My heart went racing very fast because of TELLING LIES and I made a wish that the officer wouldn't find out. Maybe they could arrest you and take you to prison for that. I pinched the skin under my thumb. The officer turned his head to look at Dad. He was still in the same place in front of the car, like he was frozen in ice. He opened his mouth to say something but just then the officer lifted up his arms, and two boys came running toward him.

Dad watched them. He wiped his hand down his face and then he slowly climbed into the Jeep.

At the lights, he checked the mirrors. First the one in front, then the sides. He did it at the next stop again.

"Who are you looking out for?"

"No one."

"Is that officer following us?"

"No."

He kept checking the mirrors.

"He's going to follow us," I said. I turned to look back down the road. I felt like throwing up. "It's because I told a lie," I said.

"What?"

"He's going to chase after us because I told him something that wasn't true."

Dad turned around. "What did you tell him, Dolly?" His eyes were two wide saucers.

"I said I had fun at Dollywood," I said. "And I didn't. Not really. Because of you getting so mad."

"Christ." Dad wiped his face. His hands were shaking.

"Are you even more mad now?"

"No, no, Doll, I'm not." He checked the mirrors again and took another pill out of the bottle and sucked it onto his tongue. He opened the windows and let the wind hit him in the face.

We drove on the empty road and then turned off at a sign that said WELCOME TO. I couldn't read the town's name because it was too dark. All I could see was that it looked murky and creepy, like it was full of bad things hiding in the trailers in the trees.

Out the window it smelled of gas and grease and rotting leaves and probably rotting dead animals too.

Dad pulled up at the HALFWAY MOTEL & LODGE. It wasn't a house like Darlene's place and it wasn't a lovely and fancy hotel like the Chambersburg Comfort Lodge with tubs in the middle of the room. Instead it was a yellowy-colored square building with most of the paint chipped away and a broken welcome sign and a few pickups parked in the lot. Next door to the motel there was a bar with one of those flashing red arrows pointing to the entrance saying COME AND BE SILLY HERE, DADS.

Dad turned to look at it as we unloaded our bags.

Clemesta's whole body shuddered.

"That looks disgusting in there."

The motel's door made a noise like bells ringing. The TV was playing a loud wrestling match between two men who were making lots of screaming and grunting noises as they crashed into each other. They looked PREPOSTEROUS, which is very strong ridiculousness.

The clerk at the front desk had tattoos all over his arms. One was a picture of a woman's face, but he also had a dragon and a human skull and a Queen of Hearts playing card. He had a pierced eyebrow and a bolt through his nose that probably got full of boogers all the time.

"Cash only," he said. "And the air-conditioning's down."

He rubbed his hand on his stomach, which was poking out of his T-shirt. It was very white. His skin was shiny and he had a row of pimples across his forehead. One of them looked like it was about to explode yellow pus all over us and I stepped away from the desk in case it decided to burst.

The elevator wasn't working so we took the stairs. Our room smelled of smoke and clothes that didn't dry. The TV was a very old box, and in the bathroom the toilet seat was broken. Someone DISGUSTING with no manners had forgotten to flush so there was a big brown lump floating in the water which Dad very quickly sent away.

"It's only for one night," Dad said, when he saw my face.

He turned the TV onto the boring news channel and watched the fuzzy screen for a few minutes before he switched it off again. He looked at me standing in the corner with my Walmart bag in my arms.

"Come here," he said. I stepped over to the bed.

"I'm not mad," he said. "I'm never mad at you."

He made his eyes big, like for a staring contest. I opened my matching ones wide and stared into them.

"Your eyes look sad tonight," I said. He blinked and I won. Nobody giggled.

"I'm ready to go home now," I said. "I don't want any more adventures. I want Mom."

Dad swallowed. He let out the air inside him and nodded. "Yeah. Okay." He rubbed both hands over his face, like it was a mask he could pull off. "We'll head back." He went to use the bathroom. Even though the door was shut, I could hear him peeing. It lasted forever.

I pressed my hard balloon stomach and sat down on the bed. It squeaked and squished in the middle like it was one hundred years old and dying of tuberculosis. The carpet was full of cigarette burns and there was a big brown stain right near the bed. Blood, I bet.

I yawned three yawns in a row. "Is it bedtime?"

"Yeah." Dad unpacked the bag that had our toothbrushes and my pajamas and set it all out.

"You want to wash up?" I looked at my hands. My finger-nails were dirty and everything felt sticky, but I didn't want to go into the disgusting bathroom. I bet brown slime was going to come running out of the shower instead of water. Probably the brown lump had come swimming back too.

"I'll do it tomorrow." I pulled the pajama top over my head and looked at the smelly covers.

"Just one night," Dad said again.

"Are you going to sleep?"

"Uh," Dad said. "I need to take care of a few things. I'll be right here, or—if I'm not here, then I just slipped out to the car for a minute to get something. Okay?"

"But I don't want to be here alone."

Dad shook his head. "You won't be. I'll be here."

"Promise?"

"Yeah."

"Pinkie promise."

"Sure. And if I'm not, then I just went to get something from the car. Remember."

I climbed under the covers. They felt heavy and dirty and I didn't want them anywhere near my mouth in case I sucked up tiny particles of disgustingness. I lay back and looked up at the ceiling. It was spotty with mildew. My skin went crawling, and the bedbugs started licking their lips.

I didn't ask Dad to tuck me in. I just looked at him standing over by the window, staring out at the street.

"I wish we were already back home," I said to Clemesta.

The wish wasn't jinxed with saying it out loud because saying a wish to Clemesta isn't the same as saying it to a regular human person.

She kissed my cheek. "Oh, Dolly," she said. "I don't think we're going home at all."

I closed my eyes and everything went blank for a long time. I woke up to use the toilet. The room was dark but there was still some brightness coming from the streetlights, and I didn't turn on the light to find the bathroom. When I came out, my hand accidentally went to the wall and flicked everything on. "Sorry," I said, because I thought maybe I had woken Dad. But Dad wasn't there. His bed was still made up.

"Dad!" I called, even though that was silly because he couldn't be hiding anywhere. I peered behind the net curtain that was stained brown with a dead moth still hanging from it, and I looked to see if the Jeep was parked outside. It was right where Dad had left it, but he wasn't inside getting anything.

"He's at that bar," Clemesta said. "I know it."

I looked at the neon sign and the red arrow pointing in the direction of DOOM.

"He promised," I said.

"He always breaks that promise." Clemesta sighed.

"I wish I could punch him in the face."

"Me too," Clemesta said. "And kick his ankles and do a Chinese burn on his arm."

"He deserves that. If he had a gold star chart, I would take away EVERY SINGLE STAR and make him start again."

"It's okay if you want to cry," Clemesta said. "I'm crying a little myself."

I climbed back under the covers. "I'm not crying because I'm scared," I said. "It's because I'm MAD AS A SNAKE."

Clemesta stroked my cheek. "Oh, Dolly. He doesn't deserve a best girl like you."

I stuck out my lip. "I'm not even going back to bed," I said. "So there."

I switched the TV on and went flicking through the channels. There was a scary movie and a movie about two grown-ups doing SEX. I didn't switch channels even though it was DISGUSTING. Disgusting and gross and repulsive, which are all the things YOU KNOW WHO is.

"Really everything is his fault," I said to Clemesta. "He is to blame for everything bad."

"Dolly," Clemesta said. "I think that's only part of the story. And I think you're not remembering the rest on purpose."

I shut my eyes. "Shush," I said. "Close your eyes. We're going to do a magic vanishing trick to get us out of here. Look, now we are back home in our bed under the blue covers with the white clouds. Clemesta?"

"I'm doing it."

"Good. Now imagine we're lying in bed and our tummies are nice and full because Mom made a delicious dinner."

"Spaghetti?"

"Yeah. And ice cream for dessert, the one with three flavors in one tub."

"I like that one, but the strawberry best."

"Ditto. Anyway. Imagine we already put all the dolls in their beds, and we finished our stories. Now we snuggle down and Mom gives us bedtime Mom-cuddles and the special good-night-sleep-well-with-no-bad-dreams kisses. Do you remember the recipe for those kisses?"

Clemesta nodded. "One Eskimo rubbing noses kiss, one

Butterfly blinking eyelashes kiss, and one Mom kiss on the cheek."

"Excellent. Now we're very sleepy."

"I am feeling sleepy." Clemesta yawned.

"Yeah, so look up at the glow-in-the-dark stars and planets that Mom stuck up on the ceiling for us."

"I only see mold."

"Because you didn't do the trick like I said. Now try harder, and look up at the ceiling that's really the one from home and say, 'Good night, lovely universe, and thanks for shining all night and watching over us.' Say that and then we will fall asleep."

Later, the door made a loud crashing noise and I woke up again. It was Dad. He wasn't even standing up properly, he was just falling all over and he STANK like the garbage truck when it's sitting in the street waiting to gobble up the trash.

"I hate you," I hissed.

"Dolly," Dad said, but his eyes were only half open. "I'm such a fuck-up, baby, I fucked it all up. I try not to but I always do. My whole life, I always fucking do. It's all I fucking do." He knocked into his bed and fell on it. His eyes were shut and he covered them with his hand. "I'm gonna make it right, you'll see. You and me, we're gonna have a new start, Doll. Everything's gonna be better. Everything's gonna be great."

He stopped talking and started snoring, with his clothes on and his feet still on the carpet.

Tuesday

In the morning, Dad was sleeping and snoring and still wearing his clothes from the night before.

"It's morning," I said, VERY LOUDLY. "Wake up."

Dad opened one eye and groaned. "Wake up," I said. "It's time to go home."

"I gotta get some more sleep," he said. "My head."

"Stupid Dad." I threw one of the pillows to the floor.

"He was very drunk," Clemesta said. "Alcoholic and drunk."

"I know."

"That's not responsible grown-up behavior. Not at all."

I nodded.

"That's DISGRACEFUL DISGUSTING behavior. Mom was right. We shouldn't be around that."

I pulled the covers over my head so everything would be dark. "Now I'm a butterfly inside my caterpillar cocoon," I said. "I'm about to be born fresh. When you see my wings, you have to gasp because they're so beautiful."

Clemesta tugged at the covers. "But Dolly, don't you understand?"

I went silent in my lovely dark and warm cocoon. It was quiet and peaceful and it felt nice to be a safe and snug little caterpillar instead of a girl in the middle of the worst and strangest parts of America.

"Something isn't right," Clemesta said. "I feel it."

She knocked my cocoon with her hoof. "Dolly. Remember we saw that sign on the ice-cream truck last week? It said, 'If you see something suspicious, report it.'"

"Mm."

"I think this adventure is suspicious. Suspicious is bad. Dolly!"

I cracked open my cocoon and climbed out. My beautiful wings were broken forever and they would never ever fly. "You spoiled it, Clemesta!"

She made a sorry face but it was mixed with a worried face.

I found my hairbrush and combed out my hair. "I'll do yours too," I told her.

"Ouch," she said. "You're brushing too hard."

"Yes," I said. "I'm in a thundercloud mood." I looked at Clemesta's shining mane and her little horse bones underneath. I made her tail into a braid. I tried not to pull. "That's very beautiful," I said. I picked her up.

"Anyway, we're going home when Dad wakes up so everything will be good again soon."

Clemesta bit her lip. "I don't think we can."

"What do you mean?"

"I don't think Dad wants to go back. I think he's too mad. And, something else too."

I shook my head. "My brain hurts. My stomach hurts too. I bet it's the scurvy, from all the JUNK and NO NUTRIENTS and just sitting in the car all day long. Or maybe it's the homesickness disease."

Clemesta held her stomach with her horse-hoof. "I feel a little sick too."

I looked over at Dad. I didn't feel sorry for him anymore. I felt sorry for Mom, for having to live with him and Mr. Angry Bear inside his chest. And now he had taken me away on an adventure and she was back from her girls' weekend and we were still gone. Probably when I got home she would say, "OH DOLLY, MY HEART, I missed you every second." She would go on her knees and say, "I'm so sorry for my silly-stupid plan and I'll never do anything like that ever again and now everything can go back to how it was before." Then she would hug me and I'd smell her Mom smell HONEYSUCKLE MARSHMALLOW and her hair would tickle my cheek and she would give me a million kisses and I wouldn't feel sick anymore, I would feel like I was floating on a cloud.

I shut my eyes tightly so I could send her some telepathic love puffs, which are zaps that go straight to her heart. They say, "Dolly loves you" and they make Mom very happy.

"I wonder what Mom is doing right now," I said. "Probably her fitness. Then making herself beautiful for the day and taking a picture to put on her phone so everyone can write STUNNER and GORGEOUS and OMG. I bet it will be a good day with lots of messages and burning fire pictures. She likes those."

Clemesta was staring into OUTER SPACE.

"What?"

"Nothing." She shrugged. "I'm trying to solve a puzzle."

• • •

DISGRACEFUL DISGUSTING Dad's snoring was getting louder. His breath smelled of strong medicine. *ALCOHOLIC* rhymes with *FROLIC* rhymes with *BUBONIC.* That was a plague and it killed millions of people and they all got chucked onto a cart and thrown in the fire to be burned.

Dad would sleep for one million hours and I would have nothing to do all day long, not even play on his phone which was thrown into the bushes like a banana peel because that's how ridiculous he was. I sighed loudly.

"BORING," I said to Clemesta. "Snoring is boring."

Dad didn't budge.

I found the remote and switched on the TV. I turned it up EXTRA LOUD. The channels were all news and more news and commercials. I flicked back to one of the talk shows because THAT BITCH was sitting on the chair laughing with her whole mouth open. THAT BITCH used to be Mom's best friend in Hollywood but then she went and STOLE A ROLE that Mom was meant to get. It was a famous TV show with eight seasons so far and Mom already had a contract but THAT BITCH stabbed her back with a hundred knives and took it. Now she wins prizes on award show nights and Mom glares at her through the screen trying to make her trip on her way up the stairs.

I like those nights because Mom and I dress up in her prettiest Florida dresses and she does my makeup and hair and I get to wear some of her jewelry and we pretend that we are also invited to the theater. We applaud when nice actresses win but we boo for THAT BITCH and say how ugly she is and how she is losing her looks and getting too old and also running out of boyfriends.

Dad doesn't play the awards night game. He hardly plays any of our games. He just plays the dad. When he sees me in Mom's makeup and sexy sparkly dresses he gets mad and says it's INAPPROPRIATE. Mom says, "What do you know about appropriate?" and he leaves the room and sometimes the house.

I didn't want to see THAT BITCH anymore. I flicked off the TV. I had nothing to do. If I was back home in my bedroom I would have a million things to play with, like my collection of archaeological discoveries from the backyard, from the cavemen and the dinosaurs, and my seashells from the beach and my jar of BEST TREASURES and my leaves that have secret messages written on them that only I know how to decode. One leaf comes from the Planet Nefaria, and it says YOU HAVE BEEN CHOSEN. I have to wait for the next one to find out the rest.

I also have my whole doll's house, which Savannah says is better than her Lego Hotel because it's special and the only one of its kind in the whole world. Dad built it for me out of pieces of wood because Mom said there wasn't money to buy the real one in the toy store that I saw and put on my Christmas wish list for EXTRAORDINARY GOOD BE-HAVIOR. That one was made from plastic and it had a pink house and a white roof and it had lights that could switch on FOR REAL.

Dad took forever to make my wooden one because he is good at being DISAPPOINTING. He only did it after a big fight with Mom and after that, he set aside a whole weekend and didn't come out of the basement until it was done. The house has two stories and four rooms and one day when Mom was being a BEST MOM, she made all the furniture inside. She used little pieces of card, and she painted the windows with flower boxes and she stitched cushions and curtains from scraps of her old clothes. That was a good day and I didn't need to do any vanishing tricks.

Inside my house, I have a Mom and a Dad who are actually Monster High Vampires from last year's birthday. I also have a little girl who is a beautiful Barbie. There's no magical horse queen because we didn't find one yet, so instead I cut out a horse head from a catalog and stuck it onto a pair of Lego man legs. That's only TEMPORARY so Clemesta doesn't mind.

The Mom and Dad in my house kiss and make smooching sounds. They don't ever fight and they never have to pay any bills because everything is free. Everyone plays hide-and-seek together and the little girl is excellent at tennis and reading books. Every night before lights out, I put them into their beds and close the curtains so they will have sweet dreams. They don't have a dream catcher but they never get nightmares anyway. They won't have had anyone to tuck them in for so many nights and probably they are crying all day long. That's Dad's fault too.

I threw off the covers and climbed out of bed.

"I guess I will have to entertain myself." I said it very loudly. I went over to the Walmart bags and emptied them all out onto the carpet. I scrunched the bags so they would make lots of annoying noise. I took out the notepad and the pencils and I drew a picture of a bald eagle and another one of a tiger biting a man in half. I gave the man sad brown eyes and a VALUE MOTORS badge. If Mom was with me she could have helped. She is very good at making pictures and we like to do them together. She calls them our COLLABO-RATIONS. She is excellent at drawing hands and shoes and animal faces and I am excellent at the rest.

My first–best collaboration of ours is called MAGICALAND and we spent two whole weeks making it. We colored the pictures and sprinkled glitter into some of the flowers for fairy dust and we stuck paper beaks onto the toucans and it was so beautiful that Mom put it inside a frame beside her bed. Probably so she could look at it on her CAN'T GET OUT OF BED days and feel cheered up because it's impossible to stay sad or mad if you stare at glitter long enough. The sparkles jump into your heart and make you feel shiny, but I didn't have any glitter with me or actually ANYTHING that could cheer me up.

The tip of the red pencil broke off. I couldn't finish coloring the blood of the man the tiger was eating. I took all the other pencils and broke their tips too. They were dumb pencils anyway and nowhere near as nice as my ones at home.

I looked at all the new clothes Dad had bought me. I didn't like any of them. I just wanted my old ones. I picked out my purple leggings and put them on, even though they had chocolate smudges on the front and they didn't smell of fresh flowers anymore.

I spotted Dad's map lying on the floor beside his duffel bag. I tried to read it. Somewhere called Toluca was circled.

"That's Mexico," I whispered to Clemesta.

Her eyes went wide. "That's a whole other country."

"Well, we can't go there. It will take forever."

Dad's duffel bag was on the floor. It was unzipped and I could see a shirt peeking out and also one of my sweaters from home. I pulled it out. It smelled of home, of Mom and the laundry detergent she uses for our clothes. I gave it a hug. I wished Mom was here to give me a hug too.

I looked inside the bag, and my eyes went wide. Dad had piles and piles of money rolled together in bunches.

"That's a million dollars," I said.

Clemesta took a look. "Why does he have all that?" Her worried face got even more SUSPICIOUS. "What else is in there?"

I put my hand inside and felt something hard. I pulled it out. It was the framed photograph of Dad and Mom and me as a baby that normally lives on the bookshelf in our living room, next-door neighbors with a bowl I made in pottery class when I was five. "Why did he bring this?"

Clemesta looked at the photograph and then looked away. "He wants to keep the memory close."

"Mom is so beautiful," I said. The shower started dripping suddenly and it gave me a fright. I put the frame back.

I went over to the other Walmart bag instead. "Look," I said, "I forgot all about the tutu."

I pulled it over my head and did some dance practice to see how it would feel wearing a floaty skirt.

"You look like a professional ballerina," Clemesta said. "But I want us to focus on remembering something else."

"I still can't do an air split."

"Probably you'll do one next week. But Dolly, listen to me."

"Not now," I said.

I did ten jumping jacks and ten sit-ups. Mom usually does one thousand and that's why people call her SMOKING.

Dad opened one eye and looked at me. "You're great," he said.

SHUT UP, I said to him in my head. He rolled over and went back to snoring.

I walked around the room but there was nothing interesting to do. I finished the last of the Twizzlers. I went to brush my teeth. In the mirror, I could see the loose tooth getting more and more wobbly. I bet the tooth fairy would be mad if the tooth fell out in the stinky motel, because then she'd have to come collect it. Probably she'd only leave a few small bills and her note would say PLEASE NEVER STAY IN DISGUSTING MOTELS AGAIN. PS: YOUR TEETH ARE EXCELLENT AND HEALTHY, GRATEFUL THANKS.

Dad sounded like a pig who belonged in a pigsty instead of a bed. He didn't deserve any love or kindness from me and I kept it all to myself. You can do that and no one can force you not to. Like no matter how many times Mom BEGGED me to be friendly to YOU KNOW WHO when I saw him, I just made myself into a tiny frozen block of ice every time.

"She's adorable," he told Mom, but in my head I was actually chopping him into pieces with an invisible and deadly sword.

He wasn't even supposed to be a person in our lives but then we went and bumped into him in Manhattan one day on one of our TOP SECRET MISSIONS. The elevator doors opened and he said "Anna Kalina!" and Mom's eyes nearly popped out of her head.

"Well, my goodness," she said. "It's been forever."

She smiled hugely with all her white teeth and her eyes sparkled and we went into the lobby so that YOU KNOW WHO and Mom could chat. I drank a soda and tore the pieces of the coaster that it came on into confetti. Mom was laughing and tossing her hair and leaning in very close the whole time to touch his knee and afterward YOU KNOW WHO gave her a big hug and held her in his arms for a hundred minutes and said, "I'll call you," and Mom said, "Please, don't say that if you don't mean it."

On the train home, Mom was floating on a faraway cloud and shining big smiles at everyone. "Oh, Dolly," she said, "wasn't that just fate working its magic!" I didn't think there was anything magical about YOU KNOW WHO but I pinkie promised when Mom said, "It's going to be our special secret." Then I shoved the secret into the secret-secret box but first I spat on it because already then I knew he was a BAD OMEN, like a curse or a plague that steals away your precious beloveds or makes them do stupid things.

I looked at the clock on the table by the side of the bed. It said 11:17. My stomach was hungry even though it was also a big hard ball from no number twos.

Dad had left a bunch of bills on the table, all scrunched up like old tissues. Next to them was a pack of cigarettes with half missing and probably sucked up into his lungs. They would be black and rotten forever. SERVES HIM RIGHT.

"I'm taking some money," I said to Clemesta. "There's a

vending machine downstairs. We'll have to have more JUNK for breakfast but if we don't we'll starve to death."

"SHAME ON HIM," Clemesta said. She narrowed her eyes and stared a curse into Dad's skull.

The motel hallways smelled of ashtrays and dirty carpets with lots of things stepped into them, like gum and beer and pus. There was an ice machine at the end but someone had stuck a note on it saying OUT OF ORDER. Everything around here looked broken so I wasn't even one inch surprised.

I walked down the stairs to the main office. The clerk from last night was wearing the same too-tight T-shirt from before and talking to a woman who was yelling and trying to shush her crying baby at the same time.

"I already told you," the clerk said. "You gotta check out every twenty-eight days. Law's the law."

"We don't have anywhere to go," she said. "The baby. The fuck am I supposed to do with the baby?"

The clerk shrugged and the woman kicked over the trash can and stormed out with her suitcase and her baby dangling from her hip. I went up to the desk.

"Um," I said. "Do you have a vending machine?"

"There." The clerk pointed. He came over to pick the trash off the carpet. When he bent over, his butt made a face at me. I shut my eyes and walked away very fast.

I stood in front of the machine and tried to push the bill into the slot. It spat it back out. I tried again and it did the same thing, like someone sticking their tongue out at me.

"It won't take such a big bill," a voice said.

I looked around. There was a girl standing watching me. She had her arms folded and she was leaning against the wall. Her ponytail was in her mouth and she was sucking on it like it was a piece of candy instead of ratty old hair that Mom would call MOUSY-COLORED. Mousy is the exact opposite of lustrous and chestnut-colored hair, and probably it shouldn't be found on people, only mice.

"I'm Crystal," the girl said. "I can help you change that bill for something smaller if you want."

I stared at her. She was skinny-bony and she was wearing pointy shoes that were too big for her feet and her knees were grazed like she had fallen on gravel and bloodied them up.

"Well, come on," she said, "I don't bite."

I thought of Dad upstairs, snoring and being revolting and not even caring about hurting our best love with lies and broken promises AGAIN AND ALWAYS. It would serve him right if he woke up and I wasn't there. It would serve him right to be worried and scared like I was last night. Dad gets FLAMING MAD if he thinks that he's going to be left alone so HA and SO THERE and SO WHAT, because that's exactly what he deserved.

"But it's not responsible," Clemesta said.

"Who cares?" I slipped her under my arm. "Nobody in this whole family is being one inch of responsible."

I followed Crystal outside into the parking lot. She was walking very quickly, even in the too-big shoes. Her knees turned in as she walked, like they were trying to kiss each other. There were a load of cracks in the sidewalk and I tried hard to keep my toes away from the trolls.

"You here long-term?" Crystal said. Her ponytail bounced as she walked. "We've been here since November. It's better now that it's getting warmer."

"What's long-term?"

"Like, you live in the motel room," Crystal said. "Like it's your house."

I shook my head. "We're only here for one night."

Crystal shrugged. "Then I guess we can only be friends for today."

"Where are we going?"

"First we're going collecting," she said. "It's on the way. Here." She handed me a trash bag and led me under a fence and into a park. The grass was brown and dead and full of weeds, and most of the equipment in the play area looked broken and rusted and dangerous. There weren't any kids playing or anyone walking their dog or doing yoga. It was just us with the trash bag.

"You didn't tell me your name yet," Crystal said. She threw two empty cans into the bag.

"I'm Dolly."

"Pleased to make your acquaintance, Dolly."

We shook hands like you're meant to do when you meet someone new and friendly.

"Are you a climate change warrior?" I said.

"Say what?"

"Is that why we're collecting trash? To make the planet nice and clean again?"

Crystal frowned. "It's for the recycling money. Five cents a can. Some weeks that's fifty dollars, but we have to do a ton of collecting, like, all day long."

"Oh," I said. "I didn't know you could get money for that."

"Uh-huh. All you have to do is collect it, and it's, like, free money."

I peered under a bush and picked out a can. "Lucky people are LITTER BUGS."

Crystal went scratching in the trash. She was still chewing her ponytail which was wet with her spit and sticking together in clumps.

"Why do you live in the motel?" I said. I tried not to step in any of the poop lying around that NO ONE HAD SCOOPED.

"Mama lost her job last year," Crystal said. "So we lost our house. Well, we didn't lose it like we couldn't find it. The bank took it away."

She pushed her bangs out of her eyes. They were bright blue and glassy and sharp, like she was an ice princess. Or a lady wizard.

"It was a nice house. We had a yard and a kitchen table for doing homework. Now I do it on the floor while my brother Charlie watches TV. He likes the show about home renovations." She shrugged. "Anyway, it's okay, I guess. This place is better than the shelter we were in before. Those are the worst. The food is so disgusting." She made throwing up noises and spat for real in the dirt. "Hey, watch out for those," she said. "If you get pricked you can die from the junkie disease."

I looked down at my shoes. Three plastic injectors with very SHARP AND DEADLY needles were lying right there. A can of Mountain Dew was sitting beside them, but I didn't pick it up and neither did Crystal.

We walked around the other side of the park.

"Why are you skipping school?" she said.

"Um, I'm on an adventure with Dad."

"What kind of adventure?"

I sighed. "A dumb one. But we're going home today. My mom misses me a lot."

Crystal stopped to pick at a bite mark on her arm. "This is why I'm not in school," she said. "They had to shut it down to kill all the bugs. There was an infestation. Some kids got real sick."

I looked closer and saw a whole row of tiny red bites along the underneath part of her arm. Some of them had been scratched raw and bloody. "Does it hurt?"

"It itches like a bitch." Crystal clawed at the skin and then dabbed spit on it.

"I do that too," I told her. "It's a good cure."

She bent for a can and tossed it in the bag. "How old are you?" she said.

"I'm seven years and almost three months."

"I'm seven and a half. But everyone says I'm small for my age. I should probably go to the doctor."

"Maybe you have scurvy," I said.

Crystal shrugged. "I had the chicken pox before. I still have a scar."

She showed me her cheek and the little crater sitting by her nose.

"I have a scar from burning my arm on the oven once," I said. "My mom was baking cookies but she fell asleep and forgot and I tried to get them out before they burned. It didn't hurt so much. Only a little. And I got to eat the cookies afterward."

Crystal clutched her hands to her stomach. "Stop," she said. "Now I want cookies. A hundred cookies."

"A thousand cookies!" I said. "I could eat a thousand."

"With milk!" Crystal yelled.

"And ice cream!"

"With caramel chunks!"

"And a billion chocolate sprinkles!"

We were screaming louder and louder and then we fell to the patchy grass and laughed in STITCHES. Crystal's blue eyes were sparkling at me in the sun and it felt very nice to have her for a friend.

I dusted the grass off my knees. "Do you know ballet?"

"Uh-huh," Crystal said. She got up and showed me her pirouettes. Her long skinny legs could stay very straight and perfect.

"You're so good," I said. I felt a pinch of jealous but then I decided that she deserved a SPECIAL TALENT because of losing her house.

"I'm better at the jumps," I said. I set Clemesta down and showed her the one I had been practicing.

"That's pretty," Crystal said. "And your tutu is real nice."

I smoothed it with my fingers. "It was a bargain," I said, "that's the only reason Dad bought it. I'm not spoiled or anything."

Crystal looked at Clemesta who was resting on the grass. She petted her mane.

"She's my most special-precious thing," I said. "She's magical. Also she talks, but only to me. She's my guardian protector angel. But also a horse queen."

I waited for Crystal to call me a PANTS ON FIRE LIAR

or a baby like the girls in my class usually do, but she just nodded. She stroked Clemesta very gently so she wouldn't feel frightened. Clemesta liked her. "I have an old stuffed lion of Charlie's," Crystal said, "but he doesn't talk."

"Lions are good protector animals. He'll keep you safe."

"I hope so."

We collected a few more cans and tossed them in the bag. The sun was burning in the sky and a plane passed over us. Its white trail stayed behind in the blue, two long lines to show you the way.

"One day I'll be a pilot," Crystal said. "I'll fly people to their vacations in Hawaii."

"I like your name," I said. "I forgot to tell you before."

Crystal slung the garbage bag over her shoulder. "It's because I came out bright and shining like a crystal. That's what Mama says. Charlie calls me Crystal Meth but he's a jackass."

Someone called out, "Who's your friend, Crystal?" and Crystal jumped. She stopped smiling right away.

"What do you want, Shayna?"

Shayna was much bigger than us, maybe even older than Lucy, my old babysitter. She was wearing a tight dress and scuffed cowboy boots. Her hair was mousy like Crystal's and shaved on one side and long on the other. She reached over and yanked Crystal's ponytail.

"Stop sucking that thing," she said. "I told you, it's nasty."

Crystal flicked her hand away.

"Introduce me to your friend," Shayna said.

Crystal looked at the grass. "This is Dolly," she said.

Shayna smiled. "Well, hey there, Dolly," she said. "I'm Crystal's big sister, Shayna."

She snatched the trash bag out of Crystal's hands and looked inside. "This all?"

"We didn't finish yet."

"We were playing," I said.

Shayna looked me up and down. She had beady black eyes like a cruel and hungry shark.

"We're leaving now," Crystal said. She took my hand and tried to pull me away.

"Where to?" Shayna asked.

"Crystal is going to help me change my bill for the vending machine," I said. "It's too big."

Shayna's eyes went wide. "Is that so?" She smiled. "Well, I guess I better help with that. Since I'm the oldest."

"No, Shayna," Crystal said. "Please just leave us alone." She looked like she wanted to cry.

Shayna smiled at me. "Give me that bill, Dolly."

I looked at Crystal. She shook her head but only a little so Shayna wouldn't see. I crossed my fingers behind my back.

"I don't have it," I said. "I left it at the motel."

Shayna squinted her eyes. "You sure?"

I nodded.

"Well, I hope you know it's a sin to lie, Dolly. And we don't like liars around here. Isn't that right, Crystal?"

Crystal stomped her foot. "Pleeeease, Shayna," she said, but Shayna ignored her. She put her face so close that I could feel her breath on my cheek. It smelled rotten. She smiled a MEAN WITCH smile with her pointed yellow teeth.

"Give over the bill, Dolly."

I reached into the top of my leggings and held it out.

"That's a good girl," Shayna said. She snatched it out of my fingers and turned to walk away. "Come on, girls," she called, "keep up."

Crystal didn't speak as we followed Shayna into the town. We passed a hardware store and a bait shop and a diner. Everything else was shut up and the windows nailed with wood. There wasn't even one grocery store or deli or flower store, so probably no one around here could ever buy stuff like that, even on Mother's Day. One house we passed had a big sign stuck over the door that said CONDEMNED PROPERTY. I didn't remember what that meant, probably something like DAMNED or CURSED. Everything looked damned and cursed around here.

One of Crystal's shoes came off and she stopped to stick her foot back inside.

"Stupid shoe," she said.

"Wendy's is a good place to break that bill," Shayna said. She touched her stomach like it was talking to her. "Yeah, I'm feeling Wendy's."

Crystal didn't answer and I didn't either. We just followed Shayna across the street. At the counter, Shayna ordered bacon cheeseburgers and chicken nuggets and chili cheese nachos and fries and chocolate Frostys. She paid for the food and when the lady behind the counter gave back the change, Shayna slipped it inside her pocket.

"That's mine," I said.

"I'll give it to you later." She winked, and I already knew it was a lie.

We carried our trays to a table in the corner. The restaurant was full of old men in faded T-shirts and baseball caps. Also there were lots of women with big stomachs and kids all around them, shoving fries into their mouths and staring at the TV in the corner.

Shayna ate like she was a starving stray dog who hadn't seen food in a hundred days. Crystal only picked at some nuggets. She didn't want to look at me.

I tried to stare DAGGERS into Shayna's skull for spoiling our fun, but she didn't seem to notice. Probably she was so evil that she was IMMUNE. I ate my fries and pulled the bacon off my cheeseburger. It was pink and shiny, like a tongue.

When Shayna had finished all her food, she sat back in the chair and patted her stomach. "Well, that's better. Isn't it, Crystal? Way better than that garbage from the food bank."

Crystal scowled at her.

"Don't be like that," Shayna said. "I'm looking out for you." She turned to me. "Crystal's skin over bone, isn't she, Dolly? You can count all her ribs."

I didn't know what to say. I squeezed Clemesta. "That girl is trouble," she said. "We should get back to the motel."

I finished my Frosty and wiped my hands on a napkin. "I have to go now," I said. "My dad is getting worried."

"Suit yourself," Shayna said. "We're in no rush."

"But," I said, "I don't know the way back."

Crystal stood up. "I'll walk you," she said, but Shayna grabbed her arm.

"Hold up," she said. "You want to make sure that's worth your while."

Crystal tried to wriggle away but Shayna kept her trapped.

She looked at me and the tears started to fall down her cheeks. She was very ugly when she cried.

I swallowed. I wanted to cry too but I held everything tight inside my tears pouch.

"What do you want, Shayna?"

She smiled again, that stupid fake and phony smile. I wished she would get EATEN BY WOLVES in very slow and tiny bites that would hurt a LOT.

"Well, now," she said, "I'm a reasonable woman. I'll keep your change. And Crystal will take that tutu off you."

We walked to the motel without saying anything. We must have taken a different route because I didn't recognize even one thing and I would have definitely gotten LOST FOR-EVER if I had tried to find my way back alone.

We passed a big fence with KEEP OUT tape all around. Everything inside was burned and black and crispy. It looked like it was a fairground once upon another time when the town wasn't filled with mean BITCHES like Shayna. Prob-ably one day everything got set on fire. I bet lots of bad people got burned too. I was glad. Someone should have set fire to Shayna.

She sang the whole way back. She tried to do some dance moves but she was a horrible dancer and just looked preposterous with her stupid broken-heeled cowboy boot clicking against the sidewalk. Crystal's recycling cans jangled like cowbells and the tutu floated around her bony legs. She had to keep stopping to hitch it up so it wouldn't fall off her tiny waist.

As soon as we reached the motel, Shayna skipped off.

Crystal stood looking at me with her teary blue see-through eyes. She didn't say anything. She didn't give me my tutu back, either.

I walked away BOILING.

"What a witch," I said to Clemesta.

"Probably a SLUT too," she said. "A mean witchy bitchy slut."

We stomped upstairs and banged on the door. Dad opened up right away.

"Jesus Christ, Dolly, where the hell have you been?" he said.

He was showered and his hair was slicked back and he didn't stink of cigarettes and medicine anymore, he smelled fresh and fruity, but his face was twisted and angry and also pale and ghostly, like he had the biggest fright of his life.

"I was freaking out," he said. "I didn't know where you'd got to. I was thinking something awful happened, that you'd run off or someone had got you or the police—Jesus."

He rubbed his hands over his face and sank onto the bed. "I thought you were gone."

I looked at him and I felt so mad that I couldn't even speak one single word, I just sucked it all inside me and shut my mouth and ran into the bathroom and slammed the door behind me.

Stupid Shayna. Stupid Dad. Stupid adventures. I looked at my reflection in the mirror and gave it a WHACK. Stupid everything.

I wished Clemesta was with me but I had dropped her on the other side of the door.

I spoke to her using telepathy and she answered right away.

"I want to go home," I said.

"I know," she said.

"I want everything to go back to how it was before."

She sent me telepathy hugs. That made me feel a little better, but my stomach was cramped up like someone was twisting it with their two fists.

Dad was knocking on the door, saying, "Let me in, Dolly."

I didn't say a word.

"Please, Dolly." He wasn't yelling anymore, his voice was soft, like when he's SORRY DAD full of promises and asking for another chance and saying, "It will be different" and "I will try harder."

"I'm sorry," Dad said. "I was just so scared. I can't lose you. Understand? I couldn't live if you were taken from me, Dolly."

His voice cracked. "You're the only thing that matters to me in this world. You're what I live for, Doll, you're the only thing."

I opened the door, but only a tiny bit.

"Can you forgive me?" Dad said. He touched a hand to my cheek and I didn't jerk away. His eyes went dark and he touched my forehead.

"Jesus," he said. "You're burning up."

"I'm mad," I said. "That's why." I wanted to tell him about Shayna but my voice sounded strange, like the words were stuck. "I'm mad at you too," I said. Dad went spinning around the room and I tried to catch him in my eyes.

"Jesus, Doll," he said. He scooped me in his arms when my legs went to Jell-O. My stomach jumped and then there was throw-up everywhere and I started to cry because of the bad taste in my mouth, Twizzlers and fries and something sharp and burning. Dad opened the toilet seat and moved my head over the bowl. "I don't want to go in there," I said. I threw up twice more and then I went blank.

I blinked and I was in the bed. Dad was holding me and pressing a cool cloth to my head. The water trickled down my face.

"I'm on fire," I said. "I'm on fire."

Dad's eyes were frightened eyes again, like the coyote in the trap. I remembered that he didn't survive with only three paws. The other coyotes ate him up. "It's a fever," Dad said. "We'll bring it down."

I still tasted throw-up in my mouth. "I need medicine," I said. "Mom gives me medicine for a fever. The purple one."

Dad pressed the cloth but my skin was turning the water into hot lava.

I cried. "Call an ambulance," I said. "Call the doctor." I started shivering but I was sweating too and everything felt wet around me. Dad put his head in his hands and shook his head. "Fuck, fuck."

I cried some more. "I need Mom. She'll know how to make me better. You don't know anything, not anything." My voice croaked and the tears went backward down my throat instead of out my eyes. Everything was heavy and invisible.

Dad nodded. "I know, sweetheart, I know. I'm sorry. I'm so sorry."

"Are you crying too?" I said, and then it all went blank again.

When I opened my eyes, Dad was standing over me with a glass of water.

"Drink this," he said. He put a teaspoon of something into

my mouth and I swallowed. He had his shoes on. My pajamas were wet from sweat and Dad pulled them off and slipped one of his T-shirts over my head. Everything was dizzy and spinning but my body was made of bricks.

I shut my eyes and and let everything go dark.

"I'm sorry," said a voice. "It's all my fault."

I couldn't tell if that was Dad or me.

Wednesday

Dad was sitting on the floor in the corner of the room. He was very still, and he seemed far away even though his body was right there.

"Good morning," he said. His eyes were red and shining, and they looked at me with WORRIED-AFRAID-TIRED-SAD-I-LOVE-YOU written inside them.

"Were you watching me sleep?" I said.

"Yeah."

"All night?"

He nodded. "Most of the night. I wanted to make sure you were okay. That the fever didn't come back."

"Oh. Did it?" Dad shook his head.

"You slept through."

The curtains were pulled shut but there was a line of light sneaking through. It made the dust dance.

"I was very sick," I said.

"I know."

"I was scared."

"Me too." Dad came over to the bed. He touched my forehead, stroking it gently like I was a very delicate baby bird.

"Do you feel better?"

"A little."

"And—and how's Clemesta doing?" Dad asked.

"Clemesta?"

"Yeah."

I looked at Clemesta, who was tucked in beside me. Dad must have put her there after I fell asleep.

"Good morning, Clemesta," I said. "My best-treasure horse."

She opened her eyes.

"Dad wants to know how you are."

"Humph!" she said. "He's just trying to get on our good side. To make up for all the disgraceful and bad stuff he's done."

"I like when he's trying," I said. "He's nice when he tries."

"No, I don't think he's nice at all."

She folded her horse-hooves to sulk. I flipped the covers back over her head. Dad was watching me with his shining eyes. He was paying me every bit of his attention, like I was his most special-precious thing.

"Clemesta's fine," I told him. "She's ready for breakfast. And we need REAL FOOD from now on. Nutritious and with hundreds of vitamins and NO MORE JUNK."

Dad smiled. "All right," he said. He took my hand in his and held it over his heart. "I'm going to take much better care of you from now on," he said. His brown eyes were big and serious. "I promise," he said. "See?" He stuck out his little finger for a pinkie promise. I shook my head.

"No," I said. "Those don't work with your fingers."

I went into the bathroom to wash up. My face was all blotchy and splotchy from getting sick, and my hair was fuzzy from sweating out all the fever juice. I was glad that

Dad was being SORRY DAD who remembered that I was his EVERYTHING and felt destroyed with shame for not looking after me properly. I still had some mad left in me, and I tried to get it out like Mom does on the days when she practices her meditating exercises. Breathe in love, breathe out all your mad and sad and bad. That's how it works, and afterward you are brand-new and happy and you can forgive people when they hurt you. Unless it's THAT BITCH or YOU KNOW WHO. You don't ever have to forgive people like them.

The Motel Disgusting had one tiny bottle of shampoo and no conditioner and no soap, but I did plenty of rinsing to clean my hair, and after that I combed out all the tangles, and then I brushed my teeth and after that I was SPOTLESSLY CLEAN AND FRUITY FRESH. I felt better in my stomach after being sick but there was a new feeling inside there now, like a big rock was sitting at the bottom making everything heavy. Especially I felt it sinking every time I thought about Mom back at home without us.

"That's because you're remembering," Clemesta said.

I put the towel over her head. "Here," I said, "dry yourself off."

I dressed myself in the new shorts. They felt tight around my legs, and I tried to pull on the edges to stretch them so they wouldn't pinch. Probably I was putting on PILES of weight from all the junk Dad was feeding me. Mom would be mad at him about that. And the other stuff too.

"You look nice," Dad said, when I came out of the bathroom.

"The shorts are too tight. Or I'm too big."

"You're perfect," Dad said.

"I'm not," I said. "I'm not perfect at all."

I watched as Dad packed up the Walmart bags and zipped up the duffel with all the money inside. He slipped the pack of cigarettes into his jeans even though it belonged in the trash.

I looked at him. "I want to call Mom," I said. "I need to speak with her." Dad nodded.

"Yeah," he said. "Of course you do."

"Can we call her now?"

"Well, this phone doesn't work. I tried yesterday."

"Oh."

"We'll stop somewhere. Find a pay phone."

I nodded. "Because Mom doesn't like not hearing my voice for so long."

Dad's sad eyes blinked. "I know, sweetheart."

"What about Miss Ellis?"

"What?"

"Does she know I'm missing more school? Today is three days I'm not there. Monday, Tuesday, Wednesday."

"Oh, yeah," Dad said. "I told her on Monday that you'd be out a couple of days. She doesn't mind."

"But I'll miss so much."

"You can catch up. She said so."

"Probably because I'm advanced."

"Exactly."

I pressed my fingers into my stomach. I picked up Clemesta and folded her against me.

"And we're going home now, right? That's what you said."

Dad nodded. "Yeah, we're going back."

. . .

The clerk at the front desk was running his tongue around a doughnut, licking off all the pink frosting. He was wearing the same T-shirt AGAIN but I forgot to check if his face pimples had burst. His head was turned to watch the TV screen hanging on the wall. The voice said IN THE LATEST ON THE ABDUCTION OF—and the man's eyes went from the TV to me. His mouth dropped open just as I felt Dad's hand push at my back very hard and shove me out the door.

He grabbed hold of my hand and dragged me to the car and didn't stop when I said OUCH or nearly tripped over my feet. He pushed me inside and jumped in front to start the car and he didn't put his seat belt on or set our bags on the seat, he just raced out of the parking lot with everything still on his lap and the seat belt reminder screaming loudly in our ears.

As the car spun us away, I could see the clerk standing outside. Shayna was right next to him and I heard her calling after us, "I told you that was Dolly Rust."

Dad drove very fast, screeching the brakes and then racing off again. We came to a red light and he drove right through it. Clemesta and I held on tight to our seats and said a wish not to crash into a pole.

"He's mad because I told Shayna and Crystal my real name," I said. "Now he'll get in trouble for taking me out of school."

Clemesta shook her head. "It isn't that."

Dad swerved and we went sliding on the seat. He tried

to unfold his map but he couldn't get it to lie flat with one hand.

"Here," I said. I reached over and smoothed it out and set it on the passenger seat.

Dad was looking in his side mirrors, watching the cars behind us. His eyes were wild.

"Are you mad at me?" I said. "Because the guy from the motel knows my name?"

Dad shook his head. "I'm not mad at you, Doll. Not ever."

He turned off at the next exit and then we were on a road with no other cars, just trees thick and green on either side. Dad was still going very fast and I had that feeling inside me the same as when the superstorm was about to hit New York. Everyone had to stay home and buy flashlights and food and keep safe indoors and I was scared that the storm would destroy everything, that it would flatten the whole neighborhood and crush it to pieces until nothing was left.

In the end, it wasn't even scary, because Mom and Dad and me got to spend all day in our pajamas and Dad made big bowls of popcorn that he refilled every time we ate it up, and we watched movies and played board games and when the power went off, we lit candles and went around in turns to tell ghost stories. Mom and Dad fell asleep on blankets on the living room floor, all twisty and curled in each other's arms. Clemesta and I made a bed next to them and we all stayed just like that until the morning came and the storm had passed.

"Probably this will turn out fun too," I said. "It feels scary now but soon it won't be. Isn't that right?"

Clemesta put her hoof into her mouth and bit her horse-nails. "Dolly, it's bad."

I watched Dad's eyes in the mirror. He was back to no blinking.

"What's *abduction*?" I said.

His hands on the wheel were shaking. "It's like stealing," he said. "Stealing a person."

I tried to catch hold of his eyes in the mirror but he didn't look back, he just stared ahead.

I kicked off my shoes. The Jeep's windows were starting to get dirty. It made the pictures outside blurry.

We drove through two more boring towns, past ugly broken houses with no one mowing the lawns or picking up the empty beer cans they'd tossed out onto the grass. Most of the houses weren't even real houses, they were just old trailer homes on cement blocks.

Abduction, abduction.

I picked at the scab on my leg.

"Don't," Clemesta said. "You'll make it bleed again. It will leave a scar."

"Maybe I want a scar," I said. I lifted the rusty skin part till it came off in my fingers. The blood oozed out and the skin underneath yelled at me.

"Dad. Are we still going home?"

"Uh-huh."

I watched the blood on my leg slowly trickle away.

We passed by a man sitting on his porch, drinking a can of beer and watching the cars. He was scratching inside his dirty jean shorts and the sofa he was sitting on had all its yellow stuffing oozing out. There was a Confederate flag on his porch, waving its blue X in the breeze.

I combed my wet hair with my fingers to help it dry, and then I took the plastic comb and brushed all the tangles out of Clemesta's thick mane.

"You look beautiful," I told her. "Even if you can be a nag sometimes."

"DITTO," she said. "And I'm only looking out for you. That's my job."

"I know," I said. "You're a very good protector horse. Except you didn't protect us from Shayna."

Clemesta hung her head.

"But don't worry. I bet she catches the bubonic plague from a rat."

It's all right to wish bad things on people who are mean because they deserve it.

DEAD POSSUM.

FLAG FLAG FLAG.

GOD SEES EVERYTHING.

"Does he? Even inside my secret-secret box?"

Clemesta looked at me. "Why? Did you remember what's there?"

"No."

"I think you're lying."

"Am not."

"Are too."

WELCOME TO ALABAMA it said on the side of the road.

"Hey," I said. "This is another state. Why aren't we going back the way we came?"

"It's faster this way," Dad said.

I tried to remember the world map we have hanging up in the kitchen. It shows all the countries in the whole world and all the states of America, but I couldn't figure out if Alabama was up or down from where we were. When I was back home again, I would stick pins into the map, marking all the places we'd been on the adventure. Then I would take it to class to show Miss Ellis and she would say, "Gosh, Dolly, you are a real world traveler."

Alabama, I said in my head. I like the word very much, because it makes your tongue curl back in your mouth and it also sounds like a poem.

Alabama, I said, *Alabama.*

There used to be a girl in my school called Alabama, but she moved with her family to Los Angeles because her big sister became a famous actress on a TV show. Mom and I watched an episode once, but Mom turned it off when we were only halfway through.

"If that's talent, I'll eat my shoe," she said.

Los Angeles is the place where DREAMS COME TRUE. That's how Mom explained it. That's what YOU KNOW WHO said too.

"You'll love it," he told me.

"I hate you," I said back. I stuck out my tongue even though that's RUDE and rude girls don't get gold stars.

YOU KNOW WHO said he had just the part for Mom on his new show and she would be famous again and we wouldn't have to worry about bills and Mr. Angry Bear anymore.

"I've spent all these years waiting for things to get better,"

Mom said. "Waiting for him to pick up the pieces and get back to the man he was when I met him."

"It's never going to be different, Anna," YOU KNOW WHO said. "You must know that."

Mom sighed. "He can't even look at me," she said. "All I do is remind him of everything he's lost. The life we had. Well." Mom pressed her eyes and switched on her smile. "And now you're here," she told him. "Like my knight in shining armor."

YOU KNOW WHO took her hand and I put my best-worst curse on his head.

"Where is that damn waiter?" he said. "I told him to bring the dressing on the side."

Just thinking about YOU KNOW WHO made me so mad that I squeezed my hands into two fierce punching fists without even trying.

"It's all right, Dolly," Clemesta said. "He can't ruin things anymore."

"Why don't you look happy about that?"

She picked at her hooves. "What if we were wrong about him? What if he was really trying to be her friend?"

"Silly horse, moms can't have friends who are boys. And YOU KNOW WHO is definitely and certainly and for surely the WORST. Rita even warned Mom about him. She said, 'Watch out, Anna. That man is full of promises but he's never been the most sincere. And this isn't asking him to get you into that damn members' club you're so obsessed with; it's your lives.' See? Everyone can tell he's a monster."

She knitted her horse-brows together into a *W* for *WORRY*.

"I don't know, Dolly," she said. "I think we might have made a mistake."

Dad looked back at me in the mirror. He smiled but it was like a smile that hurt his face. "We'll . . . we'll pull over in a bit. Get something to eat."

I frowned. "Are you very sure this is the right direction for going home?"

Dad kept his eyes on the road. "Yeah," he said. "I'm sure."

I rubbed the skin on my arms, which was changing color in the sun. Probably back home it was still cold and rainy. Mom would be saying, "Perfect weather to be a duck," and I would be wearing my rain boots, which are blue with yellow bottoms. They are made of rubber to be waterproof against splashes and puddle-jumping, which is the best fun, especially in the garden where the water gathers in very deep pools. Sometimes Mom puts on her rain boots too, and then we have a SPLASH-OFF COMPETITION and we get so muddy that we have to throw all our clothes off at the back door before we can go inside the house. Sometimes Mom even strips NAKED and we do the crazy naked dance right outside with our bare bottoms shaking in the rain. Mom doesn't care if the neighbor Mrs. Mistry sees us and tattletales to Dad.

"I don't think she's doing too well," is what Mrs. Mistry told him last time. We were outside in the drive getting ready to go to the park and practice my bicycle riding tricks, but she came over to us and whispered her NOSY NEWS to Dad. It put him in such a bad mood that by the time we got to the park, he just sat on a bench and didn't help me ride. When we got back home, Dad pulled Mom to him and stroked her face and said, "I'm here, I'm here," and she laid her head on his shoulder and closed her eyes and melted. Dad's arms around her were big and solid, like one of those Life Saver floats you throw to a drowning person in a lake.

My stomach made a noise and I pressed my hands into my belly button. That's the place where a baby is joined to its Mom when it's inside her stomach. That's called GESTATION and if you're a baby elephant you spend twenty-two months in there but if you're a baby human it's only nine months.

Mom keeps an album of photographs from when she had me growing in her. In one of them, she looks very beautiful and smiley in a long blue dress with no sleeves and a big straw sunhat that covers half her face. She has her hands cupped around her belly WHICH IS ME and she's cradling it like it is something very precious.

"Were you excited for me to pop out?" I asked her.

"Yes," Mom said. "It was a very happy day."

"Did you know already that I'd be a girl?"

"No," Mom said. "But I hoped you would be."

"Did you love me right away?"

"Oh, yes. And forever and always to come."

I like the photo very much.

I wondered if Mom felt something in her belly when I was far away from her, like an ache of missing and loneliness, or a special stomach-voice that said, DOLLY IS GONE, DOLLY IS GONE, SOMETHING IS WRONG BECAUSE DOLLY IS GONE.

"Something is wrong," Clemesta said.

"It isn't," I said. "We're going home now."

Clemesta shut her eyes. I think she was trying to meditate out the bad.

Dad pulled up in the parking lot outside a strip mall. It was all square and concrete and flat, like there weren't any colors left to make the town look pretty.

"I'll be a minute," Dad said. "You wait here." He put down all the windows to let in the air.

"But I'll be bored."

"I'll be quick," Dad said. "And Clemesta will keep you company."

"I need to pee," I said.

"Didn't you go at the motel?"

"I need to go again. I'll go in the store."

Dad scratched his head. "Just hold it a while longer. We'll stop another place."

He looked at himself in the mirror and messed his hair so it was standing up. Then he got out of the car and pulled the plaid shirt out of the Walmart bag. He put it on and lifted the collar and hunched over like something was wrong with his neck.

At the entrance to the store, I watched as the doors swallowed him up.

I jiggled my tooth. It was still holding on. I hung my arms out the window and felt the hot metal of the car against my skin. There wasn't any breeze.

A woman pushed her stroller in front of Dad's car. I watched her lift the baby out to put him in his car seat. The baby's eyes were black and wobbly and his head was flat on top, like it never finished growing into a circle. He made a funny moaning sound as the woman strapped him in. She slammed the car door shut and climbed in front. Then she just sat there with her head on the wheel. Probably she was napping.

Dad was still gone.

"Maybe he's leaving us behind," Clemesta said. "Like running away."

I shook my head. "He would never leave us. Never ever." I yawned, but not from tired, from bored. The woman with the flat-head baby pulled away. Now it was only the Jeep and two other cars left.

"Hello, hello," I called out into the empty parking lot. I wanted to see if it echoed. I sang the words from the song Mom loves best. A man pushed a shopping cart to his car, but he didn't stop to listen.

"Pretend I'm on stage," I said. "Pretend you're the judge and you say, 'Dolly Rust, you will be a sensation.'"

Clemesta shook her head. "I'm getting tired of pretending the whole time."

Dad came back to the car with two bags in his hand. He scratched in one of them and pulled out a baseball cap. He put it on and turned to look at me.

"You like it?"

I gave him two thumbs up.

"I have one for you," he said. "Here."

"Not now," I said. "My hair is lovely and shiny. It wants to stay loose."

Dad took a pair of glasses out of the bag and snapped off the plastic tag before putting them on.

"You don't wear glasses."

"I need them for driving."

"LIAR," Clemesta said.

Dad passed a pack of crackers to me, and then a box of cereal and a couple of granola bars. "It's a breakfast picnic," he said.

"There's no milk."

"Are you kidding? Dry cereal is the best."

"I said only healthy food. Like green smoothies and fruit."

"There wasn't any," Dad said. "But granola bars are kinda healthy."

"No. Mom says they're packed with sugar, it just hides in there like a sneaky cat burglar."

"Oh. Well."

We drove through a long stretch of trailer homes and they howled at us to look away. All the trees had thorns and all the windows had eyes.

"Are you definitely and certainly sure we're going in the right direction?"

Dad nodded.

"Because it doesn't look right at all."

I glared at Cap'n Crunch's face on the box. "You aren't nutritious," I told him.

He cackled. "I know," he said. "I'm full of sugar too."

I opened up the box and took a handful anyway. I crunched a few bites and wiped my sticky hands on the seat. I stared at Dad's head in the new cap, watching the road ahead. He turned on the radio and we listened to the voices crack and scratch.

ABDUCTION. ABDUCTION. I kept thinking of the clerk's pimply face watching us drive away. DOLLY RUST, Shayna had yelled, but I never told her my last name.

"Exactly," Clemesta said. Her eyes were shining.

"Have a nap," I said. "You look like you have a fever." I set her under the seat.

Dad slowed the car near a gas station. Behind it, there was a parking lot full of rows and rows of rusty old heaps parked out in the sun. They looked like they were in a car cemetery for dead cars that would never move again. Most of them were rusted brown. An old yellow school bus was sitting on bricks. Probably someone stole the tires. Maybe they took the schoolchildren too.

Dad pulled up. I opened the window because Clemesta had accidentally let out a fart that was stinking up the car.

A voice called out. "Can I help you, mister?"

Dad spun around. A woman was standing in the doorway of the store. She had a cigarette in her mouth and she didn't even take it out to speak.

Dad gave her a wave. "Thank you," he said. "Be over in a minute."

"You look funny with your glasses," I said.

He nodded. "I need you to put the cap on," he said. "Tuck your hair up and put it on."

"I don't want to."

"Dolly," he said. "Do it."

I pressed my fists into my stomach to feel the rock. "Are we in disguise?"

"Kinda."

"Why? Are we in trouble?"

Dad wiped his forehead. "A little bit."

"Because of skipping school?"

He nodded. I kicked my sneakers into the seat. "Well, it wasn't even my idea," I said. "And you never asked me, you just scooped me up and left."

Dad looked back at the woman waiting for us at the store. "I know," he said. "I'm sorry. And you aren't in any trouble, only me. We just need to be careful for a couple of days."

I looked at his brown eyes. "Until we get home?"

"Yeah."

I threw off the seat belt and shoved the cap on my head. My hair was too thick and lustrous to stay hidden away for long, and it all popped back out. Dad didn't notice, he had already grabbed his duffel bag and he was walking ahead.

The woman didn't smile at us. She walked with a cane and one of her legs was bandaged up.

"You lost?" she said. Her words came out very stretchy, like in slow motion.

Dad pulled his new cap down low over his face. "No, ma'am," he said. "Just interested in your cars."

His words sounded funny too, like he was playing a game of pretend.

"You looking to buy?" the woman said.

"Looking to trade the Jeep."

The woman narrowed her eyes. "That sounds to me like trouble. Are you in some kind of trouble?"

Dad tugged on his cap and I squeezed Clemesta. "No, ma'am," he said. "And I mean none for you." He was suddenly being very polite and using his best manners, and the woman didn't even deserve them. She just scowled at us like we were fleas. Dad unzipped his duffel bag and pulled out two bills. "Would this help?"

The woman curled back her lips like she wanted to eat the money. Her teeth were pointy and brown at the edges. She started to cough, probably from LUNG CANCER. She pulled a handkerchief out of her bra like a magic trick and spat into it. She peered down at me and then back at Dad.

"Do I know you?" she said. "You look familiar."

Dad shook his head. "We're passing through."

"Well," she said. She reached for the money and slipped it inside her bra where the dirty handkerchief and probably twenty other things lived. "You seem like nice folks, don't you? Wait here." She disappeared inside the store and left Dad and me squinting our eyes in the sun.

As soon as she was gone, I turned to Dad. "What are you doing? Those cars are DISGUSTING and we have the best car already. It's called the Jeep Renegade, in case you forgot!"

Dad click-cracked his jaw. "I know, Doll. Just trust me."

"I don't trust him," Clemesta said. "He's full of big fat lies."

"Clemesta! Don't say that."

"But it's true," she said.

I looked at Dad. "And stop speaking in that voice. I don't like it. It doesn't sound like you."

The woman came back outside. "Follow me."

Dad took my hand and we walked behind her. She hobbled on her cane and we had to stop twice so she could catch up her breath to her body.

Finally she pointed to a rusty blue car. "Take the Ford," she said. "She's a real solid ride."

She started coughing again and I watched for the handkerchief trick but this time she just spat her goopy phlegm onto the ground.

Dad stared at the car and then turned to the woman. "You can't be serious," he said.

"All we have," she said. "Without proper paperwork." She lifted her cane and pointed it at Dad. "I'm guessing you don't want any of that."

Dad opened the car door and looked inside.

"Like I told you," the woman said. "She's a nice ride."

We walked back to the Jeep and didn't wait for the old woman to catch up. Dad popped the trunk and took out the Walmart bags, and then he climbed in front and scooped everything out of the glove compartment. He held onto his duffel bag very tightly and I kept my eyes on it too, to make sure it didn't leak any money. The old woman would FOR SURE not put it into the Lost and Found box. She would steal it for herself and hide it in her bra.

Clemesta was in a RAGE.

"I don't like this one bit," she said.

"I know."

"But think, Dolly, think!" she said. "Your advanced brain must be SOLVING it."

The woman hobbled over, wheezing.

"You done?" She was sweating in the sun and there was a pool of wet under both of her arms.

Dad handed her the keys to the Jeep and she slipped them in her pocket like it was hers all along.

It stank inside the new-old car like something was rotting. The seats were sticky and scratchy and the stitching was coming apart. Only one of the seat belts in the back would buckle, and the fabric part was half-torn.

"It's only for a few more days," Dad said. He started the engine, and it made a chug-a-chug-chug noise. I secretly hoped it wouldn't start, but it did and then we were back on the road, winding around in the rusty old Ford.

My shorts had cut two lines across my legs. They looked like sad faces.

"Why did you take me out of school for this dumb adventure?" I said. "We could have gone over Spring Break, or the holidays."

Dad made a fist. "I wasn't . . . I'm sorry. It was a mistake. I didn't think it through." He took a sip of water and splashed some over his face. It wet the seat but he didn't care because the car was already in RUINS.

"Well, now we're in trouble. Mom will be fuming at you. I'm a little fuming too."

Dad swallowed. "It will be okay. We'll be . . . home soon."

I took a deep breath and tried to let out some of the fuming parts. I counted to five and then backward from five.

"Do we have to stay in disguise until we're home?"

"Yeah."

"Is it like a secret mission?"

Dad nodded. "Exactly."

"I can keep secrets," I told Dad.

"No, you can't," Clemesta said into my ear.

The rock in my stomach went spinning.

The car wouldn't stop spluttering, like it also had a bad cough from smoking too many cigarettes. I bet the old woman was spitting up all over our Jeep. I thought of Mr. Abdul back home, who never made such disgusting coughing sounds even though he smoked too.

Probably he was missing me a bunch. Everyone from home was missing me, but most of all Mom. I bet she was crying a lot and looking at my photograph and kissing it and trying not to get it wet with her tears. Poor Mom. Probably it was the worst time in her whole life, and every day since I was gone was a CAN'T GET OUT OF BED DAY. I sent her a telepathy kiss, and one from Dad too.

There, I said, *now we are all friends again and no one needs to be mad.*

I opened the windows all the way down so I wouldn't have to smell the car. Outside it smelled of fresh air and trees, and smoke when we passed by a house with a firepit burning trash in the yard.

"I still need to pee."

"We'll find somewhere," Dad said. "We'll stop soon."

I lifted up Clemesta.

"I remember the word I was looking for in my brain. It's *METAMORPHOSIS*. That's when the caterpillar becomes a butterfly."

Clemesta sighed. She stroked my cheek. "You don't want to figure it out, do you?"

She kissed my eyelids and stayed close. Something popped into my head about another secret mission and a pinkie promise with Mom, but I shoved it inside the NOT NOW box in my brain. Then I locked it and threw away the key.

Dad mumbled something to himself and then he pulled the car over to the side of a field. He could have stopped it right in the middle of the road and no one would have noticed since there weren't any other cars around. It was just us in the whole state.

Dad checked something on the map. I looked outside. There was grass and trees and a wooden cross painted white. A black bird was sitting on one of the arms.

"Do you see that bird?" I said to Dad. "That bird is a bad omen."

"How do you know?"

"Clemesta told me."

He marked something on the map with his finger and then folded the paper around that spot.

"It's a black-hearted ravenator," I said. "It means that someone is lying."

We drove off and the bird pierced his dark eyes into my soul.

"Yes," I told him. "I know."

I shoved my hand into the cereal box and ate another sugary mouthful of Cap'n Crunch. "I hope I don't get scurvy," I said to Clemesta.

"It's probably already too late," she sniffed. "Thanks to this dumb adventure."

"Yeah, and no one ever asks me what I want. They just make plans and drag me along."

It's for your own good, Dolly. That's what Mom said about her plan. Or maybe it was YOU KNOW WHO.

Dad reached back to squeeze my knee. "Everything will be okay," he said. His hand was clammy and hot.

ABDUCTION. *Abduction* rhymes with *production*. YOU KNOW WHO is a producer. Producers produce productions. Producers produce abductions. The best way to make someone cry is to steal something they love. I once stole a plastic turkey from Lina's house when I went there for a playdate. I only wanted it so I could give my dolls a lovely Thanksgiving feast, but as soon as I got back home, Lina's mom was on the phone saying I had to return it. I could hear Lina crying in the background, like she was being ripped apart with sadness. She had two different turkeys, but I still had to return the one I took the very next day.

We didn't have any more playdates after that.

Dad took an exit and snaked around a road which had trees growing thick on either side. Actually it felt like the road was going to get squeezed and squeezed, maybe until everything went dark and it disappeared forever.

"What are we doing here?" Clemesta asked.

"I don't have ONE CLUE. But we're in the wilderness now for sure."

Dad took another turn and parked the car at a small wooden cabin. NATIONAL PARK, it said on the sign. He pointed to my new cap, which was lying on the seat. "Can you put that back on?"

"My hair pushes it off."

He frowned. "Yeah. Put it on anyway. And... we should pretend we have different names. If anyone asks."

"I like my name."

"I know. It's only pretend. For the secret mission. I'm going to be Mike. You be?"

"Margot."

"You should be a boy. So the disguise is really good."

I stared at Dad with his cap and glasses. "Your disguise is excellent," I said. "I don't recognize you at all."

Dad scrunched up his forehead. "Please, Doll."

I opened the door. "I'll be Joshua," I said.

Inside, a man in a National Parks uniform was rapping and grabbing his jeans at his private parts. When he saw us he stopped and clicked something on his phone. "You caught me," he said. His eyes were very bright, and he seemed excited to have us inside his cabin.

"Welcome to the most beautiful place in the South," he said.

He was very tall and thin like a pencil.

"We'd like to camp tonight," Dad said.

"Well, sir, you came to the right place for that," he said. He told us his name was Travis and he was a National Parks Ranger, and that meant he knew the park like the back of his hand. I looked at the back of his hand, which had a heart tattooed on it and the letters *L-O-V-E* written on his knuckles. He was moving his hands a lot as he talked.

"You coming with a trailer or fixing to pitch a tent in one of the campsites?"

"Do you rent tents?" Dad asked.

Travis shook his head.

"No, sir, afraid we do not. The cabins are real nice, though. Costs more but you got a kitchen and a bathroom and no need to mess with setting up a tent. I prefer that way myself," he said. "For the convenience. Anyhow, park's near empty tonight. You can take your pick."

I held Clemesta behind my back because she was frightened of Travis's wild eyes.

Dad walked around the store picking up wood and matches and candles and marshmallows.

"You don't have any vegetables," I said.

Travis shook his head. "Vegetables aren't camping food," he said. "If you ask me, they aren't anytime food."

He laughed, and I thought he probably had scurvy with that attitude.

Dad took two tins of beans and sausage and added it to the pile at the checkout.

I caught him looking at the beers all piled up on the shelf. I watched him LIKE A HAWK with DAGGER EYES that could slice him in a second.

"I won't," he said. "I swear."

"That's good," I said, even though that's his favorite promise to break.

Travis gave us a map that showed you where to find the camping cabin, and then he marked some hiking trails with a red pen.

"But you can just drive up there," he said. "Save yourselves all the walking. Lot of folks do that."

I looked down at his hand. The word tattooed on his other knuckles was *F-E-A-R*.

•   •   •

"Why are we camping?" I said. Dad and I climbed back in the car, and he set off down the narrow path.

"We need a place to sleep," he said. "And I thought you'd like it here. It's nice and quiet, with no one around."

"I never went camping before."

"I know."

"Did you ever?"

"Yeah. Not far from here actually. It was a long time ago. I was just a kid."

We arrived at the cabin, which was really just a pretty house made from stone and wood and set in the middle of trees instead of a street. There was a porch you could sit on to watch the stars, and a fireplace ready for building a fire and right on the doorstep there was the forest and nature. It was very still and you could hear the birds chatting to each other and the bugs scratching away in the leaves. I liked it much better than anywhere else we had been since the Chambersburg Comfort Lodge, and Dad must have felt the same because he stood at the door and looked around and breathed in the air and smiled for the first time that whole day.

Inside the cabin it was exactly like a real house but tiny, with one room that had the bed and the kitchen and the table and a very small bathroom with a tub that was only the size of a shower. I raced inside to pee. It was very yellow, which was probably Cap'n Crunch's fault.

After we unpacked the supplies, Dad pulled out Travis's map and looked at the different trails.

"How about we explore a little?" he said.

"Really?"

"Sure, it will be fun."

I smiled. "Yes, let's go back to having fun. And can I keep the map for a souvenir? I want to keep it with the Dollywood map and your driving map and then I will have all the maps of America and I'll always know how to find all the places and all the people in the country."

Dad's face scrunched up with lines.

"What?"

"You're wonderful," he said. "That's all."

The hiking path was rocky in some places and smooth in others. I set my shoes inside Dad's footprints. I looked around in all directions. We climbed up a steep path and then we went winding around in a circle and then we stopped to tie my laces.

"This is a good part of the adventure," I said.

"I think so too."

"You can say *DITTO*. It means *ME TOO*."

Dad smiled.

"Is it like when you were a kid?"

Dad squinted his face back at me. "I'm not sure," he said. "Things always seem so different in your memories."

"How different?"

"Sometimes better. Sometimes just far away."

I stepped over a fallen rock. Everywhere smelled of soil and wood.

"Who took you camping?" I said.

"My parents," Dad said. "Your grandma and granddad. And Joshua came along, of course."

"Did you have fun?"

"Yeah," Dad said. "It was one of the best things we ever did. We stayed a week, went hiking and swimming in the lake and had cookouts and roasted marshmallows and watched the stars. Me and Joshua walked every inch of the park. We pretended we were pioneers."

"What's that?"

"Like, that we were discovering the country for the first time. That everything was unspoiled and possible and just for us." He looked out at the view of the valley. "Those were good times."

"Why didn't you ever come back?"

"I don't know," Dad said. He bent over to pick a branch off the path and threw it into the trees. "I moved away for college. Then I stayed away. That's life, sometimes. It runs away with you."

He went quiet.

"You never tell me stuff about when you were a kid," I said.

"Mm," Dad said.

"Didn't you like it?"

"I did," Dad said. "I just wanted so badly to get away. To have a different kind of life from how I grew up."

We had climbed to the top of a steep hill and he was out of breath. I still had lots. I took his hand to pull him along.

"Why different?"

"I don't know... better. I wanted the kind of opportunities other people had. The kind of life I'd be proud to have, instead of just...." His brown eyes looked very light in the sun.

"I can spell *opportunities*."

"Because you're so smart."

"Advanced. Yeah." I thought about what he'd said. "Will I have to leave home for my opportunities too?"

Dad gave me a smile, but it was a sad one and far away in another time. My stomach rock sank a little more.

"Look over there." Dad pointed.

Like magic, we were standing above a beautiful and sparkling lake, a pool of blue shimmering in the sunlight, and spotty with the reflection of the trees.

"Wow," I said. "It looks like paradise or something."

Dad smiled. "It sure is beautiful."

I stood at the edge and held out my arms. "Hello America, your loveliness!" I yelled, and the noise echoed all the way into the clouds.

Dad laughed and took my hand to help me down to the shore. Around the lake, it was full of tiny round pebbles. Dad's face lit up. He looked real happy, not just pretend-happy like usual.

He started pulling off his shoes and his jeans and his shirt. "Come on." He left everything in a heap.

"I don't have a bathing suit!"

"It doesn't matter," Dad said. "No one's here to see us."

He was right. It was like we were the only people on a deserted island, or at the end of the world.

Dad waded into the water in his boxer shorts. His skin prickled from being scared of the cold but he kept going.

"Wait for me." I undressed and held out my hand so he could help me over the stones. We walked deeper and deeper into the cool water and then we flipped over on our backs and floated, staring up at the sky. It was as big and wide as forever.

Dad shut his eyes. He held out his arms and drifted on the water and I watched him start to float away from me. I touched a hand to him and he took it and held me so that we could stay together.

We will always stay together, I said in my head-voice.

I closed my eyes but not all the way. I watched the sun flicker on my eyelashes like little diamond sparkles. The water smelled of salt and it was silent apart from the ripples of the fish below us swimming back home for their dinner.

Dad and I floated and floated, like two snow angels on the water.

I saw Dad flip over. He put his head under the water and when he came back up, he let out a scream. It was so loud I clapped my hands over my ears.

"What are you doing?"

"Joshua and I used to do that," Dad said.

He sank under and splashed up and screamed again, and the noise jumped off the water and came flying back at us. "Try it," he said.

"But what are you screaming about?"

"Everything," Dad said. "Everything."

He screamed again and I screamed too, and Dad's screams and mine mixed together until you couldn't tell whose voice it was, it was just one long cry that the forest would keep forever like a secret in the trees.

The sky started to turn hazy. We climbed out of the water and shivered on the shore and Dad used his shirt to dry me off. He sat down to put his shoes back on and waited while I tied my laces. He scratched his hands in the pebbles.

"Look," he said, "this one is shaped like a heart."

He put it in my fingers. "You should keep it. I bet it brings you luck."

He looked at me with that funny-strange expression on his face, not exactly happy and not exactly sad. Somewhere in the middle of good and bad.

"Doll," he said, "being your dad makes me the happiest man in the world. You know that, right?"

My heart felt warm and happy and only a little afraid.

"I hope you'll always remember it," Dad said. "That you're my whole world, and the best thing I ever did in it."

I touched his face. "Your eyes look funny," I said. "Watery."

He wiped them with a finger. "They're okay."

"You look soft."

"Soft?"

"Yeah, like you're melting." His eyes crinkled up in a smile and then he looked at me again and made them wide. We locked eyes for a staring contest and I giggled and we held them tight and I stared into the brown and the sad and the melting-with-love for as long as I could.

Afterward, I slipped the heart-stone into the pocket of my shorts, and we followed the trail back to the cabin.

It was almost dark when we arrived. Dad built a fire with the wood we'd bought from Travis and then opened a soda. We sat on the porch and laid back our heads to look at the stars.

"Stars make shapes in the sky called constellations," I said.

Dad smiled.

"That's Orion's Belt. And there's the moon. It's very, very

far away from us, even when it's so big. We can't reach out and touch it, not even from an airplane. I wish we could."

Dad looked up. I watched his eyes. The light from the fire made his whole face shine.

"And there's a man in the moon, but you'll never get near him either," I said. "He only watches you. He watches over all of us and he's lonely because he's by himself with no one else there. He eats cheese. Every day he wishes on shooting stars. His wish is to get to earth and have a wife and a daughter and friends and a pet Doberman. I think he used to be a mortgage broker too."

Dad reached over and laid a hand gently on the back of my head.

"I wish we'd done more of this," he said.

"What?"

He stood up.

"Just this."

He went inside and came back out with the tinned beans and a metal pot and a spoon. He showed me how to hold the pot over the fire without burning my fingers, and I stirred the dinner until it was ready.

"Beans have to be cooked *al dente*," I said. "I learned that on a cooking show."

We ate our dinner from the pot. Dad drank another soda and I drank a bottle of water because of being healthy and responsible and trying to stay hydrated.

After we scraped out the last of the beans, Dad said it was S'MORES TIME.

"This is the best part," he said.

He taught me how to roast the marshmallows spiked on a stick, and then how to build them into a sandwich with the crackers and the chocolate squished inside so it could all get melty together.

"My mouth is watery," I said.

"Wait till you taste it."

They were hot so we blew to cool them and then I licked the melty oozing chocolate part and the melty oozing marshmallow part and then I ate the whole thing. It was the most delicious of everything I ever ate in my whole life and that is one hundred percent FACTUALLY TRUE.

"One more," Dad said, and we made second helpings, and then one more after that and then we stopped so no one would explode with throw-up again from too much junk.

We sat and watched the moths fly into the light. I listened for the sounds of the animals calling out to each other, the owls and wolves and rats who are NOCTURNAL because they like the nighttime better than the day.

The fire was making my skin warm and my eyes droopy.

"Is this the part where we tell campfire stories?" I said.

Dad yawned. "Or maybe it should be bedtime," he said. "It's been a long day."

"No, stories," I said. "Like when you were a kid. It has to be the exact same."

He smiled. "Do you have a story for me?"

"You have to tell me one."

"I don't know a good one."

"Tell me something more from when you were a kid."

"I can't remember all that."

"Try!"

Dad laid his head back against the chair and closed his eyes.

"Okay," he said, "I have one. Joshua and I used to race cockroaches."

"What?"

"We used to find them in the house and put them in jars, then we'd line them up in the bathtub and race them."

"How did they know when to start the race?"

"Well," he said, "we'd give them a little poke and they'd take off."

"Tell me another one."

"I used to shoot at pigeons with a toy pellet gun that I won at the state fair. I'd build a fire in the backyard and cook the birds up for me and Joshua to eat for lunch."

"Ew!"

"It was really good," Dad said. "I might make it for you sometime."

"NO!" I yelled, even though I knew that Dad was just kidding around. He was smiling and relaxed and it made me think he should probably always live out in the woods. Then we could all be happy like this the whole time, Mom and Dad and me.

"Was this the best place?" I said.

"What do you mean?"

"For the adventure. You said we were going to the best place. I think it's this."

Dad nodded and smiled and then went quiet.

"Don't be sad," I said. "We can come back soon. We'll bring Mom next time."

Dad nodded again. He closed his eyes a minute, like he

was making a wish, or sending Mom a telepathy kiss and a message. I LOVE YOU, ANNA. I LOVE YOU TILL THE END OF ALL TIME.

"I liked your stories," I said. "I wish you could tell me all of them."

"Not all my stories are good ones."

"Why not?"

Dad rubbed his eyes. "Sometimes life was tough."

"Like how?"

"Just, tough. For our family. We didn't have much. After your grandad got laid off we . . . well, we survived, I guess. We were so poor, one year I didn't have money to buy new shoes. My feet wouldn't fit any of the old pairs, so I tried to steal a pair from Mr. Hobson's store in town."

"Stealing!" I said. I didn't like thinking about Dad doing bad things that were AGAINST THE LAW. I didn't like thinking that he could steal shoes because then maybe he could steal other things too. Like people.

His feet kicked the dirt. "Anyhow, Mr. Hobson caught me with the sneakers under my jacket. He let me keep them, but I had to come by to clean his floors every Saturday for three months."

"Was your dad so mad he had smoke coming out of his ears?"

"I never told him," Dad said. Then he went quiet again. He tilted his head back and finished his soda.

"I never met any of them," I said. "And all of them are dead. Everyone from your life is dead except Mom and me."

Dad stared at the fire.

"Why don't you ever want to talk about them?"

Dad sighed. "I don't like thinking about all the things that are gone."

"Like Joshua."

"Especially Joshua."

"Why?" I said.

Dad cracked his jaw. "Because I'm to blame."

"For what?"

"For everything."

"Like what?"

He sighed again. "I was the one who brought him out to Florida to work with me. Him and his fiancée, Karlee. I taught him how to—how to do things that weren't totally honest. You really want me to tell you all this?"

I nodded.

"A lot of people lost their homes," Dad said. "Their savings. We lost everything too. Joshua owed a lot of money. He'd taken money from Karlee and her sister and her folks, and there was talk of fraud charges—"

"What's fraud?" I said.

Dad shook his head. "It's like telling big lies. It was all a mess, see? Everything."

I looked at him. "Then what happened?"

"Joshua couldn't face it, he just couldn't." Dad rubbed his eyes. "But you know that part."

He stared into the fire, not even blinking. The wood crackled and a piece broke off. Everything turned to ash.

Dad shook his head, and then he turned to face me. "You look like him," he said. "I see him every time I look at you. It's like he's right there."

I pressed my hands together. Dad kept looking at me. The sad in his eyes was bigger than the brown.

"I only ever wanted to do right by my family," Dad said. "Instead..." He shook his head.

I turned to watch the last lick of flame try to keep itself alive. It flickered twice and died.

In the trees, the owls were hooting. That was a warning for all the animals to go and hide. It meant the NIGHT PREDA-TORS were getting ready to catch their dinner. They have glow-in-the-dark eyes exactly for finding you in the night.

I was happy to go inside and shut the door.

I changed into my pajamas and brushed my teeth. Dad stood next to me and brushed his too. We spat at the same time.

"Let's see that loose tooth," he said.

I opened my mouth to show him and he felt it with his finger.

"I bet it comes out soon," he said.

"Maybe it will get stuck in an apple. Or maybe I'll sneeze and it will shoot right out. Like ACHOO, PLONK."

Dad smiled. He stroked my hair.

"Joshua didn't get to have kids of his own," he said. "But he sure would have loved to know you."

He pulled back the covers and we climbed in. I gave Clemesta her good-night kisses.

"Eskimo, Butterfly, and Mom."

She smiled but not with all her teeth. "That's nice," she said sadly.

Dad switched off the lamp and lay against the pillow.

"We didn't get to call Mom," I said.

"Yeah," he said. He closed his eyes. "Tomorrow." Then he was snoring.

Clemesta nipped at my ear.

"What's wrong?" I said.

"Everything," she replied. "Everything about this whole adventure."

Dad's body was warm in the bed and I touched a hand to his chest. I could feel his heart beating, alive and warm and full of blood.

Good night, Mom, I said inside my head.

Outside, the hungry night beasts started their hunt, and the whole forest shivered with fear.

Thursday

I slipped out of the bed very quietly LIKE A MOUSE. I looked at my clothes lying in a heap on the floor and pulled them on.

Dad was sleeping with his whole body curled up like a baby. I felt bad for him for needing to leave home for his opportunities and for having no shoes and for losing his company and his mom and his dad and Uncle Joshua, but I also felt mad that he did stuff that made Joshua want to die.

"I'm mad at him, too," Clemesta said. She chewed her horse lip. "Because I think he's trying to run away with us."

"He is not. He's taking us home."

"I don't think so. I think we are going the farthest from home we have ever been and I think I know why," she said.

I brushed out my hair and tied my sneakers very carefully. "Hello, you," I said to my laces when they made two friendly bunny ears.

"Have you remembered yet?" Clemesta said.

I shook my head. "Not yet. Come on," I said. "Let's go out and explore the lovely woods. We can pretend we're pioneers."

The door to the cabin creaked open. Outside, our marshmallow roasting sticks were lying beside the firepit. The moths were all dead. Their bodies were dropped around the ground like petals when they fall off the flowers.

The air was fresh and cool and lovely. Actually you could smell real trees instead of just cardboard ones hanging from car mirrors. I breathed them into my nostrils and I swatted away a tiny bug who wanted to buzz inside there too.

I tried to imagine Dad as a little boy waking up in these same woods.

I only ever saw one picture of him when he was a child. He had floppy hair and a missing front tooth and he was very skinny with long legs and big sticking-out knees and he was wearing a dirty striped T-shirt with a hole in the front. He had a stick in his hand and he was scrunching up his eyes with the bigness of his smile. He looked happy, like nothing bad had ever happened and no bears lived inside him yet.

I once asked Mom why Dad never talks about where he grew up or his mom and dad, and she just sighed and said, "It's a long story," but she didn't tell it.

Grown-ups are good at that. Anything they don't want you to know, they can lie about or pretend that it isn't true, or they can just never talk about it. They don't even get into trouble.

"Actually sometimes they do," Clemesta said. "And also, you are good at pretending, too."

I touched a hand to the trunk of the biggest tree. "How do you do?" I said to it.

Clemesta shook her head.

The woods were waking up. If you listened carefully you could hear the frogs saying good morning to each other and the lake swishing over the pebbles to turn them into hearts. The NIGHT PREDATORS had full bellies, and they were snoring in their caves. All the other animals were safe to come out. Some were crying because their beloved ones got eaten in the dark.

Clemesta and I walked around the cabin and to the edge of the trail.

"We can't go past that line. There might be some DANGER LURKING."

Clemesta frowned. "I think Dad is where the danger is."

"Clemesta! You are trampling on ALL MY NERVES."

I stomped off to examine another tree.

"This one is a million years old," I said. "It has a house for a family of squirrels over here. Their names are the Nutskovitzes."

I felt in my pocket for the heart-stone Dad had given me.

"He loves me very much," I said. "With his whole heart and forever."

Clemesta nodded. "Too much."

"No, the perfect right amount."

"We need to go home, Dolly," she said.

"We are going home. How many times do I have to tell you? Now come on, be a pioneer. Say, 'Look, we discovered all this brand-new land' and 'Isn't America lovely?' and then say, 'I do declare this land is ours, and let all who go here go in great merriness and peace.'"

"Look at lovely America," Clemesta said, but only with HALF her heart and not acting like a real excited pioneer at all.

"Let's build a fire, my pretty pioneer wife," I said. "I will go and gather sticks while you prepare us a tasty dinner." I picked up two sticks and a leaf for the kindling.

"Dolly," Clemesta said. "Have you looked in the NOT NOW box in your brain? I think you should."

"Hush, horse," I said. "Everything is just PEACHY PIE fine so stop letting your imagination run away with you to crazy-town."

"Dolly, please. If you just let yourself THINK, you'll remember."

I kicked a rock with my foot and sent it tumbling over the edge of the mountains.

"STOP IT, CLEMESTA! Just stop with your silly tricks trying to get me to remember." I plonked her on a tree trunk.

"There," I said. "I'm ignoring you because you're being silly and you need a good long TIME OUT to think about your behavior."

I gave up being a pioneer. Instead I sat down and scratched around in the dirt for stones, hoping to find another magic love heart. Maybe I would give it to Dad and maybe I would save it and give it to Mom instead when I saw her again. Maybe she deserved it more. Maybe she was sorry enough for her stupid silly plan, and anyway it was all YOU KNOW WHO'S idea, NOT HERS. I know that's true because when Mom first started talking to him, she said she never ever wanted to take me away from Dad.

"I always thought it would be too cruel," she said. "She idolizes him so. He barely notices us most days and still he can do no wrong in her eyes." She sniffed her tears and YOU KNOW WHO squeezed her hand.

"Well, maybe it's the lesser of two evils," he said, and that's when he planted the worst and most evil idea into her brain like a POISON SEED that grew into a dark and thorny and evil tree.

I tried to chop the tree down, but maybe only in my dreams. Mr. Angry Bear was there too. I think he ate YOU KNOW WHO and then threw him up in the toilet. It left a big mess.

I took another rock and threw it as hard as I could. It went rolling down the mountain, maybe knocking an evil forest-rat on the head. That would be a very good service to the whole National Park and they would throw a party. I kicked my foot over another rock to loosen it for throwing. Some litter bug had thrown two empty beer cans in the dirt.

I heard the door to the cabin open. Dad's voice called my name and I ran over to him.

He stretched his arms over his head. "Did you sleep okay?"

"Yeah."

"Good."

I watched Clemesta out of the corner of my eye. I felt the wiggly loose tooth with my tongue.

"I'm ready to leave," I said. "We can start driving home right now. I promise I won't complain about driving all day and being bored in the back."

Dad rubbed the scratchy stubble on his chin. He looked at the fog kissing the tops of the trees. "I'm sorry to leave here."

"We have to. We're going home."

Dad nodded. "Sure we are."

"Promise?"

He nodded again.

The rock in my stomach went sinking down. Clemesta on her time-out tree sent a word into my brain with her telepathy powers. *LIAR* is what it said. I put that in the NOT NOW box and went inside to get my things.

Before we left, Dad grabbed his baseball cap and the glasses.

"That's your secret mission disguise. To get us home extra fast," I said.

"Exactly." He started up the car and we drove back the way we came.

"Goodbye, Your Loveliness," I called to the mountains.

"DEAD SQUIRREL," I said, looking at the red blood smeared like paint on the side of the road.

"That's probably Mrs. Nutskovitz," Clemesta said.

"No!" I said.

She shrugged. "I'm just being honest. Honest is good. Not honest is bad."

"I'm honest," I said.

"Ha!" Clemesta turned her horse nostrils up in the air.

Dad knocked his hand against the dashboard and then said we needed to make a gas stop.

"I hate this stupid car," I said. "It really is PREPOSTER-OUS and LAMENTABLE and INCOMPETENT."

Dad filled up the tank and then peered at me through the window. "Wait here," he said. I tried to make my eyes roll in my head.

I kicked off my sneakers but not my socks, because I didn't want my bare feet touching the yucky carpet which was for sure INFESTED with bugs or some kind of contagious and deadly diseases that I could catch through my toes.

Dad came back with bottled water and two newspapers and one banana full of black spots. He shoved the papers on the floor of the passenger side, but I could read the words *DAUGHTER MISSING* before he folded it over.

"Probably the daughter is missing her mom," I said.

"Oh, for heaven's sake," Clemesta said. She folded her horse arms and turned to look out the window.

Dad handed me the banana. "It's as healthy as I could find."

I took it from him and set it on the seat. "It's rotten," I said. "It will give me food poisoning."

Dad took the winding back roads again. I missed driving on the interstate. At least there was more to see. Here it was only trees and silence and a million miles of blank road. The road, the road. The road knows. The road knows everything, probably. It hears everybody talking and it collects secrets.

"Like you," Clemesta said.

"I hate secrets," I said. "I don't want to collect them anymore. Now I'll only collect seashells and butterflies."

Dad wasn't saying much. He kept looking back at me in the mirror and catching my eye in his. Then he'd look away.

We passed through a stretch of trailer homes, all hidden away in the trees and surrounded with piles of trash. One looked like every single thing from inside had been tipped right out onto the lawn. There was a sofa and a refrigerator and a knocked-over barbecue and an inflatable pool that was leaking out its air and filled with leaves. A chained-up dog ran up to the fence as far as he could get without snapping off his neck. He barked at us with angry yaps and said, "GET AWAY, FOREIGNERS. YOU DON'T BELONG HERE." A little boy in a white T-shirt went over to him and flicked his ears to shut him up. Then he went back to dragging an old lawn mower over the dirt like it was lovely green grass and not just a pile of stones.

I looked back at him through the window. "I don't think this is America anymore," I said.

The dog started barking again and Clemesta put a spell on him to make him disintegrate within a week. I bet no one would miss him ONE LITTLE BIT.

Further down the road, there was a stuffed toy lying facedown in the mud.

"Why didn't anyone pick her up?" I said. "Poor little bear. I hope you get home soon."

"She can't," Clemesta said. "She's dead."

Dad was driving slowly. He followed a road that went no-where, with nothing around it except for weeds and dirt. The car crunched over the stones and then stopped. Dad turned around.

"Dolly," he said. "We have to do something now. And you're not going to like it."

His face was not joking and not laughing and not smiling. My heart went thumping and everything else went frozen.

Dad scratched in one of the shopping bags from the day before and pulled something out.

"Why did you buy scissors?"

"Because we need to cut your hair."

"We don't," I said. "My hair is healthy and lustrous."

Dad nodded. "I know. And I promise it will grow back."

"What do you mean *grow back*?"

"I mean that we need to cut your hair," Dad said.

"But I don't want to."

"I know," Dad said. "I wish we didn't have to do it, but we need you not to look like Dolly for a while. Just a short while."

"But I *am* Dolly."

"Dolly," Dad said. "Please listen."

"You're scaring me." Clemesta held my hand tightly. She was scared too.

Dad got out of the car and opened the back door.

"Please let's not make this any more difficult than it already is."

"But I didn't do anything wrong."

"I told you," Dad said. "I need you to not look like Dolly. Just until we're safe. Until we get home. It's very important. I wouldn't make you do it if it wasn't."

I didn't move. "I'll wear the cap," I said. "I'll wear it the whole time."

"It's not enough."

He reached his hand to my seat belt to unbuckle it. He took my arm and started to pull.

"You're hurting me."

He didn't let go.

"Come on," he said. "Just stand still and let me do it and then it will all be over. Just a few minutes and we'll be done. And then a few days more and you can be Dolly again. I promise."

"You keep promising me stuff," I said. "I think you're just TELLING LIES. Big ones. Bad ones."

"Please, Dolly."

He was still gripping my arm. "I'm sorry, sweetheart." He looked at me with eyes that were begging and pleading and desperate. "Please, Dolly. I know it's a lot to ask but it's for your own good."

I looked at the scissors in his hands. I pulled my arm away and rubbed it where it was red and burning.

I turned my back so that my hair would be hanging down in front of Dad.

I heard him take a breath. Then he started to cut. I held my hands over my ears so I wouldn't have to listen to the sound of the scissors chopping away my beautiful chestnut hair. It came floating down to the ground, falling and falling and then landing on my socks. I kicked it away.

I bit down on my lip to stop myself from crying.

Dad brushed my shoulders with his hand, flicking off the hair that was sticking to me.

"All done," he said. He rested his hand on my neck and I moved to get away. I didn't want him touching me. Maybe EVER again.

I looked at him with my flaming angry eyes and then I bent to look at myself in the rearview mirror. I didn't feel like me anymore. I felt a little bit like I was broken into pieces and a little bit like I was made from steel.

Dad cleared his throat. "I have some new clothes for you too," he said. "You should put these on."

He held out a T-shirt and a pair of shorts. The T-shirt was green with THE INCREDIBLE HULK stuck on the front.

"Boy clothes," I said.

"Yeah. Just for a while."

I pulled off my clothes and threw them onto the gravelly ground. I put on the shorts. They were too big and I had to roll them up twice. Dad looked at me and he nodded.

"Yeah, that's good."

"No. All the good is gone and you took it."

I climbed back inside the car and pulled the door shut with a loud bang.

Clemesta looked at me. I saw that she'd been crying.

She spoke some words into my ear.

"Are you sure?" I said.

She nodded her head. She insisted.

"All right," I said.

I opened the door and stuck my hand out.

"Here," I said to Dad. "You have to do Clemesta too."

Afterward, Dad sat behind the wheel not moving and not driving.

"Thank you, Dolly," he said.

I didn't say anything back. I watched my chopped-off reflection in the window. I could see my hair in a pile on the grass, lying there like another dead animal on the side of the road. My clothes were there too, not like a dead animal but like a child who got vanished by bad magic.

Dad set off, the same way as before, keeping us off the interstate and driving on the empty roads. The wind was blowing cold on my bare neck. I liked feeling cold on the outside. Inside it felt like there was a firepit.

I touched my hair. It felt like it belonged to someone else

now. It was sharp and spiky, like a Stegosaurus. Clemesta's was too. She had some clumpy parts on her head and other parts where the plastic was peeking through. She didn't look like a magical horse queen anymore, but I didn't tell her that. I just held her against my chest. Her heart was angry and pounding.

We passed another town and then a stretch of fields with a few trailers hiding in the trees. The blue *X*'s of all the flags were waving to us as we went by, reminding us that everything was all wrong.

"I hate it here," I whispered to Clemesta. "I hate every-where we've been."

She nodded. She held my hand and sent kisses to my sad heart.

Dad kept looking back at me in the mirror, like he was checking to see if I was still there. He didn't say anything.

I hate you, I said to the back of his head.

We kept driving. Just driving and driving. I felt like I would never get out to stretch my legs and run and play and feel the ground under my toes, or go to class and ask Miss Ellis all the questions I had been building up in a big pile of head-notes.

Like how come young girls like Jolene can sit in front of the TV all day instead of going to school, and what's the tree called in Virginia with the purple blossoms, and what does the bumper sticker WHITE PRIDE mean? I bet she would have all the answers. She always does.

BUCKLE UP BUTTERCUP it said above a sign for the next exit. Mom likes a song called "Build Me Up, Buttercup."

Sometimes we sing it in a duet when we play the America's Got Talent game. We have a good dance for that one, and we do it like synchronized showgirls which means we do the exact same moves at the exact same time. Mom is very good at dancing, just like me, so I guess that's one talent I got from her as a gift.

I watched the sun fall behind the clouds and then disappear completely. The sky turned cloudy and dark. I shivered in the back and my skin went goosey.

Dad took a right turn and we drove through another town. There was one diner with two trucks parked out front. A woman was standing outside, blowing smoke circles through her mouth. She turned her head slowly to watch us pass by.

I hugged my knees and tried to be a small ball that could bounce away. I would bounce out the window and all the way back to Crescent Street. I tried to make it happen with magic but it didn't work.

The rain came down hard and the windows fogged up with our breathing. You couldn't see outside anymore. You could only see till the end of your nose.

I'M SORRY, I wrote in the foggy glass. I drew a heart. That was a message for Mom.

My stomach rock hurt and Clemesta stroked my cheek with her hoof.

"I wish we never went on this stupid adventure," I said.

"It was never an adventure." Clemesta wrote her own word on the window.

ABDUCTION.

I held my arms tight against myself. The wipers scratched loudly across the window.

"Imagine if you had brain-wipers. They could wipe away all the things you didn't want to remember."

"Dolly," she said. "You can't keep saying you don't know. It won't make it go away."

I closed my eyes.

Clemesta nudged me. "Dolly. I'm trying to keep you safe."

"I know that." I counted something on my fingers. "Six days since we were home. That's a long time."

"Too long," Clemesta said. "That's why they're looking for us."

"Who is?"

"The police."

"For skipping school?"

"No. Because Dad stole us."

I looked at the back of Dad's head. Dad who loved me and wanted to keep me safe. Dad who loved me so much because I saved him once upon a time and I was his whole wide world and the best thing he ever did in it.

"He didn't steal us, Clemesta, you lunatic *equus ferus*. You can't steal someone who's already yours."

The rain stopped falling but Dad forgot to turn the wipers off. Screech-scratch, screech-scratch. I watched the raindrops on the window dry up one by one until they had all disappeared.

We passed three wooden crosses. Each one had a white cloth hanging from it, like a dead angel had fallen over with her beautiful broken wings.

I started feeling hungry and so did Clemesta. Her stomach made a loud growl asking for food. That made Dad turn around.

"Hungry?" he said.

I didn't want to talk to him.

"I'm hungry too," he said. "We could probably stop. Looks deserted enough around here."

I bit down on my lip so I wouldn't let any words out.

"Dolly," Dad said. "I'm sorry. I'm so sorry about your hair. I told you that. Please understand, I had to do it. I had no choice. Forgive me, sweetheart, please. I just want to get you safe."

SAFE SAFE SAFE. Everyone wants me safe.

"Mom wanted us safe too," Clemesta said.

Dad's eyes were shining at me in the mirror. "You're my brave girl, Dolly," he said. "My brave girl."

Brave was good. Better than anything else you can be, like beautiful or famous or rich. Brave is the best of all because you can't ever lose it or have it stolen from you or leave it behind. It can follow you to the end of the world.

I picked at the scab on my leg and made it open again. The blood came out. The new skin was angry because it didn't even have a chance to heal.

TOO BAD, I told it. *That's life.*

Blood tastes red and like old garden tools left out on the lawn all winter.

Blood rhymes with *flood* but not with *hood* or *good.* That's because English is full of CONTRADICTIONS and that means things should follow the rules but don't want to.

RULES ARE FOR FOOLS. That's graffiti someone wrote on the wall near my favorite park. As soon as we get back home, I'm going to go there with Mom and we'll have a picnic on the lawn and we'll go on the swings and swing so high we almost touch the clouds. The clouds will be in the shape of hearts and the sun will be shining. Everything will be JUST PERFECT because we will be safe and home and Dad will be sorry and Mom will be sorry and two sorrys make everything all right and that means YOU KNOW WHO can't ever bother us again.

"I think he's the reason we aren't safe," I said.

"What are you talking about?" Clemesta said.

"Probably Dad had to take me away because I put a curse on YOU KNOW WHO and... and then I bet he called the police. Remember?"

Clemesta looked at me with her blank face.

"Remember that time we met him in Central Park? He and Mom were talking and I was walking in a circle around the bench to make a violent curse on him.

"Mom said, 'I don't know how I'll ever be able to thank you for all you're doing for us,' and he said, 'Oh, please, if it wasn't for you, I'd probably still be in the closet, convinced the world would end if I ever came out.' Then Mom rested her head on his shoulder and he said, 'You were always my favorite beard,' and they laughed like it was so hilarious even though it wasn't."

Clemesta frowned. "No, I don't think that's it."

"It is. And Mom never should have let him out of that closet. She should have locked the door and bolted it with steel and left him inside forever so he could never ever get anyone to make silly plans again. Then I wouldn't have had to curse him and Dad wouldn't have needed to take us away to be safe."

Clemesta sighed. "I think you know the truth but you don't want to look at it."

I squeezed my eyes. They were puffed up and the eyeball part felt pinched and itchy from wanting to cry.

"No. We just need to go home," I said. "Everything will be fine as soon as we're home." I found Dad's eyes in the mirror. "We can be friends again," I said. "I know you are just looking out for me."

He put his hand across his heart. I guess it felt warm again.

We drove through two more towns before Dad slowed the car near a place with a pig's head hanging over the door. Someone had written *BBQ* in big letters on the side of the house, which was really just another one of those trailers. I put my cap on without Dad asking.

Inside, no one was there and there weren't any menus to read, just a chalkboard with six different things to eat. None of it was healthy and whoever wrote it down was very bad at doing their spelling homework. They wrote *BISCITS* and *TOMATOS* and those would get you a big fat red *X* if you were in Miss Ellis's class.

A girl came out a door in the back. "What can I get you?"

She had long hair hanging right down her back, and a fat purple bruise on her arm.

Dad and I took a seat outside. The table faced out onto the road. There was a falling-apart wooden house around the side. Probably that's where the girl lived or where they slaughtered the BBQ piglets to turn them into dinner.

The girl set our food down without saying anything. I picked up one of the ribs and took a bite. The meat tasted sweet. I set it back down and ate the fries instead. They were oily and burnt. I drank my soda and felt the bubbles fill me up like a balloon.

The rain had stopped but everywhere there were puddles of water and the sky was still gray and heavy and saying STAY AWAY to the sun. Dad was picking at his food. Every time I looked up, he was staring at me with his sad shining eyes. It felt like they wanted to eat me up.

I went inside and asked the girl if I could use the restroom. She pointed to a door. I washed my hands with soap and looked at my chopped-off hair in the mirror. It was ragged and messy and you couldn't even tell that it was actually the color of chestnuts anymore.

Do not cry, Dolly, I said to my face. My eyes were misty but the tears stayed away. There wasn't anything to dry my hands with, so I left the restroom and went back over to the girl.

"Can I have a napkin, please?" I said. She handed me a couple, and I stared at her bruise. I couldn't help it. It was very dark purple and that meant her blood was sitting right there under the skin, boiling and angry at whoever did it to her. I watched it pulse and quiver. It was trying to tell me something important.

"Mr. Angry Bear," it said. "It was Mr. Angry Bear."

I swallowed. The rock in my stomach turned.

The girl touched her sleeve and moved it to cover the bruise. There was another one on the inside of her arm, but it wasn't so fresh. She looked at me and her chin wobbled. I bet she heard a lot of SORRYS after she got her bruises. A lot of crying and begging and PLEASE FORGIVE ME and NEVER AGAIN that really meant UNTIL NEXT TIME.

She didn't know about the special vanishing makeup that you can paint on any bruise to cover it up. Mom keeps some in the bathroom cabinet next to the jar of face cream that eats wrinkles. It's called FULL COVER FLAWLESS and it smells like candy.

The girl opened her mouth like she wanted to say something, but then she shut it again.

"You have pretty hair," I said. She blinked, and her bruise stopped yelling at me.

Dad paid the bill and the girl stood in the doorway watching us leave. She looked very small and alone.

"Safe travels," the pig's head called. He was trying to be nice, even though someone had chopped off his body and roasted it for dinner.

I saw a dead possum lying on the road but I didn't call it out. I wasn't in the mood for any more dead and gone things.

We passed a few road signs and Dad said a curse word.

"What happened?"

"I took a wrong turn," he said. "Fuck."

"You shouldn't say *fuck*."

"Yeah, sorry."

"Are we lost?"

"Yeah. We need to stop," Dad said. "Then I can figure out where we are."

He made a turn in the other direction. I watched the road, the endless rotten road that was taking forever to get us back where we belonged.

"When we're home we won't be lost," I said. "We'll be

found." I made a wish to make it true. Clemesta stroked my cheek.

"Oh, Dolly," she said. "My dear and sweet Dolly."

The car made a beep beep beep noise and Dad said, "CHRIST, WHAT NOW?"

"What's happening?"

Dad shook his head. "I don't know, I don't know."

The car kept on beeping. In the movies that's always the sound a car makes before it stops and everyone gets stuck and the zombies come and eat them.

"We shouldn't have given that coughing woman our Jeep," I said. "This one is just a heap of junk. It's CRAP," I said. "CRAP." All my mad had come back and I tried to breathe it away.

I looked out at the murky sky and the nothingness and the no houses and the no people and the no lights. Who would help us if the car broke down? How would we call someone to come and get us?

Brave, I said in my head, *remember how you are brave.*

"Come on," Dad said. "Come on."

He banged the steering wheel like it would help the car to keep going but the car just made a gurgling spluttering sound, like it was a person running out of air and coughing out the last breath it would ever take. Then it gave up altogether, right in the middle of the road. Dad tried to steer it off to the side but the car wouldn't budge.

There were no more beeps. Everything was DEAD STILL except the noisy old crickets who were laughing at our bad luck.

Dad said FUCK and FUCK again and I said FUCK too because I could and no one would even care out here in the middle of America's nowhere.

Dad banged the steering wheel, but really fiercely this time, with both his fists. I could hear him breathing through his nose, loud and angry.

"Goddamn," he said. He sat back in the seat and rubbed his face.

He made a sound, like he was laughing or crying or choking, like it was the worst thing or the funniest, being stuck in the middle of the road on the darkest night.

I listened to the sounds of the frogs. They weren't mean like the crickets, they were worried about us because there weren't any other cars and probably no one was going to find us. Maybe ever.

"I've got to move the car out of the middle of the road," Dad said. "My brave girl, do you think you could help?"

I had to sit up front in the driver's seat and hold the wheel, like I was driving the car for real. Dad went behind to push, and I kept both hands very strongly on the wheel. Dad pushed and pushed. I could hear him grunting and then I felt the car rolling. Dad called STEER TO THE RIGHT and I steered and the car moved and Dad pushed us into a patch of field that was wedged against a wire fence. I kept my hands on the wheel until Dad leaned in the window.

"You did great," he said.

"Probably I saved the day," I said. My hands were still shaking.

Dad nodded.

"I'm very brave. And smart. Because I'm only seven and I can already drive."

"How about that," Dad said.

He walked around to the back of the car and opened the trunk. He poked around and then he slammed it shut again. "Piece of shit," he said. He banged on the roof with his hand.

"Yeah," I said. "That stupid woman. Maybe she'll die tonight of coughs. That would serve her right for giving us this rusty old heap."

Dad sighed. "I think we're going to have to spend the night out here. It's getting too dark to go walking around, and I can't leave you. So we're going to have to stay where we are until morning."

"Oh."

"We'll do our best to protect you," the frogs croaked. The Frog Princess was called JUSTICA RIBBIT and she said she liked helping people, except French ones who were after her legs.

Dad climbed into the back to see if he could make the seats go flat like a bed. He yanked at them for a few minutes but nothing happened.

"Looks like these don't go all the way down," he said.

He covered the seat with one of his shirts and made me a pillow out of a pile of rolled-up clothes. Then he handed me his sweatshirt to use as a blanket.

I lay down on my car-bed and Dad banged the door shut.

He climbed into the front and leaned over to remove something from the glove compartment. Then he opened up the car door again.

"I'll be right here," he said.

I watched him out the window. I could see a small orange light near his mouth, and a cloud of smoke glowing white against the black sky. I didn't like him smoking cigarettes but I liked watching that tiny light shining in the dark. It reminded me of my glowing universe on the ceiling back at home. The real Alabama sky was wide and forever too, sprinkled with bright and twinkling stars. I didn't want it to be beautiful, but it was.

I hugged Clemesta in my arms. "You're very silent," I said. "I'm very tired."

She still smelled of the bubbles from the Chambersburg Comfort Lodge, but now that was mixed with other smells, like greasy-food diners and National Parks and throw-up and tears.

I heard a noise and it made me jump. I wondered if there were any wild mountain lions nearby, because they can smell people and track them and then creep up and eat them if they're feeling hungry. I didn't know any lion greetings, except HELLO, SIR LION.

Dad was still outside. His cigarette was finished but he was just standing there, his arms folded, his eyes looking out to the road, staring at nothing.

LOOK AT THE STARS! I wanted to tell him. *Look up and see the lights right up there in front of your eyes!*

But he just kept looking out at the dark.

"I wonder if Mom is asleep yet," I said. "I wonder if she can even fall asleep when she misses me so much." I slipped my hands inside the pockets of my shorts and squeezed them into two tight fists. "Oh," I said. "My heart-stone from the

National Park." I searched both pockets but it was gone. "I think I left it behind in the other shorts."

Clemesta sighed. "Well, that's another forever lost thing."

I tried not to cry.

Dad climbed in and we all shut our eyes.

I lay very still in the back. I pressed at my loose tooth with my tongue, trying to make it hurt.

"We'll be okay," Dad said.

We all woke up when the window went BANG BANG BANG. I thought for sure it was the lion and that it was going to smash the glass and gobble us up but then I saw that there was actually a very bright flashing light and a voice outside saying, "YOU CAN'T BE HERE."

My heart was racing so fast it felt like it wanted to run away. I pulled Dad's sweatshirt over my head, but not before I saw the face at the window like a ghost.

I heard Dad say something, but the person was still knocking on the window.

"Sir, sir," it said.

I poked my head out to have another peek. Dad wound down the window.

"Sorry, Officer," he said, "our car broke down earlier. It was already dark out and I didn't want to—well, I have my kid with me so I couldn't leave. I didn't have a phone to call for help."

"I'm no police," the voice said. It sounded deep and scratchy.

Dad held his hand to his eyes and squinted them against the light.

"I'm no police," the voice said again. "But you can't be out here all night sleeping in the car. Especially with your little one in the back."

I sat up. The man was older than Dad but not as old as Pop. He looked strong, with enormous wide shoulders and bulgy muscles and a very thick neck. His eyes were friendly like a cartoon dog who licks your hand and chases naughty cats up trees.

"The car's dead," Dad said. "We can't get anywhere else tonight."

The man shone his flashlight toward the back to look at my face, and then turned it back to Dad.

"Where you headed?"

"A little further south," Dad said. "Texas."

"That's a couple hours yet. You'll need to rest up."

The man looked at me again and I looked back. I tried to make my face look EXTRA ADORABLE so he would help us.

"Well," he said, "you better come with me."

His name was Harlan D. Ingram, but he said no one called him that except on his birth certificate and we should just call him Hank. He told us to gather up our things from the car and then hop into his pickup, which was parked up ahead.

I liked Hank right away because he was like a magical genie in a storybook who flies down and grants you your special wish. My wish was to not sleep in a broken car on the side of the road, and he was making sure we didn't have to. Maybe because of his muscles he was more like Batman than a genie, but Batman doesn't actually grant anybody their wishes, he just solves crimes.

Anyhow, Hank said he lived nearby in a big old house with plenty of room to spare, and that the side of the road wasn't a safe place to be at night.

"There are some bad types around here," he said. "Everywhere, really. But these boys ride around looking for trouble. And they sure don't care for strangers."

He didn't tell us what kind of trouble the boys look for, but I bet it was nowhere near as bad as lion trouble.

Hank's truck was enormous and all three of us could fit in the front without even touching legs. He had a hula girl on the dashboard who danced her hips around as the car moved.

"You're a very nice person to help strangers," I said.

Hank looked at me. "Well, it's the right thing to do."

"I'm Joshua," I said.

"I'm very pleased to meet you, Joshua," Hank said. "Where are you folks from?"

"New York," I said. "It's very far away."

"You bet it is." He turned to Dad. "You're not from there, though, are you?"

Dad shook his head.

"I thought so," Hank said. "Accent always creeps back. Soon as you cross state lines."

"We crossed a lot of state lines," I sighed.

We didn't have to drive too far before Hank said, "Home sweet home."

It was very dark, but I could make out a house tucked away behind a lot of tall trees. The house was wooden and painted white. It didn't have a lot of windows but at least the ones it had weren't nailed shut. There was a porch light to help us find our way up the front steps.

"Watch yourself," Hank said, because the wood on one step was cracked in half.

Inside, the house was messy, with a million things everywhere, like heaps of old newspapers at the front door and a brown armchair that looked broken and two TVs on the floor and a guitar and a hundred cardboard boxes and a pile of books spread open with different parts of the writing underlined in red pen even though writing in books is TREASON.

A German shepherd ran into the room barking loudly. Hank said, "DOWN, BIRNEY," and the dog immediately lay down and whimpered at his feet like a very obedient SIDEKICK HOUND.

"He's very excitable but he won't harm a fly," Hank said.

"Can I pet him?"

"Sure can," he said. "Only he won't leave you alone if you do."

I bent down and scratched behind Birney's ears, which is exactly where dogs like to be scratched best. He licked my hand.

"We will be excellent friends," he said. "And by the way, Hank is a very nice man and he won't chop you up and cook you into human soup."

Hank patted a wooden chair with a ratty green cushion.

"Make yourself at home," he said to Dad. "I'll fix you a drink. Looks like you could use one."

I shot FIERY WARNING DAGGERS at Dad and he shook his head. "Better not, thank you."

"How about you?" Hank said. "I believe I make the finest hot chocolate this side of the Mississippi."

"Oh, yes, please," I said, with my lovely manners.

"Come on then," he said. I followed him across the hall into the kitchen.

There was a long table in the middle of the room, but only a small part of it wasn't covered with more books and newspapers and dishes. There were old pots and pans hanging on the walls and two olden-day guns and three hats and a chopping ax. Probably Hank was a lumberjack or a hunter.

He scratched through his cupboards and pulled down a small red saucepan.

He wiped it with a kitchen towel and filled it with milk. Then he took a slab of chocolate and broke off a couple of pieces to stir in. He poured everything into a blue striped mug and held it out for me. His eyes were eating me up.

"What did you say your name was?" he said. I took the mug and looked into the steam.

"Joshua," I said.

LYING CUNT. That's what dads call moms who tell them lies to their face. Lies make Mr. Angry Bear wake up. He gets so mad he explodes and turns to fire. The fire burns everything up and the whole world turns red, like the color of blood.

"I'm glad you found us," I told Hank.

I carried the hot chocolate very carefully with two hands and sat on the living room floor with Birney. Everything in the house was dusty and it itched my eyes and tickled up my nose. I sneezed two times but number three wouldn't come, so none of my wishes were going to happen.

Hank went back into the kitchen and fetched a soda for Dad. He lit himself a tobacco pipe and sat in the broken chair.

Dad sipped his soda. He looked very, very sleepy. He took off his pretend glasses and rubbed his eyes. The circles underneath were growing into two dark pools.

Hank watched Dad very carefully. He took a puff of his pipe and kept his eyes on him until he had blown all the smoke out of his lungs. He set the pipe down and then he turned to me. "Why don't you say good night to your daddy, and I'll show you to your room."

Dad stood up. "I should probably go too, in case—"

"You sit," Hank said. "I believe we have a few things to discuss."

Dad swallowed. He raised his hands. "We can leave," he told Hank. "We can leave right now."

Hank shook his head and shot Dad a sharp look. "See, I can't let you do that, Joseph," he said. He stared at Dad and Dad stared at him. It was like they were having a contest but no one was smiling.

"Sit down," Hank said, and finally Dad did. I didn't know how Hank had guessed his real name but I was happy we didn't have to leave. So was Birney. He licked my hand and said I tasted very kind and brave.

"Come on," Hank said. He led me down the hallway. I could see stairs at the end winding down to a basement. Inside, a light was shining.

"Who's down there?" I said.

"Me, most of the time," Hank said. "I'll show you around tomorrow."

227

"Is it a den for playing Xbox? Savannah's brother has a whole basement to himself for his games. We aren't allowed down there."

"Nah," Hank said. "No games down there."

He opened the door to a bedroom. Inside was a small wooden bed and a desk and a closet.

"Whose room is this?"

"Just anyone who needs it," Hank said.

"Where's your room?"

"Oh," Hank said. "I'm not much of a sleeper. When I do, I stay down in the basement."

He took covers from the back of the closet and I helped him make up the bed with blue sheets.

After Hank closed the door, I lay awake, staring up at the ceiling. I stroked Clemesta in the place where her mane used to be and felt the beige plastic poking through.

"You're still beautiful," I said, "because of your kind and shining heart."

"Ditto," she said. She nuzzled my neck. Her breath was warm. She'd forgotten to brush her teeth after the hot chocolate but I didn't say anything about Gerry Germ.

"We're being very brave," I said, "aren't we?"

"Yeah." Clemesta sighed. "But I'm tired of it."

"Well, we don't have much longer to go. We'll be home very soon."

Clemesta made a face. "Dad told Hank we were heading to Texas. Texas isn't home."

My stomach rock went sinking and I pressed it with my hand.

"Dolly, did you hear me?"

I looked at the ceiling. It didn't have any stars.

• • •

In the night, I woke up to use the bathroom.

I crept down the hallway. The toilet seat was made from wood and it wobbled loose when I sat down. I wiped but I didn't flush because I thought it would make too much noise and wake everyone up. That would be inconsiderate and bad manners and I didn't want Hank to regret helping us.

I looked in the mirror above the washbasin. It had a big crack down the middle, which everyone knows is seven years' bad luck. *Poor Hank,* I thought. Poor everyone who breaks mirrors and gets bad luck. Or gets bad luck without even breaking anything.

As I walked back to my bed, I heard voices. It was Dad, talking with Hank down the hall. I could see Dad's legs and shoes, and Hank standing in the doorway.

"I wasn't thinking," Dad was saying. "I was blinded with it. Blinded. She's having an affair, planning on running off with my kid, taking her across the country. Something broke in me." He rubbed his hands on his knees and then he leaned forward in the chair. "I just panicked and left," he said. "Grabbed her and ran."

Hank walked across the room. I heard glasses clinking with ice. "Drink up," he said. I saw Dad's arm lift a glass of the golden stuff that comes in the glass bottle.

LIAR LIAR PANTS ON FIRE. Another broken promise.

"I thought we could disappear," he said. "Start over. Never come back. I have an old friend in Mexico, Diego. One of these people who knows people. He could help us out. Get the right papers, make sure we stay vanished."

Hank's boots creaked against the wood as he went to sit back down. "Not much of a life, being on the run."

"I know," Dad said. He took a long sip of his drink. "I know."

No one said anything for a while. Then Hank let out a long sigh. "Someone helped me once," he said. "Got me out of a bad situation, a very poor decision I made. I almost certainly didn't deserve help but I got it all the same. So I'm going to help you, Joseph. I'm going to help you on your way."

There was no more talking after that, just ice clinking against glass. I waited in the dark. I could hear my heart thumping inside me like someone trapped in a box banging to get out.

Dad made a strange coughing noise.

"I'm not a monster," he said. "I'm not."

Birney barked twice, and I crept back to bed. I climbed under the covers and whispered everything I'd overheard to Clemesta.

"I know," she said. "I remember."

She nipped at my ear with her sharp horse-teeth.

"And Dolly," she said, "you're remembering now too."

Friday

Birney woke me in the morning. I felt his tongue licking my face and it tickled till I opened my eyes. Hank called, "Breakfast!" and I followed Birney down the hall to the kitchen. He told me he had guarded the door to my room all night long to keep me and Clemesta safe.

"You're a marvelous dog," I said.

"I don't do it for everyone," he said. "Only special and brave people who I like very much."

I circled my hand over his head. "Dogs don't usually live for very long," I told him, "but with this special blessing, you will live forever."

Birney was very pleased.

In the kitchen, Hank was dressed in clothes like he was a soldier in the army, with heavy black boots on his feet. His sleeves were rolled up and he had a kitchen towel tucked in his back pocket.

"Morning," he said. "Sleep okay?"

I nodded.

He was standing at the stove flipping bacon in a pan. The whole kitchen smelled of breakfast and my stomach rumbled loudly. I hadn't eaten real food for a long time.

Hank looked over at the table covered with stuff and

frowned. "I guess I'm not used to company," he said. "Why don't you move that over to the side so we can sit and eat together like civilized folks."

"Is Dad still sleeping?"

Hank shook his head. "Your daddy's out back, taking a look at the car."

"What car?"

"My old Chevy," Hank said. "It's been sitting out in that garage gathering dust for years. I told your daddy he should take it."

"To get us home," I said.

"Right."

I slumped in a chair. "I think we're still too far away." The bacon was sizzling and Hank took the pan off the heat.

I pushed everything on the table to the opposite side. It left behind marks in the dust and I rubbed them away with my finger.

I watched Hank drop eight eggs into another pan. He broke them right in his hand, without cracking them on the side of the bowl first like Mom does. Probably because he was so strong. He had a tattoo on the bulgy part of his arm, but it wasn't a picture. It was just numbers. *2.5.2011.* Maybe that was somebody's birthday and he put it there so he'd never forget.

"Are you a for-real army soldier?" I said.

"Used to be."

Hank threw Birney a piece of bacon and he caught it in the air and gobbled it down in one excited bite.

"What are you now?"

"I work as a trapper," Hank said. "Bird removal, mostly."

"Why do you have to remove birds?"

Hank wiped his hands. "If they're stuck in a mall, or nesting in a grocery store, I go get them and take them away."

My eyes went wide. "You kill them?"

"Oh, no," Hank said. "I set them free. That's the idea."

He laid the food on the table and pulled up a chair next to mine.

I wanted to ask him about the things Dad had said last night, but I didn't want him to know that I was an EAVESDROPPER who listened in on other people's private conversations. Eavesdropping is a bad habit and it causes a lot of trouble because probably you don't always get everything one hundred percent FACTUALLY CORRECT and then people say, "That's not true," but other people say, "Bullshit," and it's all a great big confusing mess.

I looked at Hank's enormous arms that could definitely break you in two without even trying very hard. "Did you know that killer whales are really dolphins?"

He shook his head. "That's an interesting thing to know."

"I know a lot of interesting things. I'm like a knowledge collector. It's all in my brain."

Hank smiled.

"I missed a whole entire week of school. That's a lot of knowledge I didn't get to collect and it's Dad's fault." I pinched my skin with my fingernail. "He took me away," I said. "I think it's called abduction."

Dad came through the door and Hank nodded at him.

"Morning," Dad said. He washed his hands at the sink and sat down with us.

I watched him from the corner of my eye like a good

detective. He'd shaved his stubbly beard and he was wearing fresh, clean clothes. He must have borrowed them from Hank. He didn't smell of the golden stuff from the night before but maybe he only had a little this time.

He piled a plate with eggs and bacon, and reached over to grab a fork.

Hank drank his coffee. "How's that engine?"

"Got it working fine," Dad said. "I siphoned the gas from the truck like you said. Tank's half full, and that's plenty to get us on our way."

"Good," Hank said. "That's good."

He threw more bacon for Birney to catch in his teeth. His gums were black and pink, so probably that meant they were half-rotten.

Dad poured himself more coffee and Hank held out his mug for more too.

"You aren't eating any breakfast," I said.

He shrugged. "Me and Birney mostly eat out of a can."

"Why?"

"You get into habits, I suppose."

"Well, it's nice to have a healthy breakfast FINALLY." I scowled at Dad but he was busy looking out the window.

"It's a beautiful day," he said.

It looked like an ordinary and regular day to me, with the sun waking up and the fog moving out of the way and the birds flying around getting worms for their breakfast, but I guess Dad saw something else.

"Life sure is strange," Hank said, "isn't it?"

I let Birney lick my fingers under the table with his long, wet tongue.

• • •

After breakfast, I followed Hank down to the basement. It looked like a hardware store down there, with a workbench and ONE MILLION tools and a chainsaw and a welder and a huge pile of wooden planks and metal wire fencing all rolled up and three big tubs of paint sitting on the floor.

"What do you do here?" I said.

"This and that," Hank said.

"Like craft projects?"

"Well," he said. "Come see."

He walked over to the wall. It had an American flag pinned to it, and below that a photograph of two army soldiers with their arms around each other's shoulders. They both wore sunglasses and red bandannas on their heads.

"Is that you?"

"A long time ago."

Hank pressed down against a lever and suddenly the wall became a big metal door and it opened up to a whole entire SECRET HOUSE hiding away on the other side. Inside, there were two armchairs and a bed and a shelf filled with rows and rows of canned food and hot sauce and toilet paper and bottled water and soda and batteries and flashlights and candles and a huge enormous TV and a wall with HUNDREDS of guns and another shelf of books and a chessboard on a table and an exercise rowing machine and a bunch of dumbbells on a rack. My eyes were darting around trying to see everything but there was too much to catch it all up.

"What is this?" I said.

"It's called a bunker," Hank said.

"Like a secret hiding place?"

"Sort of."

"Like a hurricane storm shelter," I said. "For staying safe." I looked at Hank in his army clothes with his giant muscles and his stomping boots that could kick you to Mars. "But who could ever hurt you?"

Hank shrugged. "You never know who or what you might need to protect yourself from."

"Like strangers?"

Hank rubbed his chin. "Not just strangers. Sometimes people you know. The world can turn upside down pretty quick."

"And then what happens?"

"Then it's real good to be prepared."

I sat on the bed. It was only big enough for one person. "Won't you be lonely," I said, "if it's just you down here?"

Hank smiled. "I don't mind lonely so much. I mind it less than I mind people, to tell you the truth."

"Why do you mind people?"

Hank made a face. "They have a way of disappointing you."

"Yeah," I said. "And they do stupid things."

"They sure do," Hank said.

The bunker smelled of fresh paint and cement. There was an empty glass on the floor beside the bed, and a book lying open next to it.

"You slept here last night."

Hank nodded. "I test it out sometimes."

"To see if you like it?"

"To see if I have everything I need."

I looked around. There was a birdcage hanging from a

hook in the ceiling that I hadn't noticed yet. Inside, a teeny tiny bird perched on a swing.

"That's Lester," Hank said.

"Why is he here?" I walked over to get a better look.

"I think he likes it," Hank said. "I got called out to remove him from a building site but he wouldn't go anywhere. Wouldn't fly away. I keep him as a pet now. He seems to like the quiet down here."

"How do you know his name is Lester?"

Hank held a finger out and the bird pecked it with kisses.

"I knew a Lester once," he said. "He wouldn't leave my side either."

I watched Hank stroke Lester's bird beak. Probably they had unconditional love between them. That's the love which never stops no matter what bad stuff you do or how many secrets you spill from the secret-secret box. I bet Hank would do anything to keep Lester safe. Probably die for him. Or kill for him.

I looked at Hank. "My name isn't really Joshua," I said. "I'm really a girl. I'm sorry I told a lie."

He shrugged. "You're all right."

I bit my lip. "Hank, is Dad in big trouble?" He looked at me and puffed out his lips. Then he let out a long sigh.

"What I know is that your daddy loves you very much," he said. "More than anything. More than life itself." He shook his head. "I also know that life isn't always black and white. Things get messy sometimes. Good people do bad things by mistake. We have to remember that. Life is complicated. Love is complicated."

"Why does it have to be complicated?"

"It just is."

"I wish it wasn't complicated. I wish it was just love." My throat went tight and I swallowed down as hard as I could.

Hank cracked his knuckles, first one hand and then the other. We stood watching Lester in his cage, pecking his beak at the metal bars. Maybe he didn't want to be there anymore. Maybe he wanted to get out and fly away home but he wouldn't ever be able to tell that to Hank. He'd just stay trapped forever.

"Come on," Hank said. "I think your daddy will want to get on the road."

"Can't I stay down here? Where it's safe."

Hank ran his hand over his bald head. "Stay a few minutes more," he said. "But mind those guns."

I listened to him climb back up the creaky stairs. I went over to the armchair and sat down. Hank had a gas mask hanging on the wall, and two guns and something else that was probably a cannon or a zombie-destroyer.

I moved to the kitchen part of the bunker and looked at all the cans lined up on the shelf.

"Spaghetti and meatballs," I said to Clemesta. "That's what we would have on Monday nights. Corn on Tuesday, chili con carne for Wednesday, macaroni Thursday, Friday back to spaghetti. Soda on weekends only."

I ran my hand over the rows of toilet paper and paper towels and the big tubs of salt and sugar and coffee. Everything was very neat and tidy and stacked in perfect lines.

I touched the knight on the chessboard but I didn't move him in case Hank was in the middle of a game.

"We'll learn chess," I told Clemesta, "and bring books and

craft paper and puzzles, and we can watch TV and go to sleep at regular bedtime so we aren't too tired. Survival probably isn't that hard."

"Mm," Clemesta said.

A black spider was spinning its web in the corner of one of the floorboards. I stomped it dead with my shoe so it couldn't make a web and hatch lots of spider babies that would bite Hank and Birney one night while they slept.

I sat back down in the armchair. "It's nice down here," I said.

Clemesta shook her head. "I don't think so."

"It is. You're safe from the whole world and nothing bad can happen to you. It's like our hurricane storm shelter at home."

"You know that isn't true," Clemesta said.

"It is."

She shook her head. "No, it really isn't. You remember."

"I don't remember. It's all fuzzy up there. Like someone is making scrambled eggs with my brain."

Clemesta stroked my head. "But if you try and make it clear it won't be fuzzy anymore. You'll solve it, like a detective mystery."

"I don't want to be a detective. I want to be a bird trapper. I will go and rescue them from trees and buildings and I'll bring them home and they will sing happy songs and eat seeds from my hand and they will come to me when I call them with a special whistle."

"Time to go!" I heard Dad's voice from upstairs.

Clemesta pierced me with her eyes. "Dolly, I know you worked it out. I know you're afraid, too."

I closed my eyes. I covered my ears. The capital of Denmark

is Copenhagen. The capital of France is Paris. Two times four is eight. Foods high in vitamin C include bell peppers, dark leafy greens, kiwi fruit, broccoli, berries, oranges, and tomatoes.

"Dolly," Clemesta said. "We can't go with Dad. We need to tell someone where we are so they can come and get us."

"But I don't know how," I said. My voice whimpered like a scaredy-cat even though I was meant to be brave.

"Well," Clemesta said. Her eyes were wide. "I saw a telephone. It's right in Hank's basement. And you remember Mom's number, don't you? It's in your sponge brain."

I nodded slowly. "Yeah, it's in there."

"Good. So we just have to go over there to the other side of this wall and dial the number and . . . and that's what we'll do."

I swallowed my scared. "Okay," I said. We went creeping quietly out of the bunker and over to the phone. It felt like stealing even though it was just one phone call and Hank probably wouldn't mind. I lifted the phone and closed my eyes to remember Mom's number. I dialed and it started to ring. Once, twice, three times and then suddenly there was someone on the other side and I whispered, "Mom! Mom!" but it wasn't her. It was another woman and I thought I had mixed up the numbers, but then she said, "Dolly, Dolly, is that you?"

"Yes," I said. "It's Dolly and I want to talk to Mom."

The woman said, "Yes, Dolly, just a second, okay? Honey, can you tell me where you—"

"Come on!" Dad's voice was coming closer and Hank's boots were pounding down the stairs.

I dropped the phone and ran up to meet him. My heart was racing and I begged it to stay quiet.

"Come on up," Hank said. "You have a long drive ahead."

He looked over my shoulder. I couldn't tell if he saw the phone hanging from its cord. He didn't say anything. He just led me back up the stairs to Dad with his enormous hand on my arm.

We said goodbye at the back door. Birney jumped up to give me a dog-hug, and Hank shook my hand.

"Good luck to you," he said.

Dad and I walked across the lawn to the car. He tried to take my hand but I didn't want to hold his. I jerked away and pretended that I needed to scratch my arm instead.

I waved to Hank and Birney one last time. Hank threw a stick and Birney chased after it. As we pulled away, I saw Hank's flag waving us off. The blue X looked like a bird trying to fly away.

Hank's Chevy was a much better car than the PILE OF JUNK from before. It didn't smell bad, and there weren't any cigarette burns in the seat and it wasn't beeping and spluttering the whole time like it was dying.

Dad was wearing his baseball cap and his glasses. Hank had loaned him a new map, which he folded out on the seat.

We drove without talking. I pressed the loose tooth with my tongue. I pushed it back as far as it would go, till it lifted almost all the way off the gum. The part underneath felt cold and smooth. The new one wasn't pushing to get out yet, like when my front tooth fell out last year and the replacement tooth was already waiting. I pressed my tongue against it, harder and harder even though it was hurting.

"Stop," Clemesta said, "you'll make it come out before it's ready."

"Who cares?"

"You'll bleed."

"I don't care if I bleed. I'm not afraid of blood."

Actually when I thought about blood, my stomach made a flip-flop. I tasted my breakfast, sitting upstairs in my throat.

I watched Dad in front of me, his hands stiff on the wheel and his eyes staring ahead at the road. He didn't even notice that the back of his head was crawling with snakes.

We passed green fields and farms and two signs for *plantations.* That was a new word but I didn't collect it. We passed two trailer homes. One was getting crushed by a big tree that had fallen over it. Maybe the people were still inside. They would be trapped for one hundred years and no one would stop to let them out.

I looked down at my clothes. They were covered with Birney's muddy paw-prints. All of me felt dirty and tired and wrong, like that stuffed toy in the mud nobody cared to scoop up and take home.

I pressed my tongue harder against the tooth.

A billboard said WELCOME TO MISSISSIPPI. IT'S LIKE COMING HOME.

No it isn't, I said inside my head.

"Mississippi is another state," I said. "You're going the wrong way. This is the wrong road for home."

Dad shook his head. "It's not far now," he said. Clemesta shoved me with her hoof.

"LIES," she hissed.

I kept pressing the tooth. "Who picked up Mom's phone?" I said.

"Probably the police," Clemesta said.

"Because they want to help Mom find us."

Clemesta held her breath.

"What?" I said.

"I don't know, Dolly."

Dad looked at me in the mirror. "You know, Joshua and I came to Mississippi every summer," he said. "We'd come for shrimp season. We had an uncle out here who ran some boats. He paid us well. That's how we saved up for college."

I didn't say anything. I didn't want to hear any more stories about Dad when he was a kid, or about dead Uncle Joshua who would have liked to meet me if Dad hadn't made him want to die.

I stared out the window. Mississippi was flat and swampy, full of marshes and thick trees and places to get sucked into forever with no way out. It looked just like on the nature documentary about alligators that I watched. Alligators like to live in the rivers, bayous, and swamps of the southeastern United States, and they have lived on earth for millions of years and their blood is cold, which is because they are mean.

I watched the show with Mom that afternoon when I had the flu. She made me a mug of soup from the packets that have tiny baby alphabet noodles inside, and tucked the orange striped blanket around me on the sofa, and then we sat together and watched anything on TV that I wanted to watch, and she never got bored and she never said she had to go and paint her nails or check her emails for callbacks or do her exercises or rehearse lines, she just sat there beside me and stroked my hair and it was a very lovely day even with being sick and having a temperature of 103 degrees.

That was before we bumped into YOU KNOW WHO in Manhattan. Everything that came after that was THE WORST because he is THE WORST.

"He isn't, Dolly," Clemesta said. "He wanted to help Mom get away."

"From what?"

"From Dad," Clemesta said. "So we'd be safe."

I still had my tongue pressing at the tooth and suddenly I felt it pop all the way out. The tooth dropped to the bottom of my mouth like a stone. I tasted my blood that was half of Mom and half of Dad and all of me. I swallowed it down.

I didn't tell Dad. I just kept the tooth under my tongue like another secret.

"Spit that out," Clemesta said. "It's a CHOKING HAZ-ARD."

I didn't want to and I didn't.

We drove and drove, and the roads were very flat and everything around was flat too. Concrete strip malls and drive-throughs and gas stations and swamps and then the same things all over again.

Dad reached his arm back to squeeze my leg.

"You're very quiet back there. Do you have any stories for me today?"

I shook my head.

"Should we play the signs game? There's one. ELITE GUNS. DIAL 555-GOD'S TRUTH."

"Don't," I said. "I don't want to play."

"WAFFLE HOUSE," Dad said.

"I said STOP."

"Okay." Dad switched on the radio and the music filled the car.

"Turn it off," I said, after a while. The song was called *Mercy* and *mercy* means *forgiveness* and I didn't want to think about that or anything like it.

"Turn it off," I said again, and Dad switched the station. It was the news, and he switched that off too.

I sipped some water. My head was jumpy, with too many pictures bouncing around inside. The NOT NOW box was open, and everything was tumbling out.

I closed my eyes. There was my bedroom, with all my things inside. Dollhouse, dinosaur collection, rescued baby animals. The bed was unmade and clothes were lying on the floor. That meant it wasn't going to be a gold-star day.

The kitchen table was still covered with dishes from the last dinner we ate before we left, grilled fish and steamed vegetables. Mom hardly touched her food because she was VERY DISTRACTED with other things. She must have been too distracted to clean up afterward, or maybe that was something else.

My *Exotic Birds* coloring book was on the coffee table with all my markers. My school bag was waiting in the hallway for

Monday with the class dictionary packed inside to give back to Miss Ellis. Mom's bedroom door was shut and I didn't peek inside.

I put my tongue in the empty space in my mouth. It was strange how something could be there and then be gone, just like that. There and gone, there and gone. The empty space hurt, but it wasn't from being sore. It was from missing something.

I watched Dad's head. I slipped the tooth out of my mouth and into the pocket of my shorts.

Clemesta was being very quiet. "Say something," I told her.

She shook her head. "I can't. It feels like all my energy is used up."

In the car next to ours, a girl made a face at me as they passed. I gave her THE FINGER and her eyes went wide from shock at my DISGRACEFUL RUDENESS. *Too bad,* I thought. Her mom was driving the car. They would have a lovely afternoon together and I would be stuck all day driving with Dad.

I looked at his hand on the wheel, the dark hairs sprouting out of his fingers like someone had planted them there. The gold from his wedding ring wasn't shiny, it was dull and worn out. It didn't look like anything precious anymore.

I wanted it to be precious. I wanted it to be beautiful in the light and shining, and Mom's too. She had put hers inside a little box on the top shelf of the bedroom closet. "I want a better life for you, Dolly," she'd said.

Better wasn't in Queens, and it wasn't a gold circle on her finger.

•　•　•

I pulled Clemesta into my lap and stroked her stubbly mane. She could hardly lift her head. She was very weak. She looked like she wanted to sleep for ONE HUNDRED YEARS. Probably she wanted to empty out her head and not think about anything or remember any memories. She just wanted to be an ordinary regular horse, not a magical horse queen with special gifts and ALL THE SECRETS TO KEEP.

She opened her mouth and licked her dry lips. "I think we're in danger," she said quietly. "I think we're running out of chances to get back home."

I nodded. I laid my head back. I kicked Dad's seat with my feet. One, two, like punches. He looked back at me. "I know you're bored," he said. "I swear this is the last—this is the final day."

"Good," I said. "I hate this adventure."

Dad nodded. His eyes were shining and he wiped them.

"What's the matter with you?" I said. "Why are you looking at me like that?"

"I'm sorry—I'm so sorry. I wish it had all been something better. Everything in your life. Everything we did together."

I crossed my arms against me and looked away. "Well," I said. "Life is complicated."

We passed a billboard with an alligator head poking out, ready to gobble someone up in his huge jaws. I remembered on the show when the enormous alligator had the smaller one locked in his mouth. He was holding her between his teeth while she thrashed her tail trying to get away. Her tail cracked like a gunshot every time it hit the water. His teeth were gripping her harder and harder, and the more she tried to get away, the more he locked her in his grip.

Mom had held her hand over my heart and pulled me close. "Don't worry," she said. "No alligators here."

The alligator held on, and after a few minutes the other one stopped moving.

"Anna, you know I can't exist without you." That's what Dad said to Mom and she was crying and he was yelling.

"I need you, I need you, I won't let you go."

Mr. Angry Bear was there too. He wouldn't stay sleeping no matter how well we behaved.

Dad looked at the time and rubbed his head. "We should probably get you something to eat," he said.

"I want Thai food," I said. "Or Chinese dumplings."

"I don't think they have that around here."

"Well, they should."

We passed a McDonald's drive-through and Dad turned the car around to go back.

"That's more junk," I said. "You told me you were going to look after me properly."

Dad called out our order and at the next window he reached out an arm and picked up our dinner. "Why don't you come up in front?" he said.

"I'm staying here," I said. I opened the wrapping and stared at the cheeseburger. I ate half of my burger first, and then the fries, and then the other half of the burger.

Dad turned around in his seat to face me.

"We eat our burgers the same way," Dad said. "I never noticed before."

"Oh. Yeah," I said.

I wiped my mouth with the napkin and sipped my milk-shake. It was too sweet and too cold. Outside the car, I could hear the alligators in the swamps gnashing their teeth. Hungry, hungry, hungry, just waiting to pounce and take you under.

Someone parked next to our car and Dad turned his back and hunched over. I chewed the last bite of my cheese-burger until I had sucked out all the juice from the meat. The lump sat in my mouth a long time before I forced it down.

When we finished, Dad scrunched up all the wrappers and put them into the brown paper bag.

"Do it," Clemesta said. "Do it now."

I looked at Dad.

"I need to use the bathroom," I said.

"Badly?"

"Yeah."

"Uh," he said. "All right. Hang on." He put the baseball cap back on my head and pulled the front low over my face. "I'll wait right here in the car," he said.

The restaurant was empty inside. I walked up to the counter. I took off the cap and held it in my hands.

"Can I use the restroom, please?" I said.

The man in the McDonald's uniform was reading a giant book called BIOCHEMISTRY, which didn't look very inter-esting. He peered down at me. His eyes seemed kind, and also tired.

"Toilets are only for customers," he said. His teeth were very white and straight.

"We are customers," I said. "We just got our dinner from the drive-through. Dad and me," I said.

"Whatever," he said. "Through there."

"Thank you," I said. I smiled at him with all my teeth and I looked at him and I waited for him to look at me VERY CAREFULLY but instead he went back to reading his book. The badge on his shirt said DARRYL 2ND ASSISTANT MANAGER.

I went ON PURPOSE into the women's restroom and washed my hands with the soap and looked at my face in the mirror. Even with the boy hair I still looked like me if you just paid some attention.

My skin felt like it was slicked with honey. I splashed water on my face and wiped my cheeks with the brown paper towels.

You are brave, I told myself in the mirror. *You are brave and you can do it.*

I went back out. The man behind the counter looked at me and I looked back at him. I took a deep breath and gathered up all my brave.

"My name is Dolly Rust," I said. "Dolly Rust. The police are looking for me. And I need to go home."

The man put aside his book and leaned over the counter. "Dolly Rust," he said.

I turned and ran back out to Dad. I slammed the door and pulled on my seat belt. Dad started the car just as the McDonald's man came outside talking into his phone and walking toward us very quickly.

• • •

We drove into the dark night. The roads were pitch black and there weren't any streetlights to show us the way.

"I did it," I whispered into Clemesta's ear and she nodded.

"Good girl," she said. "Brave girl."

It was cold in the back and everything in me felt hollow. I shivered and held my legs in my arms to try and warm them up. I couldn't see anything out the window, and all I could hear was the tires racing against the road. Clemesta and I squeezed hands.

Inside my shorts I felt for my tooth and held it in my fingers. Then I opened the window and dropped it into the road.

"What was that?" Dad said.

"My tooth," I said.

"It fell out?"

"Yeah."

"Shouldn't you keep it for the tooth fairy?"

I shut the window. "The tooth fairy is a lie," I said. Everything is a lie.

Saturday

In my dream, I was driving the blue Ford. My hands were on the wheel but the car wasn't stuck, it was moving. It was going too fast and I was very scared. I looked behind me to find Dad, and he was there, running behind the car and pushing it. He was trying to make it go faster and faster, and I cried, "Please stop!" but he wouldn't.

In the morning, we weren't driving anymore. The car was parked on a patch of dirt in the middle of nothing. There was no one around, no cars and no people. Just dry grass and tall trees and a swampy-looking river in front of us. I sat up and pushed Hank's jacket off me. Dad must have covered me in the night.

I could see him out the front, sitting on the hood of the car. He was watching the sun come up over the water, which looked very still and glassy. The air outside smelled sweet and strange, like fruit that's too ripe and a little bit poisonous.

I checked on Clemesta. She was breathing softly and still fast asleep. I kissed the top of her head and climbed out of the car. My legs were stiff again. I hoped it was from being curled up all night in the back of a car and not from scurvy.

SORRY, LEGS, I said. They hadn't had a chance to dance or exercise or play for a long time. It was one whole week since we left home. Actually it felt like a thousand years. A thousand bad years of tears and plagues and very bad things. Everything felt upside-down but not like in the fun picture where you have to spot what's wrong. This was another kind of upside-down and I didn't like any of the pictures. I wouldn't even look at them.

I climbed out.

"Good morning," Dad said.

I looked out at the water, and then back to the empty field behind us.

"Where are we?"

"Orange, Texas," Dad said.

I frowned. "Another state away from home. Did we sleep here?"

Dad shook his head. "I drove most of the night. Got lost some of the way."

"You're always lost."

Dad looked very tired. His beard was already stubbly on his skin and his borrowed clothes from Hank were crumpled. He had a bottle of water in his hands. He took a sip and wiped his mouth. "Look at that sun coming up," he said. "Isn't it beautiful?"

I glanced at the sky with its pinky pale light. Nothing looked beautiful to me. It all just looked wrong.

"Why are you paying so much attention to the sun all of a sudden?"

Dad's eyes were far away, looking into the water but really trying to look all the way back in time. Probably he didn't like the picture of now either.

"I want to remember it," he said.

My stomach rock pulled at my sides as it sank and twisted. "Why do you need to remember it? It isn't going anywhere."

Dad patted the hood with his hand. "Come sit here with me a minute."

He held out his arm to help pull me up. The car hood felt warm under my skin. Dad took a deep breath. He made a fist and squeezed it inside his other hand. The knuckles cracked. I thought of Travis back at the National Park. LOVE and FEAR. LOVE and FEAR. Maybe they weren't opposites. Maybe they were actually the same thing written in different letters.

I poked my tongue into the place where my tooth had lived. *There and not there, there and not there.*

"Dolly," Dad said, "I need to tell you something."

I looked at his sad brown eyes. They were so big it looked like they wanted to burst. I didn't want him to say anything. I didn't want him to tell me why he was sad and saying goodbye to the sun.

"Dolly," he said. He took my hand. "I did a very bad thing."

I shook my head. I took back my hand and sat on it.

"Doll, listen. I—"

"No," I said. "Stop."

"Dolly."

"Stop, Dad. Zip it up and throw the key in the water."

"Doll. I need to say it."

"No, you don't."

"I do, sweetheart. Dolly, I hurt Mom. I didn't mean to, I didn't ever want to hurt her, but I did."

"No," I said. "You didn't."

"Dolly, I did." His voice cracked and his face scrunched up and his eyes spilled tears. "I hurt her really badly, Dolly."

"SHUT UP!" I yelled. "Shut up!"

Everything in my whole head was spinning too fast and my stomach rock was so heavy inside me that I could hardly breathe.

"Dolly," Dad said. "I need you to understand. I didn't mean it. It was an accident. I was so scared. Mom was leaving, she was going to take you away. For good. I'd never see you. You'd be...I was so mad. I always get too mad and this time I couldn't stop myself."

He dropped his head into his hands and he sobbed like a big fat baby. His whole body shook and wobbled. He was disgusting, and I wanted to punch him and throw up on him at the same time.

"Take me home right now," I said. "Just take me home to Mom."

Dad looked at me with his wet eyes and shook his head.

"But, Dolly," he gulped. "I can't."

"You can!" I yelled.

"Doll, Mom is dead."

I looked at his face, smeared with red and tears and snot and sad.

"DON'T SAY THAT!" I yelled. "It isn't true."

"It is, Dolly."

"NO! No, it isn't!" I screamed with all the air in my lungs and Dad was crying and I shoved him so hard that he fell off the car and onto the grass. He lay there in a crumpled heap and I stood over him crying and shaking and breaking apart.

He pulled himself up and tried to come toward me but I pushed him away.

"I'm sorry, Dolly. I'm so sorry. It was an accident, it wasn't supposed to—"

"WHY?" I yelled. "Why did you hurt her?"

Dad looked up to the sky and let out another sob. "I just snapped," he said. "When I heard about the man she was seeing, all those secret trips to Manhattan. The divorce. When I heard she was planning to take you to LA to be with him, and—"

"Stew," I cried. "She's dead because of *him*?" I wiped both hands across my face to try and clear up the mess. I tried to stop shuddering, too, but I couldn't. I looked at Dad. He had turned white and still like a ghost.

"Stew?" he said. He shook his head.

"Yes!" I cried.

"Stew Ronson?"

"YES!" My lungs burned with all the hate I had for YOU KNOW WHO, whose name cut my throat in slices and made it bleed.

"Stew," Dad said. "Oh, Jesus. Stew." He stumbled back against the car and retched yellow water onto the dead Texas grass.

I pinched my nail into the skin until it was popped open and stinging.

"There wasn't any best place you were taking me," I said. "The best place was home and you killed it."

Dad nodded. He had his hand over his mouth like he didn't want to let any more sound out. His tears were still falling and his eyes were shut.

"What's going to happen to us now?" I said.

Dad shuddered out a long breath and then he swallowed. "I'm taking you to your grandparents. My mom and dad."

"But they're DEAD," I said. "They're dead."

Dad shook his head. "They aren't," he said. "I told you they were because I didn't have them in my life anymore and I thought it would be easier that way. If you thought they were gone."

He squeezed his eyes shut. "I know it's a lot to take in. But after Joshua died, I never went home again. I didn't speak to them or see them. They blamed me for what happened. They were right. They were right to hate me. And I didn't want to cause them any more pain."

He clicked his jaw. "Sometimes I think all I do is cause people pain."

"YOU DO!" I yelled. "That's exactly what you do." I looked at him and set him on fire with my eyes and my angry.

He wiped his face. "I brought you here so you'd be safe. So you'd be with them and you'd be looked after."

I went frozen.

"And where will you be?"

Dad turned away.

We drove in silence. Dad wasn't wearing the disguise anymore. He was back to looking like Dad.

Clemesta squeezed my hand in hers, but she didn't say a word.

We pulled up outside an ordinary-looking brick house. The yard had a big tree standing in the middle of it and a red pickup parked out to the side.

"I'm sorry," Clemesta said. "I tried to warn you, Dolly."

She was very weak. Her magical powers were almost gone. I kissed her chopped-off mane. "You'll get strong again soon," I said.

"I don't know," she said. "Maybe I won't."

My heart broke into even more pieces.

Dad turned to look at me. "You wait in the car for now," he said. "I'll come back and get you in a minute."

He got out and left the car door open so I would have some air. It was already too hot. Too everything. He smoothed back his hair with his hands and rang the doorbell.

I cradled Clemesta in my lap, and we watched the front door as it opened.

An old woman poked her head out. She was wearing a yellow nightgown and slippers on her feet and in my head I said HELLO, GRANDMA and in my stomach the rock sank and the butterflies threw up. "I'm one-half orphan now," I said, and Clemesta wiped a tear from her cheek.

"Yes?" the old woman said. She peered at Dad and then she clapped her hand over her mouth.

"Dear Lord," she said. "Is that you, Joseph?"

Dad nodded. "Hello, Mama." He sounded like a little boy suddenly instead of a dad, and he hung his head.

The grandma let out a moan and slapped him WHACK across his cheek. Dad didn't move.

"Joseph, Joseph, Joseph," she said, and then she didn't say anything else. She just stood and stared and shook her head and held herself against the door until Dad stepped closer. He put his arms around her and she collapsed into them like her legs were made of Jell-O.

She was sobbing.

I felt a great big lump in my throat and I told it to BUG OFF. Clemesta sniffed. "It's so sad," she said.

"Everything is sad," I said. "The whole world is sad and everyone is crying."

I looked at the grandma who was still sobbing and holding Dad and shaking her head. She was old but not ONE HUNDRED YEARS OLD like the grandmas in Pop's nursing home, maybe only ninety or eighty-five. I thought about her looking after me instead of Mom and that made me HATE her, which wasn't kind but SO WHAT because Kindness Week was over and it had been the worst week of my whole entire life.

The grandma pulled away to look at Dad and touch his face and feel his hair and rub his arms.

"Son, son," she said. "Whatever did you do? It's all over the news. They've been watching the house. Sheriff Carter came by yesterday. Is it true? Is it true what they're saying?"

Dad stepped back and wiped his eyes. "I messed up," he said. "I made a mess of everything."

The grandma shook her head. "Oh, Joseph," she said. "My dear, sweet boy."

I shook my head. SILLY GRANDMA. He wasn't any one of those things.

Dad looked back at the car. "I want you to meet someone," he said.

He walked over to me and peered inside the window. "Dolly, would you like to come and meet your grandma?"

I did not AT ALL want to meet her or get out of the car

but I knew that the question wasn't really a question and I didn't have any choice. I set Clemesta down and stepped out. The grandma had come over and she was standing on the lawn, watching me carefully.

"Mama, this is Dolly," Dad said.

She crouched down to look at me. Her eyes were teary and red and her skin up close was crinkly in places like an old tissue. Her eyes were the same color as Dad's with just the same amount of sad living inside them. I didn't know you could get someone else's sad from them, but I guess it's like hair or dance talent.

"Dolly," she said. "I'm so very pleased to meet you."

I stared at her face. I wished I could make her disappear. I wished we could all disappear, back in time to before everything bad happened, when the whole world was perfect and no one was sad or mad or gone forever.

"She's beautiful, Joseph," the grandma said.

Dad put his hand on my shoulder and gave it a squeeze. "Best thing I ever did."

The grandma smiled and her watery eyes watered some more. She wiped them with her sleeve. "Goddamn it, Joseph," she said. "You goddamn fool."

They didn't say anything for a while. We all just stood and stared at the grass, with the sticky Orange air sitting on our skin.

A car passed by and the grandma looked out at the street.

"Come on," she said. "We best get you two inside."

She led us into the kitchen but she didn't sit down. "Your father," she said to Dad. "I'll go and get him, but..."

She opened her mouth to say something and then closed it again.

"Well," she said. "You'll always be our son, won't you?"

Dad and I sat down at the kitchen table, which wasn't made of wood like the one at home, but hard plastic with scratches all over it. We didn't look at each other and I moved my hand away so he couldn't touch it.

There was a loud voice from the other room and then someone came crashing into the kitchen yelling, "NO SON OF MINE!" It was an old man and he grabbed Dad by the collar of his shirt and pulled him right up off his feet.

I made myself very small and hid under the table. Dad held up his hands.

"I know," he said, "I know. I'm sorry, I'm sorrier than you'll ever know. I'm just here to make it right. Please. Please."

The grandma was trying to get the old man who was the granddad but not Pop to sit down. His eyes were bulging out of his skull.

"Frank," she said, "please. There's a girl. There's a child."

He looked at me under the table and I looked back at him. He didn't have Dad's brown eyes and they weren't crying, they were SPITTING MAD. He had red cheeks and white hair and he was very tall with long and thin bones, like a scarecrow. He sank into a chair and I watched his chest puff in and out like he had just done a hundred jumping jacks. The spit in the corner of his mouth puffed in and out too, a little white balloon that couldn't ever float.

No one said anything for a million hours. The grandma and granddad and Dad just sat and stared and forgot all about me under the table until Dad patted me and told me to come out.

The grandma stood up and scooped coffee into the coffee machine. She poured a glass of juice from a carton and set it down in front of me. It was the berry kind, my first-worst flavor.

"Thank you," I said anyway, to show her that I had good manners. Mom would like that.

"How old are you, Dolly?" she said.

"I'm seven and two months and three weeks."

She smiled a sad smile and shook her head. She poured the coffee into three mugs. All of them had cat pictures on them.

"Why are you here?" the granddad said. "All these years— a goddamn grandbaby we don't even know about—and you come back now. Now, like this."

Dad swallowed. "I stayed away so you wouldn't have to look at me."

The granddad slammed his mug on the table and the coffee spilled out.

"Look at you?" he said. "You think it was better losing two sons instead of one?" His voice snapped and cracked and spit. I guess he had an angry bear inside him too.

The grandma took his hand and squeezed it.

"Please, Frank," she said. "We all made terrible mistakes, didn't we?"

Everyone went quiet again. The kitchen clock's hands went around three times. No one wiped up the spill.

"What is it you plan to do, son?" the grandma said. Her eyes were wide and worried.

Dad swallowed. "I thought about running," he said. "Me and Doll. We were heading to Mexico. But she got sick one night, real sick." He looked at me and shook his head. "I realized I couldn't do it to her. Make her pay for my mistakes. Make her suffer." His words choked and he wiped his eyes.

The grandma was watching him and holding her breath.

"I'm turning myself in," he said. "That's what I'm doing."

The grandma let out a deep sigh. She nodded. "You want us to look after her. That's why you brought her here."

Dad nodded.

"Anna hasn't got anyone left?"

"No," he said.

The grandma sipped her coffee from her cat mug. The cat tried to say hello to me but I ignored it. "I'm Verena," the cat said.

"I don't care," I told her. "Not one bit."

The granddad stared down at the table. His nostrils flared, and the gray hairs inside peeked out.

I looked around the kitchen. The walls were orange. There were oranges in the fruit bowl. Oranges in Orange. *Orange* is a word you can't ever rhyme because nothing rhymes with *orange* no matter how hard you try.

Probably that was another BAD OMEN.

"You were gone a long time, Joseph," the granddad said. "You damn near broke your mother's heart."

"I know," Dad said. "I know."

The noise made us all jump. It grew louder and louder, like screams in the air.

"It's going to be okay," Dad said. "It's all going to be fine."
He tried to look at me but I turned away.

I peered out the window and saw the flashing blue lights.
Three police cars screeched to a stop on the curb outside and
the officers jumped out.

"You'll be fine, Dolly," Dad said. "Everything will be
fine." His voice was pretending to be calm but the rest of
him wasn't.

The doorbell rang and a man called out his name.

The granddad and grandma looked at each other with
frightened faces and then they turned to Dad.

"JOSEPH RUST," the police officer said again.

Dad stood up and the grandma and granddad stood too.

"You'll take good care of her," Dad said. "I know you
will. Maybe even...take her back to New York so it won't
be so..." He was looking at the grandma with PLEASE in
his eyes and he was nodding his head like he wanted her to
nod back.

"Please," he said and she nodded and he grabbed her and
hugged her. Then he turned to the granddad. The old man
made a face and groaned. He grabbed Dad in his arms and
sobbed hot and angry tears onto his neck.

We walked to the front door all together and opened it up.
There were a lot of police officers standing on the lawn. Their
guns were pointed at us. They were there to take Dad away.
Bad guys go to prison. And Dad was bad.

"Joseph Rust. Joseph Rust."

He lifted his hands up in the air.

"Come on out, sir," the officer said.

Dad started walking slowly and I followed, right in front of him. The grandma tried to pull me back toward her but I pushed her hands away.

"Darlin', can you stay on the porch?" the officer said.

I ignored him and stayed in front of Dad.

"Doll," Dad said. "Move away."

I didn't. I tied my arms around his leg so I could hold on tight.

"Let go now, Doll," Dad said, but I just held on. Tighter and tighter, forever and ever, because when Dad was gone, everything would be gone. Our whole entire family and everyone inside it, Mom and Dad and me, and our house and our neighborhood and every single thing that used to be home. When Dad was gone, home would be vanished forever, because it can't exist if the people you love most in the world aren't there. Then it's nowhere and you are nothing and the only thing you'll ever be is lost and broken.

"Please, darlin'," the officer said. "We just wanna talk to your daddy."

I squeezed Dad harder. Some of it angry, some of it afraid, some of it desperate. I was very strong, stronger than I ever knew. Dad tried to shift me away with his leg. I clamped on tighter, like a koala on a eucalyptus tree.

"Dolly. Please."

I WILL NEVER LET GO. I WILL HOLD ON FOR-EVER. I said that in my head-voice so loud it echoed.

"Sir, sir, step away from her please," the policeman said.

Everyone still had their guns pointed at us. BANG BANG and we would be dead. Dead like Mom and all together in heaven. Maybe that would be nice. Better than being alone.

I kept pulling at Dad, harder and harder. I turned my whole body and gripped him around his middle.

"Doll," Dad said. "Please."

He wobbled and I pulled and he sank down to his knees. We were face-to-face and eye to eye and I heard an officer say, "Give her a minute."

Dad blinked his eyes. "I'm so sorry, Dolly."

I looked at his face, his stupid face with his red crying eyes that were also kind love-heart eyes, but really just Dad eyes that I had seen almost every day of my whole entire life. I took my hand and I scratched his skin with my nails, clawing at him like I was a very mad cat.

"I hate you," I cried.

Dad didn't pull away.

"I know, Doll," he said. "I know you do."

I sniffed my tears and traced a finger over the blood that had burst up under the scratch marks. Maybe it would be a forever-scar on his face, to make him remember me every day. I put my hand on Dad's warm cheek and then I put my head on his shoulders. I closed my eyes.

"I don't hate you," I whispered.

"I know that too," Dad said.

I held my arms around his neck and I held and held and squeezed and squeezed, with all my might I hugged myself to him and smelled his smell and felt the warm of his skin and the boom-boom that is a human pulse and the thing that tells you someone is still alive and not yet gone from your world.

Dad whispered something into my ear and I whispered something back.

"I LOVE YOU. I love you even though you are bad. I will always love you because you are mine."

We held on tight and forever and the whole world vanished except for us.

"You have to go now," Dad said. "They need to take me away."

I shook my head.

"Please," Dad said. "I don't want you getting hurt."

He stroked my face with his hand. He looked out at the officers all around us and at the grandma crying softly on the porch. The police radios crackled and one of the officers whispered something into it that I couldn't hear.

Dad's eyes kept racing back and forth from me to everyone standing around us. He must have been hurting because his face was twisted. He kissed me and held me and put both hands on my wet cheeks.

"Go, Dolly," he said.

I shook my head. Dad looked at me with PLEASE EYES and then his face changed like he remembered something.

"Where is Clemesta?" he said.

"Clemesta." I tried to think. "I guess she's still in the car."

Dad nodded. "Then you should go and get her," he said. He wiped his sweating forehead with his hand. "She'll be scared all alone."

I imagined Clemesta sitting in the back, watching the police with their guns and wondering where I'd gone. I bit down on my lip. *I'm here,* I said with telepathic powers, but I wasn't sure if that worked anymore. She had gotten so weak.

"The thing is," Dad said, "the police will take the car away.

And she'll be stuck inside. You won't get her back for a long, long time."

He was looking at me without letting go of my eyes.

"Please," he nodded. "Go get her. Go now."

I turned away and ran as fast as I could.

Everything was very noisy and then everything was very quiet.

They took Dad away in one of the police cars and some other officers arrived to look at Hank's car and walk around the house and shake their heads. BRAVE BRAVE BRAVE went my heart as it pounded but it was sick of being brave.

The grandma took my hand and told me to go inside the house with her. She poured me another glass of juice even though I hadn't finished the first one.

"Grandma," she said. "You can call me Grandma if you like."

Then she shook her head. "Or Joy, if you prefer. That's my name."

I watched her sad eyes. Clemesta was in my arms.

"We'll be okay," she said. Her voice was so weak I could barely hear her.

I saw Dad's duffel bag on the floor by the kitchen table. I didn't remember him bringing it inside the house, but I pointed to it anyway.

"There's lots of money in there," I whispered to Joy.

She frowned. "Did he steal it?"

I shook my head.

She took the bag and slipped it inside the broom closet. Then she sat down at the table.

The granddad wouldn't come back inside the house. He just stood out on the front porch with his arms folded. One of the policemen knew his name. I heard him say, "I'm sorry, Frank. You never think this stuff happens to you."

Frank didn't say anything. He just nodded his head and stood on his porch.

Another officer came into the kitchen, along with a woman with long hair who looked like an ordinary person and not like the police because she wasn't wearing a uniform.

"Joy, this is Sandra Woods. She's with Child Services."

"Hello, Dolly," she said. She was carrying a clipboard and a pen. "I'll be going along with you to the station today."

Joy stood up. "Now is that necessary, after all she's been through already—can't she just stay with her—"

"Ma'am," the officer said, "I'm afraid that's our protocol."

"It's okay, Joy," I said. "I still have a little brave left inside me."

Sandra drove me to the station in her car. I think Joy came along too, maybe still in her slippers. Clemesta stayed with me the whole time.

At the station, Sandra led me into a room with a small table and some dolls and a pile of paper with crayons and colored pencils and stickers. The room had a big glass window, but you couldn't see what was on the other side.

Sandra sat down and pulled up a chair for me.

The door opened, and another woman came in. She was very tall and she said her name was Detective Marshall.

"Well, hello there," she said. "You must be the very brave Dolly I've heard so much about."

I looked away.

Sandra had her clipboard open and her pen in her hands. She was chewing gum that smelled like peppermint.

"You had a lot happen to you this week, Dolly," Detective Marshall said. "You think you could tell us about it?"

I looked at her. I zipped shut my mouth.

She pointed to my hair. "Did your dad do that?"

"I asked him to."

Sandra wrote something with her pen, and looked at Detective Marshall that way grown-ups do, when they want to say a lot with their eyes but not their mouths.

"Dolly," she said, "can you tell us what you remember about the day before you left home? Did Mom and Dad have a big fight?"

I stared at them. *FUCK OFF,* I wanted to say but maybe they could put you in jail for that.

Clemesta pulled at my arm. "Dolly, we really need to tell them the truth."

I shook my head.

"Dolly," she said. She kicked me in the belly with her hoof. "We have to."

"Stop!" I yelled. "Stop making me remember!"

I picked her up and threw her off my lap as hard as I could. She crashed into the wall and landed in a heap with her legs up in the air. Maybe she was dead too.

I left her there.

Sandra looked at Clemesta on the floor but she didn't say anything or run to call an ambulance. Detective Marshall wrote a note on her pad.

"Dolly, do you know who Stewart Ronson is?"

I bit down hard on my lip.

"He alerted the police a few days ago. He was worried when he couldn't reach your mom all week. He said you were headed out to Los Angeles. She was meant to be at a casting for his new show. Isn't that right?"

"He was Mom's boyfriend," I said. "He wanted to steal us away from Dad forever."

Detective Marshall and Sandra looked at each other. Their eyebrows lifted at the same time, and then Sandra shook her head.

"He wasn't your mom's boyfriend, Dolly. He's married to a man, sweetheart. His husband's name is Paul. Maybe you met him too?"

Everything froze dead and I turned into a statue. I couldn't find my breath or my heart. I bit down harder on my lip but I still didn't feel anything.

I looked at Clemesta lying crumpled on the floor. I wanted her to say something, but she just lay there.

"Dolly," Sandra said. "We'd like you to tell us what you remember."

I shut my eyes. I wanted everything to disappear but it was all there and it wouldn't go away. Mom taking me aside in the afternoon and saying TOMORROW'S THE DAY. We were going to Los Angeles and YOU KNOW WHO was going to help us get settled in. I would be starting a new school with no friends and no Miss Ellis and no Dad and no house in Astoria and no anything that was my real and best life. It was all going to be brand-new, with Mom and stupid YOU KNOW WHO, who loved her and wanted her to be SHINING HAPPY again.

I knew about Mom's TOP SECRET PLAN for three whole weeks and I had kept my LIPS SEALED and only written the secret on a small piece of paper and slipped it into my secret-secret box for safekeeping. I did not want to leave but Mom kept saying, "I'm doing this for you, Dolly," and "I'm scared of what will happen if we stay." She promised I would get used to everything that was new and in the end it would all work out and one day I would understand and I would forgive her.

Mom was packed with a secret suitcase in the back of her closet and I was meant to get packed too but I couldn't fit everything in the bag she had given me and I REFUSED to leave it all behind.

"You'll get new things," Mom said. "We'll have all new everything."

I didn't want all new anything.

I was very good at secrets but I was very, very mad.

I didn't finish packing. Instead, when Dad walked through the door, I said, "I have something I want to show you."

I opened the secret-secret box and unfolded all the secrets for Dad to read. I thought they were all one hundred percent true. I thought letting them out would fix everything and make it go back to before, when Dad was Mom's life raft and she was his shining light, and I was their whole world and YOU KNOW WHO was gone forever from our lives.

I could hear them yelling and screaming and shouting and I was very scared.

"What affair?" Mom was shouting. "Joseph, you need help."

The yelling was really really loud and they were really really mad and Mom was crying and Dad was banging his fists against the wall and it felt like the whole entire house was shaking and probably going to fall down with noise and angriness and tears, so I left the hurricane storm shelter and crept by their bedroom to say "PLEASE STOP." As I got to the bedroom door, I saw Dad's angry bear hands grabbing Mom around her neck and I shut my eyes as tightly as I could and did my best vanishing trick. I went to the FOREST OF MAGICAL FAIRIES and they fed me pollen ice cream and petal juice and they sang lullabies to take away the scared. Everything was lovely and peaceful in the forest and then everything inside the bedroom went very quiet so I said goodbye to the fairies and opened my eyes.

Dad was carrying Mom to bed and he set her down so gently and kissed her eyes to wipe up her tears. He was crying too and full of sorry and Mr. Angry Bear was back in his cave where he belongs. He had scratched Mom badly and bitten her too, because she had blood on her head and it had pooled on her dress. Dad pulled the covers up under her chin and Mom didn't move but Clemesta did. She had been in my hands the whole time, but suddenly she dropped to the floor and the noise made Dad look up. He saw me standing in the hallway and he said, "Oh Dolly. Oh Dolly."

He came over to me and his eyes were blurry. "Oh Dolly," he said, "don't cry. It was just a very bad dream."

He carried me back to bed. He got a glass of water and two magic white pills and told me to drink up. I finished the water and then I fell fast asleep. The bad dream vanished like magic.

In the morning it was all gone, and then we were gone too.

Sandra and Detective Marshall were looking at me with big eyes waiting for me to speak but I couldn't say anything. My words were all poison and they had killed Mom and sent Dad to prison and smashed our whole lives into millions of pieces that wouldn't ever be fixed. I couldn't take them back and I couldn't ever say them again.

I heard Clemesta's voice from across the room. She was using the last of her telepathy powers and her voice was only a whisper

"Dolly," she said, "don't worry. I understand."

I jumped up and ran to her. I lifted her in my arms and kissed all the places where she was hurt and bruised.

"I only wanted you to remember to keep you safe," she whispered. "But we will keep this secret forever."

"I know," I said. I held her to me and cradled her broken body gently in my arms.

Then I sat back down in the chair and looked at Sandra and Detective Marshall. I took a deep breath.

"It was an accident," I said. "Everything was an accident and no one did anything bad."

Clemesta took my hand and squeezed it with the last strength that was left in her. Sandra coughed and made eyes at Detective Marshall. They nodded. Detective Marshall shut her notepad, and gave me a smile that said POOR ORPHAN YOU.

Afterward, Joy drove me back to her house.

Frank was off the porch and sitting in the living room but when he saw me he left.

"Don't mind him," Joy said. "He'll come around."

It was almost dark. I tried not to think about Dad going to sleep in prison, or Mom being forever asleep in heaven.

Joy showed me around the house that used to be Dad's old house. It was neat and tidy. All the curtains were pulled shut. I could still hear the police radios crackling outside.

She opened the door to one of the bedrooms.

"This was your daddy's old room," she said. "Him and Joshua had bunk beds in here. They fought every night over who'd get to be on top."

"I have stars on my ceiling at home," I said. "When it's dark, they glow."

"That sounds pretty," Joy said.

"I'll show you," I said. "As soon as you take me home."

Joy looked at me but she didn't say anything.

The doorbell rang and a lady handed Joy a dish covered in foil. Joy hugged her and took the dish, and the lady disappeared across the street into another house. Joy shut the door and heated the food and we sat around the kitchen table to eat it. Frank didn't look at me. He made loud noises when he chewed and he spilled something down his shirt. Joy handed him a napkin. I nibbled a few bites and then I wasn't hungry anymore.

Joy didn't eat much either, she just kept looking at me and opening her mouth to say something and then closing it right back up.

After dinner, she ran me a bath. She left me alone to get undressed, probably so I wouldn't be shy in front of strangers. I pulled off my clothes and threw them in the trash so I wouldn't ever have to wear them again.

I lay in the bath a long time, until after the water went cold. All of me was cold too, like my heart had decided to stop beating the blood around. Probably it was too sad to do it anymore.

Joy was waiting for me in the spare bedroom. She handed me a shirt to sleep in. It was purple and smelled of flowers.

She pulled back the covers and patted the bed for me to climb inside.

"You didn't even know I existed," I said.

"Not until a few days ago."

"And now you have to look after me."

She nodded.

"Because there's no one else left. Even if you didn't want to do it."

"Oh, Dolly." She sat on the very edge of the bed like she was afraid of touching me. "There's nothing on this earth I'd rather do than take care of you," she said.

I looked at her face that was a little bit of Dad's face, and a little bit of mine. Probably she was telling WHITE LIES. Her eyes were doing a lot of blinking and she pressed at them with her fingers. I thought about what Frank had said about Dad breaking her heart. I wondered if broken hearts could be fixed, or if they just stayed broken forever.

Joy patted me with her hand. It had brown spots but it was soft and warm against my skin.

"Did you know," I said, "my middle name is Joy too?"

After she left the room, I checked on Clemesta. She had a fever of 103 degrees. She was very ill and weak. Probably she would die in the night, and then she wouldn't be a magical horse queen anymore, just a plastic toy horse with a chopped-off mane that I would keep on a shelf. I stroked her face and listened to her heart beating softly in her chest, the same exact rhythm as mine.

"Clemesta," I said. "Clemesta, my heart."

Her eyes flickered, but she didn't open them. She didn't have enough strength left for that. I nuzzled her in the neck, very, very gently so it wouldn't hurt. I breathed in her smell and stroked her soft, warm coat with my finger.

"Clemesta," I said. "You can go now if you have to. I'll be okay."

She tried to smile and I kissed her softly on each of her eyelids. They were salty from our tears. I wiped my face with my hand and lay down carefully beside her on the pillow. I held her horse-hoof in my hand and squeezed.

"Goodbye, Clemesta," I said. "Goodbye, my twin."

Acknowledgments

Thank you, my incredible agent, Amy Berkower, for always going above and beyond, and for being wise, reassuring, and wonderful at all times. Thank you, Genevieve Gagne-Hawes, whom I am lucky enough to have as both an editor and a friend, and who is magnificent at all this and more. Thank you also to Abigail Barce, Daniel Berkowitz, Maja Nikolic, Peggy Boulos Smith, Natalie Medina, and Jessica Berger at Writers House, for being endlessly helpful and supportive.

Thank you to the amazing Asya Muchnick for her insight, enthusiasm, and expertise, and for being such a joy to work with. To the entire team at Little, Brown USA, thank you for everything you've done to bring this book into the world. I am enormously grateful.

Thank you to my eternally supportive mother, Avril, and sister, Lara, for their love and encouragement. Thank you to my niece Rebecca and nephew Nathan, whose wild and wonderful imaginations gave me great insight into the minds of children (I owe you some Lego, my poppets). Thank you to my father, Norman: This one is for you, and with all my love.

Finally, thank you, Maroje, for driving me across the country to research this book, and for being the best part of every day.

About the Author

Michelle Sacks is the author of the novel *You Were Made for This* and the story collection *Stone Baby*. She was born in South Africa and holds a master's degree in literature and film from the University of Cape Town. Her fiction has been shortlisted twice for the Commonwealth Short Story Prize, and for two South African PEN Literary Awards.